A Desert Restoration

A Hearts of Woolsey Novel – Book 1

Savannah Hendricks

Grand Bayou Press

First published by Grand Bayou Press 2022

Copyright © 2022 Savannah Hendricks

All rights reserved. No part of this publication may be reproduced, stored, or transmitted in any form or by any means, electronic, mechanical, photocopying, recording, scanning, or otherwise without written permission from the publisher. It is illegal to copy this book, post it to a website, or distribute it by any other means without permission.

This novel is entirely a work of fiction. The names, characters, and incidents portrayed in it are the work of the author's imagination. Any resemblance to actual persons, living or dead, events or localities is entirely coincidental.

Savannah Hendricks asserts the moral right to be identified as the author of this work.

Savannah Hendricks has no responsibility for the persistence or accuracy of URLs for external or third-party Internet Websites referred to in this publication and does not guarantee that any content on such Websites is, or will remain, accurate or appropriate.

Designations used by companies to distinguish their products are often claimed as trademarks. All brand names and product names used in this book and on its cover are trade names, service marks, trademarks, and registered trademarks of their respective owners. The publishers and the book are not associated with any product or vendor mentioned in this book. None of the companies referenced within the book have endorsed the book.

Library of Congress Control Number: 2022902818

ISBN Paperback 978-1-7344553-3-5

eBook B09NV544NM

For Film and TV Rights – GrandBayouPress@protonmail.com

Editor: Krista Dapkey - www.kdproofreading.com

Cover ST Adobe Stock with design by Savannah Hendricks

Annually, 10% of the proceeds from the sale of this book, and all Savannah's books are donated to dog rescue organizations.

READING IS BETTER WITH A DOG ~ Savannah

Contents

Welcome to Woolsey

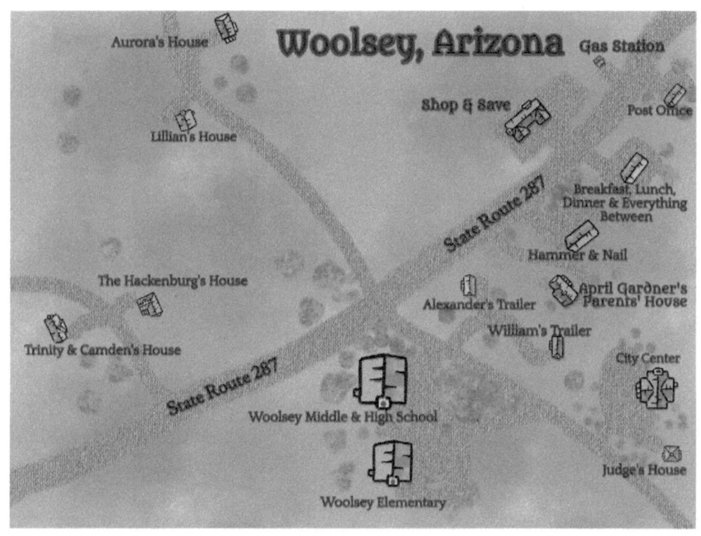

Cast of Characters

Trinity Moore - teacher
Camden Moore - teacher
Lillian Taylor - Trinity's Mom
Elizabeth Dunn - Judge
Mama Dunn - Elizabeth's mom
Gavin Hart - long time neighbor of Mama & Elizabeth

Aurora Easton - Trinity's best friend
Mike Easton - Aurora's husband
Willa Easton - daughter to Aurora & Mike
Ava Easton - daughter to Aurora & Mike
Alexander Adams - librarian
William Adams - guard at the city center
Sydney Hernandez - works at the post office
R. J. Smith - owns Hammer & Nail
Charlie Tow - owns Shop & Save
Ezra Hackenberg - firefighter
Wyatt Hackenberg - firefighter
Jasmine Hackenberg - Ezra & Wyatt's adopted daughter

Foreword

Pizza time at the way-out-fireplace.

When I wrote Camden and Trinity's story, I had no idea it would develop into a series. But I loved creating the town of Woolsey and wanted to revisit some of the characters who I felt had more to share. I also wanted to showcase more of Arizona than I could do in one single book.

I came to the Phoenix area in 2006 after never having any young adult desire to live here. But after a family reunion (usually held in California or Minnesota), I couldn't get Arizona off my mind. To this day, I'm still getting used to the heat, with only hot water coming from the faucet and not being able to open the windows from May to November. It takes a particular type of person to withstand the summers (120° F) and not freeze in the winter (35° F). I do hope that you enjoy the town of Woolsey. And most importantly, I hope that you find this series not too long, but not too short – the perfect length to visit the town, its characters, and take in its charm.

Instead of throwing an acknowledgment page in the back, I'm putting those notes here because my readers are always my first thought when writing. I've met so many of y'all via Facebook, and I can't share enough of my appreciation for every kind of comment y'all leave about every aspect of my life, my books, and Ransom.

Ransom and an approaching monsoon.

Thank you to all my readers and those who auto-buy every one of my books, and don't hesitate to pre-order the next one without even reading the blurb. Thank you to those who share their love of my books continuously (Linda Martin – girl, you're more amazing than the most extraordinary dinosaur).

Thank you to those readers who take a chance on my books and recommend them in their book clubs. Thank you for taking time out of your busy lives to read my book over anything else you can do. Thank you to those who leave reviews and write them so they make my story sound better than even I can on the back blurb.

A big long-distance hug and thank you to my ***Happy PAWS Readers*** ~ Sam Alvarez, Caroline at Page-Turners, Carol Harris, JoDena Pysher, Carrie Thompson, and Lisa Wetzel. I love to have you be the first to read my books.

Thank you to Durene Adams for your continuous support of *I Adopted My Mom at the Bus Station*. Piepie Baltz, thank you for always messaging me something you love about my books when you're reading them. Thank you, Starla DeKruyf, for being such a great cheerleader. Annette G. Anders, thank you for your support and always showing so much love for Ransom.

Thank you to all my friends and family, and my father for reading all my books, even though they don't fall into any genre that he typically reads.

Thank you to my editor Krista Dapkey, and to Kristy for doing a final double-check.

And most importantly, thank you to D.S. for keeping me safe from all those dangerously scary geckos.

Chapter 1

Trinity

As Judge Dunn's gavel slammed, Trinity flinched. Could the judge force her and Camden to do such a thing?

"Your Honor, can you do that?" Camden whined, and his voice went soprano.

"I can do anythin' I please, Mr. Moore. I'm the judge of this town. My purpose is not to grant divorces to every John, MaryAnn, Bill, and Linda who come into my courtroom. I can easily lose the paperwork and draw out this divorce request for months." Judge Dunn slammed the gavel once more for effect, her Southern accent as thick as the desert's monsoon-season humidity.

"Now, please, I beg of you two, don't complain or give me any more excuses. I must rush home and get my dear sweet mama her supper before she declares me an unfit child."

Supper? Trinity glanced at the time on her cell phone in front of her—3:42 in the afternoon. "Your Honor—"

"Ah, yes," Judge Dunn stood and started to unzip her black gown. "The terms. Listen up. I want to see the two of you back at the end of summer. Let's say September 1. Until then, don't come back to my courtroom tryin' to get me to move up the date or reconsider. Even if your house is on fire." Making her way to the door that led to her office, she paused. "In fact, go see R. J. first. I believe he still heads up the volunteer fire department. Otherwise, Mr. and Mrs. Moore," Judge Dunn grinned, fumbling with the zipper, "have a wonderful summer. But please do stop by for supper sometime. Mama would love to meet you."

Trinity crumbled into the chair that only a few seconds ago held her up by the back of her legs. Leaning forward, she lay her head on the cool wood of the courtroom table.

"Great, just great," Camden mumbled as he moved out from behind the table. "How will we manage to afford the renovations? Besides, I don't know how to reno a home. Does she think I'm Bob Vila?"

"We know I have the skill set," Trinity reminded him.

Camden huffed and threw his hands down to his sides. "Yes, we all know that, but I need to help you. *This* is going to be a nightmare."

Trinity heard the stomping of Camden's dress shoes as he headed toward the door leading to the courthouse's only hallway. *He always walks like his shoes are caked in mud when he's upset.*

The door opened with a punch of Camden's fist. Trinity leaned back in the chair, examining the empty courtroom. Only in a town as small as Woolsey could one sit alone in such a place at nearly 4 p.m. on a Tuesday. By four o'clock, except for William, the guard (who was more of a greeter than a preventer of crimes), the city center, consisting of a library and a courthouse, had long cleared out. Not that the center needed a security guard. There were no metal detectors, no security cameras, and no alarms on the doors. And if for some reason there was a threat to the courthouse's safety, Judge Dunn could easily defend herself and everyone in it. Not only did she teach the town's twice-monthly yoga class, but also the weekly karate class.

Trinity picked at the remains of her lilac nail polish on her short, squared nails. She'd painted them for the last day of school. Her preschool students always took note when Trinity added color to them. With all the work she and Camden did on their property, between the horses and their dog, the garden, and regular yard upkeep, nail polish didn't last long before it started to chip away. Yet, her students liked it enough to notice, and she wanted to make them happy. At least someone could be happy.

Trinity dragged herself to stand from the chair. The weight of the impending divorce had been bad enough, but now this. She shook her head as she made her way into the hall. *Can Camden and I live together and fix the house? All we want to do is try to start life over again, not take steps backward.* While she and Camden were by no means hostile toward each other, trying to be separated while living under the same roof might be as challenging as trying to get the house renovated.

"Trinity!" William called out, waving his hand as though he were in a crowd of people when in fact, he was alone, sitting on the stool by the main door. She'd missed him coming in since he'd been chatting with Dolores and Barrett.

"William, how are you doing today?" Trinity asked, approaching him and pushing her long mane of hazelnut hair back over her shoulder. If she didn't get a trim soon, she'd be able to tuck her hair into her jeans.

"Can't complain, my lady, cannot complain." William's words often came out with a bit of a whistle at the end.

"I know you're excited for July."

"Christmas lights time!"

William loved Christmas, and every July he turned his outside lights on for all to see. Christmas in July was a festive reminder that cooler days would return.

"Although, if I may," William stated, "I saw your husband come storming on out of here a few seconds ago. He didn't seem altogether pleased."

"Soon-to-be ex-husband." Trinity removed her Nissan truck key from her jeans pocket.

"Not until at least September 1, from what I hear," he said, placing his hands on his knees.

"William, were you listening at the door?" She wagged her index finger at him.

"Why would you assume I was listening?" William's voice cracked like a little boy caught lying.

"Because this town runs on gossip like a train runs on the tracks." Trinity smirked. "Without gossip, what would anyone spend their time doing around here?"

"I suppose." William tipped his US Army vet's hat and winked.

Trinity reached her hand out and squeezed William's shoulder. "I'll see you around."

She made her way outside, and the heat from the first week of June smacked her face as though she'd stuck it into a preheated oven. Usually, it did not get too hot until mid-June. Yet, this week had already broken triple-digit record temperatures.

Unlocking her dust-covered white extended-cab truck with an extra wiggle of the key—because it stuck every time—she popped open the driver's side door only to be hit yet again with even hotter air. Trinity didn't mind it though, since she'd grown up in the heat, and regulated it far better than Camden. He was probably already home, showering the sweat off and changing into dry clothes. She hoisted her four-foot, eleven-inch stature up into the driver's seat.

Trinity turned on the air conditioner and wrapped her hair into a bun. The drive was so short, and she'd be home long before the cab had the chance to cool down.

Radio station 96.3 was the only one on the dial which came in clearly out in Woolsey, so she listened to country music as she turned out of the city center's parking lot.

Thirty-year-old willow acacia trees lined either side of the two-lane road. To most outsiders, southwest Arizona was known as brown and lifeless. As far as she was concerned, they could keep right on thinking so. The last of the desert's spring shades were dried up. No more anywhere or pops of pinks from wildflowers sprouting up in the rocky soil or blooming yellow-and-purple flowers on trees or orange-red bursts on cacti.

The brakes squealed loud enough for Trinity to hear over the song as she stopped at one of only four stop signs in all of Woolsey. *I know, I need new brakes.* She shifted into first and crossed over State Route 287, which makes it sound like a busy highway, but with it being only two lanes, it was far from bustling.

On the right side of the road, fifteen foot tall ocotillos held blossoms of vermillion flowers. On the left side were the remains of a palo verde ripped from the ground during last summer's monsoon. The bank of palm trees remained, as they were sturdier due to their straight-down root system versus that of the palo verde, whose roots spread out like spider legs.

Trinity continued down Mountain View Road before turning onto a short stretch of dirt that constituted a driveway. She slowed the truck, shifting it into second. Camden's silver Honda sat inside the open garage; the dent on the trunk from a school kid's flyaway baseball remained in need of repair.

While she hadn't planned on Camden being able to move out right after they went to see Judge Dunn, she'd not foreseen the outcome of an entire summer together, let alone a home restoration. A part of her—probably the left side, where her heart was—had already warmed up to the idea of Judge Dunn's sentence. However, the right side of her remained rigid with frustration and doubt. They would need to find a way to cover the cost of fixing up the house. Which would mean they needed to work together but somehow not *be* together.

After parking next to the Honda, Trinity climbed from her truck and walked around to the front porch. She wasn't ready to head inside the home yet. The one-story taupe house boasted a quaint front and back porch with a jacaranda and desert willow providing shade. Trinity took a seat upon the front porch swing, which she'd hung with her mom, Lillian, shortly after she and Camden had bought the house. While Camden made all women's heads turn, his handyman skills were the equivalent, she imagined, of a royal prince's.

Trinity pushed the heel of her boot into the sun-dried wood of the porch and set the swing in motion. The way the chains moved on the hooks created a soft rubbing noise. With the sun descending behind the desert willow trees, Trinity was in the comfort of the shade as a slight breeze picked up.

She heard paws smack the inside of the front door. As it swung open, out came Anderson and Camden.

Anderson, their rescue mutt, a mix of Lab and blue heeler, crashed into Trinity's legs. "Hey, buddy." She rubbed his head and moved to scratch his ears. Anderson had a primarily black coat with tan spots on his chest and around each leg's lower part.

Camden leaned up against the frame of the screen door, a glass of red wine in hand. "At least Judge Dunn's verdict means we don't have to make our most significant decision." He pointed at Anderson.

Tears formed in Trinity's eyes as she petted Anderson's back.

"Absolutely," she mumbled, trying to make sure Camden didn't hear the sadness in her voice.

Out of all the things she and he went back-and-forth on, it was who would take Anderson. It'd not been any different than divorcing parents vying for custody of their child and wanting what was best for them.

Camden headed back inside, closing the door in near silence behind him. Trinity patted the swing and held it steady as Anderson jumped upon it and folded himself next to her. She rocked them gently as the ceiling fans came on overhead. Camden must have flipped the switch just inside the front door for them. Trinity wiped the tears as they fell, unable to stifle them. Giving up, she rested her head back on the swing and closed her eyes.

She needed to figure out how she could continue to live with Camden under the same roof until September. They still loved each other, and wanted to see their dreams come true. Trinity's thoughts drifted off to Camden's soft peppermint-and-cedar scent, his gaze that penetrated her heart, the way he never tied his basketball shorts tight enough and exposed the side of his torso.

This was going to be the longest three months of her life.

Chapter 2

Camden

All six feet, one inch of Camden fell back onto the king-size bed, his navy blue tie in hand, as he stretched over the sheets. Even after three years of living here, he couldn't get over how lax everyone dressed in Woolsey. They didn't even dress up to go to court; at least the judge had worn her robe. Without sitting up, he removed his black wingtip dress shoes with a flick and a kick. The ceiling fan hummed in a weak attempt to cool the space, and even with the air conditioner set at eighty, the room felt hot.

He thought back on when he first moved to Arizona, and Trinity told him no one in the southern part of the state turned their air conditioning lower than eighty during the day or seventy-five at night unless they were millionaires. She'd assured him he would get used to it after the first few summers.

Camden glanced in the direction of their wedding photo, still in its white frame on the nightstand. Trinity was radiant, as always, without even trying. Her spirit shone through her smile. While he wore a solid black classic tuxedo, Trinity wore a white dress from T.J. Maxx, which she'd paired with worn cowboy boots, as though they were attending a barbecue get-together. A smile formed on his face as he thought back to their wedding day and reciting their vows.

Sure, he'd been a bit grumpy in court today, but the judge had upset their plans. Sitting up like an awoken Frankenstein, he sighed. Marriage was forever, or so he'd assumed. Neither of them wanted to get divorced, but they were out of options. The best thing for them to do was go on without the other. Even if Judge Dunn had prevented it from happening today, she would have to grant it on September 1.

As he made his way into the closet to pick out jeans and a T-shirt, the antique oak box caught his eye. It'd been some time since he noticed it last, but not so long that he didn't know it was no longer in its original spot. Camden ran his palm over the top of it, recognizing there was no dust on it—a sure sign Trinity had touched it in the last few days. A layer of dust quickly coated everything in the desert in the blink of an eye. Unhooking the metal clasp, he raised the lid, and its unoiled hinges emitted a shrill.

Inside laid the items Trinity had collected with anticipation over the last three years of marriage. He unfolded the reason they filed for divorce. The fabric with yellow ducks was soft between his fingers, a onesie if he remembered the name correctly. However, he found it an odd name for a piece of clothing with three buttons at the bottom. *Shouldn't it be a threesie?*

Next, he pulled out two chunky board books and a light-gray stuffed elephant she'd picked out in Tucson during a teacher's conference. The smile on Trinity's face as she'd insisted they must buy it because their future child should never be deprived of something so cuddly was ingrained in his mind.

Outside of the bedroom, the front door shut, startling him. He placed everything back into the box and closed the lid. As he changed clothes, thoughts of a baby filled his mind. The reason for reaching their divorce agreement was a mutual decision they'd spent many months discussing. Deep down in the recesses of his heart, he didn't want to do it. They'd done everything they could, even got a second doctor's opinion, but the results were the same.

He glanced at his cropped chestnut hair in the mirror, making sure the short hairs were not out of place before heading to the kitchen. When he entered the room, he found Trinity refilling Anderson's water bowl.

"I know you don't want to talk about renovations, but . . ." Trinity started.

"I don't think either of us expected Judge Dunn to rule as she did." Camden returned to the bottle of pinot noir he'd left on the kitchen counter and held up a glass for Trinity. "Can I pour you some?"

Trinity nodded and pulled out a box of seven-grain crackers from the pantry. He eyed the linoleum floors, peeling up and separating from wall to wall in the kitchen. The laminate kitchen counters had chips randomly around the lip, and the cabinets were original to the 1970s build date. They'd purchased the house for a steal and had every intention of updating it room by room when funds became available. But their teacher salaries and surprise new roof, for starters, meant that had yet to happen.

Anderson finished lapping up his water and marked his path from the bowl to the living room carpet with a line of water dripping from his muzzle onto the floor. Camden took the glasses of wine to the sofa, and Trinity poured two glasses with cold water from the refrigerator and brought them into the living room with the crackers and cheese. When they'd first met, Trinity had never experienced a wine over three bucks. She'd preferred a beer or iced tea as her drink of choice after a long day, until he introduced her to ten-dollar wine; then she was hooked. Camden's parents had educated him long before he was of drinking age about wines, supplying him with a basic understanding of old and new world wine, including terminology and history. In Chicago, the family penthouse had a cellar, and he spent his twenty-first birthday drinking wine with his parents instead of hanging out with friends.

"Should we make a list?" Camden took a lingering sip of pinot noir.

"I guess."

He knew Trinity hated lists. She didn't like anything with a plan. Trinity was the opposite of Camden in many ways. However, it made them rather compatible because they leveled each other out.

"The only way we can work through this is with a solid plan. It might be June, but September will be here much quicker than we think." Camden took out his cell phone and pulled up his memo pad.

"For starters, the entire kitchen needs to be gutted," Trinity said. "I'd hoped we could refinish the cabinets, but the wood is cracked and split. New countertops are a must, but we'll have to go with laminate. And we won't have money for new appliances. But maybe we can finally get an island. I think it would be a nice selling feature."

That stupid island. He'd promised they could get one for the last two years. And she'd bugged him to let her build one because it would be cheaper, but he'd insisted on buying her the very best. The memory hung thick in the air, as unsure as an approaching monsoon season rain. His heart raced in both anger and fear. Anger that he had to keep living under the same roof as his gorgeous soon-to-be ex-wife. Seeing her every day, being around her, and working on restoring the house would only make it harder to let her go. And fear because he didn't know if he could live without her.

"I wanted to get you the island we loved at the store in Phoenix last Christmas," Camden interjected. "With the tin-top and drawers, but —"

"The alternator went out, and then the fuel pump."

"Don't remind me," he sighed.

"Well, now we can get it for the new homeowners."

The noise from the air conditioner and the fans filled the living room. Every movement appeared awkward and stiff between them. One moment, Camden wanted to be her husband, hold her, share his stories of the day or plans for the future. The next moment, it felt as though he needed to keep his distance to protect his heart.

"We need new flooring in the kitchen and bathrooms. I think the carpet is okay. Both bathrooms need the toilets replaced, but otherwise, the vanities only need paint and framing around the cheap mirrors." Trinity stacked too many pieces of cheese on top of her cracker.

"The house needs a fresh coat of paint—inside and out. And we must remove the wallpaper in the main bedroom. The light switches could use updating, but that might be too costly." Camden typed out the list with his thumbs. "And baseboard trim work all around."

Trinity nodded in agreement, her mouth full of a cheese-and-cracker combo. They'd installed energy-efficient windows throughout the entire home over the last two years, so they at least had that expense behind them.

Camden glanced up from this phone. "Can we demo a wall? I want to knock out a wall."

"If we make this house any more open concept, dinner guests will be able to see who's going to the bathroom."

Camden laughed softly.

Trinity sipped some wine. "This is a great bottle."

"It was on sale, so I figured we should give it a try."

He had to stop saying *we*. They might not have been granted the divorce, but they needed to act as though they had. Nothing had changed with their life just because of Judge Dunn's ruling. Once the restoration was complete, they could move forward in their own directions.

Camden found himself staring at his wife. The outside light had faded with the sunset, muting her features, but he knew them well enough to see them even in the dark. Trinity wore zero makeup, blessed with natural beauty and long eyelashes that seemed to touch the bottoms of her eyebrows. She'd removed the cover-up button-down shirt, exposing her bare shoulders dotted with freckles under her tank top straps. Regardless of Judge Dunn's ruling and what September would bring, it didn't change his feelings for her. He still loved her as much as the first day they met. Of course, he'd never admit it to his straitlaced Chicago friends that it was love at first sight.

Trinity had caught Camden's eye in the hotel lobby of the Omni Scottsdale Resort. She'd been there for an Autism Education Conference; he'd been there with his friends on an end-of-college road trip. They'd returned from dinner at one of the restaurants down the street, and there she was in jeans, a formfitting blue T-shirt, and gray boots with a black backpack slung over her right shoulder instead of a purse. When their eyes met, she'd smiled shyly.

"Remember when we first met," Camden mentioned, putting his phone aside.

Trinity rested her head back on the sofa, a smile gently forming. "Yes, you and your friends looked like something out of an episode of *Miami Vice*."

"We did not. You were checking me out because I was so handsome." Camden leaned forward on the sofa.

"Handsome and wondering what soundstage you were headed to."

Camden chuckled. Then without thinking said, "You were the most beautiful woman I'd ever seen in my life."

Trinity tried to hide her blushing cheeks behind the wineglass as she took a sip. When she lowered it, she focused on the rim, rubbing her finger around the edge and then down the stem.

"You still are," Camden added. "Nothing will ever change that."

Trinity set her glass on the coffee table and stood. "I'd better check on Starla and Stella." Her voice was tight, as though she held back a torrent of emotions.

Before Camden willed his body to stand and reach out for her, she and Anderson were already out the back patio door, heading toward the horse stable. Returning to his phone, he gulped his wine, something his parents would disapprove of. Always sip wine, they'd reminded him on his birthday. He took his phone and wine to the kitchen window and watched his wife brushing Starla, the bay they'd rescued a year ago.

Camden realized as he gazed out at Trinity that it would be nearly impossible to see her as anything but his wife long past September.

Chapter 3

Trinity

Trinity always took her morning coffee black and on the porch, even in the summer. Camden would join her in the fall, spring, and winter months. Yet, he'd been hiding out over his morning coffee at the kitchen table the last month. She knew he'd missed out on the remaining cool spring mornings because of it. This morning wouldn't be any different.

She heard the floor creaking inside and knew he was awake. Trinity stared at her mug, the last little bit had grown cold, even in the morning warmth. Then, wanting to get another cup, she leaned forward, just as Anderson whined at the door, alert to Camden.

"Okay, buddy." Trinity stood, straightened out her long-sleeve thin flannel-pattern shirt, and padded her bare feet to the door. She'd taken a sander to the patio deck and sealed it shortly after they moved in. As a child, her mother warned her about wearing shoes to protect her feet from the hot ground and critters. As an adult, Trinity was mindful, but did what she wanted.

"Good morning," Camden stated, his words hitting Trinity like sunshine peeking over the mountain range.

"Morning."

"How are you sleeping on the couch? We can switch it up, you know." Camden, still in his pajamas consisting of a gray T-shirt and gym shorts, was not a morning person and therefore never dressed immediately upon waking.

"The couch is fine." Trinity knew he would have horrid back problems if he didn't get his eight hours on the fancy mattress they'd splurged on. "We should get started on finishing the list and making sure we account for the costs of all the repairs."

Camden raised his mug full of coffee.

"After coffee, of course." Trinity held back a smile. *He is my husband. No, was. No... still is.*

Last year at this time, they were both off of work for the summer and planning their summer adventures to see new places and hike around the state. Camden made lists of what they would plant for the summer garden as the last of the spring garden died out. Then, in the evenings, they would take the horses, Stella and Starla, and ride to catch sunsets from someplace other than the porch. But that's not to say the view wasn't great from there—it was amazing. Trinity's face went solemn, thinking of all the fun times.

She couldn't dwell on the past; this was the present they had decided on together. Yet, her mind wavered. She desperately wanted to know if Camden had these same feelings, but she was not about to ask him. It wouldn't change the facts. It wouldn't change the test results. It wouldn't change their bank account balances.

"All right, I can tell you're getting antsy." Camden grabbed his phone.

"I'm not getting antsy," Trinity unintentionally whined as she poured another cup of coffee.

They gathered at the kitchen table, Anderson between them, lying on their feet.

"We'll need to get part-time jobs to cover all the costs." Camden slouched in the chair and gazed at her.

"I know. It sucks, and we're used to going out and exploring. However, I'm not sure we should be acting like a couple."

Camden nodded, his sadness hidden by his mug. "I could see if R. J. needs a hand at Hammer and Nail. If nothing else, maybe we can get a discount on all the supplies we'll need."

Trinity sipped her coffee, letting the taste linger on her tongue. She observed Camden's face as the sunlight streaked through the edge of the window on its rise over the house.

"Do you think we can do this? Can we fix this house enough for it to sell?" Camden glanced around the room.

"I think so. There are a lot of fixes." Trinity reached her hand out, resting her fingers lightly on Camden's knuckles. Shivers ran up her arms. She loved Camden. She loved this house. Life didn't always work out the way it should, even if you're a good person.

Camden gazed upon Trinity's fingers. "You're the expert. You're the handy . . . woman."

"I should probably go to the library and see what books they have on restoration." Trinity slid her fingers from his hand.

"Great idea, and what we can't find there, maybe we can search for it online."

"Those types of books don't go out of date."

Leaning against the back of the chair, Camden brought his coffee mug to his lips. His vision rested on her. "I never thought we'd be sitting at this table going over restoration plans only to sell it. I'd hoped we could have it all."

"I thought we could have kids." Trinity covered her mouth. She didn't mean for it to come out sounding like she placed blame on Camden.

"We know it's both of us, don't place the blame on either of us. We can't control it; we can't fix it."

"You were the one who didn't want me to ask your parents for money to cover adoption fees." Trinity's eyes hardened.

"I'm not fighting about this. Let's renovate the house and make it through the summer. This is hard enough as it is. I love our home and you."

"I love it, and you, too."

Drip, drip, drip.

Somewhere in the kitchen, the noise echoed, catching their (and Anderson's) attention. Then, the drip switched to a running water sound. Trinity sprang from the chair and hurried to the cabinets where the noise originated. She threw open the doors to discover water gushing out of the sink's pipe.

"Shut off the water!" Trinity shouted.

"Where is that at?" Camden yelled as he jumped from the chair, his eyes darting all around as if the shutoff would have a blinking light pointing to it somewhere on the wall.

Anderson found the spraying water to be a new game and dove under the cabinet, biting at it. He snapped his jaw open and wiggled his face back and forth over the spray. Trinity snatched the dish towel from the oven door in an attempt to wrap the pipe. "It's outside, next to the garage. On the left."

Camden darted to the garage door as Trinity grabbed more kitchen towels from a nearby drawer. Water continued to pour from the busted pipe, soaking both her and the cabinet. Finally, once the towels were all soaked, the water stopped. Sighing, she plopped down in the puddle on the floor, leaned against the cabinet, and moved her legs out into a V.

Anderson barked, and his tail wagged in disapproval of the water game ending.

"Did it shut off?" Camden swung his head around the garage door.

"Yes." Water dripped from the ends of her hair and sleeves.

Camden shook his head. "How did a pipe burst in the summer?"

"It didn't burst. The silicone seal went bad." Trinity observed the water all over her, the floor, and the cabinet. "I should have replaced it months ago."

Camden crouched beside her, taking her elbow with one hand and helping her stand. He used his other hand to move her wet hair off her face. For a few seconds, she forgot about everything around them.

"I think we have a lot more work to do on this house than we thought," Trinity whispered, only their breath between them. "Good thing you have me here." She raised her right arm and flexed her bicep, enhanced through her wet shirt.

"Good thing." Camden winked and squeezed her muscle.

Gazing into his autumn-colored eyes, she felt the same thing she had on the day they'd met. She was deeply in love.

His hand remained on her bicep until she lowered her arm, and he moved it to her waist. She could feel his hand more so with her clothing wet. *I want to kiss you, but I can't.*

This summer was going to be a challenge beyond the restoration, but it was for the best. No matter how much she loved him, she wanted children more than anything. And she knew he wanted the same thing. Their need to be parents was stronger than their marriage. Yet, as Camden's other hand touched her cheek, she doubted every dream that didn't involve staying married.

Chapter 4

Trinity

The library's rich mahogany bookshelves lined three walls and wrapped around the windows. Two plush plum-colored chairs (that Dolores had refurbished only last winter) faced the outside sitting area which was shaded with palm trees and desert willows. The middle of the library held additional bookshelves, and as soon as Trinity stepped through the building's open door, the scent of stories on paper engulfed her.

Nestled in the corner at the entrance was the librarian's desk. Alexander sat comfortably behind it, excellent posture and all, as he read *1984* for what must have been the twelfth or thirteenth time. Alexander worked at the library not only because he loved books more than anything but also to keep an eye on his father. According to Alexander, William should be home enjoying retirement, not being the city center's guard.

"Again, with that book," Trinity stated upon entering the library.

"It's a great read. I never tire of it." Alexander smiled just enough to know that he was not frowning, but nothing beyond that. "What shall I assist you with finding today?" he asked as he gently slid the bookmark between the pages and closed the cover.

"Camden and I —"

"Yes, I heard what Judge Dunn did." Alexander moved from behind the desk, his pale-blue polo shirt perfectly tucked into these jeans. "I must applaud her"—he stood next to Trinity, slipping his hands into his pockets—"nobody in town understands why you two can't make it work."

"Of *course* the entire town knows, it's been eighteen hours." Trinity placed a hand on her belt. "Every person in Woolsey doesn't need a full debriefing." Yet, as the words left her lips, she felt grateful for the collective town wanting Camden and her to stay together. Of course, it was none of their business nor did they have the ability to control it. But it was her community, and Trinity loved it beyond words.

She had no idea what she would do when the divorce was final. She hadn't even thought about what they would do if the house didn't sell. The plan had been to move in with her mom, but with them still not speaking, maybe plans would need to change. Trinity assumed Camden would go to Chicago. His parents would surely take him back with her out of the picture.

"You have books on home remodel, restoration, right?" Trinity's eyes looked around at the shelves.

"Yes, not many, but a few." Alexander led the way to the section and left Trinity to search the books at her leisure.

She tilted her head, reading the titles along the shelf. Did the library own every copy of *This Old House* ever printed? With both hands, she pulled the entire collection of remodeling books off the shelf in one swift movement. Then, carrying the leaning tower of books, she approached Alexander's desk and set the stack down with a crash.

Alexander looked up from *1984*. "I hope R.J. doesn't decide to do any fixer-upper projects on his house."

"He doesn't need any of these. Everything he knows is up here." Trinity pointed to her head. "Do you have any magazines about remodeling? Maybe something published after the eighties?"

"No, that's all at Hammer and Nail." Alexander replaced the bookmark in *1984* and closed the cover. He started with the first book, removing the aged library card from the sleeve glued to the inside cover.

"Think the library will ever update the checkout system?" Trinity almost chuckled.

"Why?" Alexander's face appeared perplexed. "This works excellent, and we all know what happens when technology takes over." His eyes drifted back to *1984.*

"It would give you more time to read and not have to check out books for every resident."

"Where is the fun in that? I'd miss what everyone is reading." Alexander moved onto the third book and stamped the date on the card. The date stamp made its *punch-click* sound.

Trinity smiled. He did have a point, and that was why she loved Woolsey so much. Small town, small charms. And everyone *did* know your name—a place where everyone cared, even if it was none of their business. In their town, time had all but stopped, only keeping the best that life had to offer.

"I've put the due date as September 1." Alexander stamped another card. "No sense in you having to return them only to renew them again and again."

"Thanks, Alexander." Trinity wanted to smile to show appreciation, but it came out weakened by the realization of September. "Do you think you need any assistance here at the library? I need a part-time job to help cover the cost of the restoration."

Alexander peered around the empty library. "To assist with crowd control?"

"Maybe it gets busier?" Trinity scrunched up her brow.

His posture slouched in sarcasm.

"Alright, what about any positions within the city center?"

Alexander continued to stamp the book's checkout cards. "Have you checked with Judge Dunn?"

Trinity's hand shot to her hip. "The judge who sentenced Camden and me to fix our house before she'll grant our divorce? The judge who is making us work together to complete something we can't afford to do?"

"That would be the judge I'm referring to, yes." Alexander stamped the final book. "I, again, agree with her ruling. As does the entire town."

"I'm aware." Trinity took the collection of books and attempted to balance them in her arms.

"Would you like me to assist you in transporting those to your truck?"

"No thank you," Trinity mumbled as her chin supported the top of the stack to keep it from falling over. "I'll manage."

Alexander shook his head and made himself comfy with proper posture in the chair and opened back up *1984*. "Camden is a lucky man to be married to such a lovely and stern woman."

Trinity would have made a snappy comeback if she'd been able to afford to take her focus off the path out the open library door without dropping anything.

"Mrs. Moore," William called out from the main entrance. She could not see much around the books, but she was heading in the right direction. "Mrs. Moore, can I help you?"

"No, William. Thank you, though." Trinity reached the door quicker than the older man, but then asked, "William, is Judge Dunn in court or at her house today?"

"It's Saturday, so she's at home."

"It's Saturday? My, how I forget my days when I'm not teaching. Thank you." Trinity slowed at the curb she knew was approaching and slid her boot around until she found it.

Once at the truck, she attempted to open the door while still supporting the books. As Trinity grasped the door handle, the pile tilted and crashed into the dirt below, sending up a dust plume.

"Great." After dusting them off, she loaded them into the truck and headed around the side of the city center on a gravel path to Judge Dunn's house.

The judge's house was as Southern as one could get in the middle of the Arizona desert. As Trinity approached the home, she took in every beautiful aspect of it. The adobe brick and cream mortar bleached by centuries of strong sunshine and a roof so flat it appeared without one. Drawing closer, Trinity noticed the faded bricks, some cracked, and others with visible mortar repairs in places.

A tan, woven sun hat popped up from behind a row of trimmed magenta oleanders. "Why, Mrs. Moore, to what do I owe the pleasure?"

Had everyone in town always called her *missus* and she only noticed it now? "Judge Dunn, I didn't mean to bother you on a Saturday." *But I have no choice because of the position you put Camden and me in!*

"Hush, I don't mind it at all. Sit, and I'll get us some lemonade. I made it for Mama for when she wakes from her nap." Judge Dunn quickly disappeared through the set of white enameled French doors with tiny glass squares which could easily be mistaken for patio doors and not the home's front door.

Trinity selected the rocking chair farthest from the door and took a seat on the edge. She didn't want to make herself right at home by sliding back into it. Above her, a ceiling fan spun and misters provided a solid ten-degree drop in temperature on the tiny patio. She sighed, upset. The blood rushed to her face, thinking about yesterday's court outcome.

"Here you go, Mrs. Moore." The judge appeared with two large, stemmed wine glasses containing pale-yellow liquid and a lemon slice floating on top. "Now, go on and tell me what I can do for you." Judge Dunn slid back into the other rocking chair. "Although I must admit, I'm surprised to see you here. I figured you'd be rather upset with me."

Trinity took a long sip of the sweet liquid. The exceptional flavor glided down her throat. "Your Honor, you have put Camden and me in a difficult situation."

The judge held up her hand. "Hush, I made it clear we will not discuss my rulin' outside of court. My rulin' stands."

Trinity rolled her eyes. "Your Honor, I was hoping you might know if the city center needed any part-time employees. Just for the summer, of course, to help cover the costs of the house restorations."

"Please, outside of the courtroom, you can call me Elizabeth." She brushed at some planter dirt on her cropped jeans, and her white Keds had seen brighter days. "I regret to say there's nothin' available there. I would check in with Sydney at the post office. I do reckon she was lookin' to head north for the summer again, but she hasn't left yet. Being a state employee, you should be able to get everythin' switched over relatively easy, as far as applyin' and hirin' goes."

"That would be perfect." Trinity beamed and stood. "I can't believe I forgot about Sydney. I know Jennifer said she wouldn't be able to cover for her this summer. Thank you so much!"

"Why, you can't leave until you've finished with your lemonade," Elizabeth instructed as she rocked in the chair.

Elizabeth had moved to Woolsey just this past winter from a small town in Jesser Parish, Louisiana. She took over the role of town judge rather suddenly when Judge Hickman up and decided to retire and move to where the city lights shone like gold in Los Angeles. Then she brought her elderly mother over only a few weeks ago.

"Mama's been here far too long for a Southerner not to know as much as she'd like about everyone in town. Even I need to learn more about the residents."

"To be fair, I figured the town had already filled you in on everyone here. No one can keep anything a secret in Woolsey."

"I would have to agree with you somewhat. I knew about your and Camden's troubles before you filed. So, there isn't a need for secrets unless it's for the greater good."

Trinity eased back in the rocking chair, letting the comfort of the curved wood hug her as she sipped more of the sweet, tangy liquid. *This is the best lemonade ever.*

"How about you and Mr. Moore come over for supper? I know Mama would love the extra company; she misses the neighbors in Jesser." Elizabeth leaned her head back on the chair and closed her eyes. "After all, with me preventin' your pendin' divorce, seems only fair I get to know the couple I will be officially breakin' up come September." Elizabeth popped open an eye to glance at Trinity's reaction. "Unless you and Camden change your minds, of course. I'm always willing to throw out a nonsense case."

Trinity gulped down the rest of her lemonade, leaving only the lemon slice lonely at the bottom of the wine glass, as she stood. It was already awkward being alone with Camden. How bad could this be? "Sure, we can stop by for dinner."

"Great, then it's settled." The judge stood. "Tomorrow night, 4:30 p.m. sharp, as Mama likes to eat early. If you're even a minute late, you'd best cancel. Mama is a stickler for timeliness."

Elizabeth took the empty glass from Trinity's hand and wrapped her arms around her in a firm hug. *Okay, so we hug now?* Taken aback, all Trinity could do was gently return the hug.

"What can we bring?"

"Yourselves will do just fine." Elizabeth opened the front door with a soft smile. "Mama is going to be simply delighted. I'll tell her when she is up from her nap."

"See you at four thirty sharp." Trinity left the coolness of the misted patio and headed to her truck with a tinge of excitement to finally meet Mama. For she was the only person in town neither Camden nor her had seen.

Chapter 5

Camden

Camden adjusted his striped tie and opened the door to Breakfast, Lunch, Dinner & Everything in Between. The remaining aroma of coffee and bacon filled the restaurant. He believed the years of grease held up the original orange floral-print wallpaper. Booths lined the walls, their tabletops level with the window ledges. In the middle were square tables with mismatched chairs. On the back wall, an exposed cutout allowed diners to see into the kitchen, and in front of it, a long countertop with a worn berry-colored top was trimmed with wood. A set of swivel stools were bolted to the step-up floor.

"You must stop dressing up, Camden. You make me look bad in my own restaurant." Luis Perez shuffled a deck of cards at the table nearest the front door. He wore a well-washed black T-shirt and a cowboy hat while a glass of what looked like tea sweated on the tabletop, its condensation leaving a ring at the base.

"Luis, how've you been?" Camden pivoted and shook his hand.

Luis motioned for Camden to take a seat at the table with him. "Waiting on the lunch crowd and doing well. What brings you by?"

"I hoped you might need some help." Camden pulled out a wobbly wooden chair. "I checked over at Hammer and Nail, but R. J. just laughed."

"Well." Luis lifted his hat enough to scratch his forehead, then pulled it back down. "April did leave me a little short-handed. Did you hear she got into the bachelor's program at the University of Washington? A full-ride scholarship, and it's one of the top colleges for library science. I can't blame her for wanting to enjoy her summer before classes start. I know Lil could use some extra help in the back, too."

Lil, as in Lillian Taylor, his mother-in-law. She'd been the cook for Luis's restaurant for several decades. If Camden were back in Chicago, he wouldn't be out begging for work, and if for some reason he needed to, he could've easily landed something within his educational expertise.

"As long as there is not an issue between you and Lil," Luis clarified.

Camden shook his head. "No issues between us. That's between her and Trinity."

"Then I could give you probably five hours a day, five-to-six days a week, with free meals during your shift. It would help with your cash flow and still give you time to get work done on your place."

Of course Luis knew about the judge's ruling. Woolsey gossip slithered around faster than a hungry rattler towards prey. A part of him—although tiny—wished he had grown up here amongst the security of the town. Nothing bad ever happened when everyone was essentially a walking video camera. Half the time, he didn't lock his car door. He and Trinity only locked the house doors after sunset each night. The penthouse he spent his childhood in had triple locks, codes, and guards in the lobby.

"Do we have a deal, Camden?" Luis leaned forward.

Camden stood and shook Luis's hand. "Yes, Luis, we do, thank you."

"I know you just finished up your school year and probably have a lot to organize with the house, so let's say you start Saturday?"

"Perfect. If you don't mind, I'll use your restroom before I head out. The water is shut off at the house. A pipe burst."

"I hope Trinity can get it fixed up."

"I'm certain she can, but I think I'll give it a try first."

Luis, who had just taken a sip from his glass, choked and patted his chest.

"Thanks, Luis." Camden smirked.

"Sorry, it's just—"

"Just wait and see." As Camden started for the bathroom, a familiar voice came from behind.

"You aren't even going to give your mother-in-law a hug?"

His heart leaped. "Lillian, you startled me. I figured you were busy prepping for the lunch crowd."

"Don't you lie to me, Cam." Lillian pulled him into an embrace that made him think he'd returned recently from a long vacation. "You're still my son-in-law. You can't go on avoiding me. Regardless of my current situation with my daughter or the whole September nightmare."

Was he lying or simply trying to figure out how to act around her?

"I'm grateful for Judge Dunn." She pulled back from the hug. Her hair, sprinkled with gray, was pulled into a tight bun on top of her head. Lillian's maroon apron and her black-and-white Converse peeked out from her jeans which nearly dragged on the restaurant floor.

"Don't start acting awkward with me now. You'll always be my son-in-law, with or without your paperwork." She winked. "Here, I packed you and Trin lunch. I can be upset with her all

I want, but she still needs to eat. Go home and enjoy lunch on the patio before it becomes too unbearably hot." Lillian kissed Camden's cheek and hurried back to the kitchen as the lunch crowd started to fill the restaurant.

"Your mother sent me home with lunch," Camden announced as he entered the kitchen.

Trinity was standing at the cabinets with a measuring tape, notebook, and pencil. "She did? Maybe she's over being so ridiculous."

Camden pulled out the foil-wrapped items from the bag as Trinity filled two cups with ice water. He removed two plates from the dish strainer on the counter and made their way to the table.

"Oh, BLTs—Mom's are the best." Trinity immediately took a bite. "She's trying to get me to apologize."

"Yours are just as delicious." Camden unwrapped his. "I'd apologize with or without the BLT. You need her."

Trinity glared at him over her sandwich.

"It would make me happy if we could all get together again before . . ."

"Anyways, there weren't any jobs at the city center, but on Monday, I'm going to go talk to Sydney at the post office. She will be heading up north soon, and hopefully, I can take her spot."

"That would be great. And I can stop by for an espresso."

Woolsey Post Office was famous for its espresso machine. Even Breakfast, Lunch, Dinner & Everything in Between hadn't sprung for something so fancy. Trinity would need to learn how to work the machine to serve the residents who stopped in for a chat and a cup.

"You don't stop in for an espresso now, do you?" Trinity went to take another bite of her sandwich but paused. "Wait, that's why you always offer to pick up our mail!"

"Took you long enough to figure it out. What's it been? Three years?" Camden covered his mouth as he laughed.

Trinity's mouth gaped open. "I can't believe it." She smiled wickedly.

"Luis gave me a job at the restaurant," Camden said, wiping the mayo from the corner of his mouth.

"Good. It sounds like we're set on both sides. And we're having dinner—or supper, I should say—with Elizabeth and her mama."

Camden coughed and reached for his water. "Excuse me?"

"It's my fault. If I hadn't gone over and stayed for lemonade—"

"You had lemonade with the judge?"

"It was divine." Trinity slumped into her chair, her eyes rolling back just thinking about it. "I've never tasted better lemonade in my entire life. Not even my mom's."

Camden shook his head, chuckling. "This town is something else. I feel like I'm in a classic movie."

"I'm a little excited." Trinity leaned over her plate. "A real Southern meal, I hope."

"I'm not completely sold since she rules the town like a fairy godmother. There must be an ulterior motive. Why hang out with the people you sentence?"

"We're not criminals."

As he pondered it, Camden realized having dinner with the judge might not be half bad. Maybe it would make granting the divorce go more smoothly in September. Or maybe change the judge's mind altogether and drop the ludicrous restoration mandate. It was hard enough sharing lunch with Trinity. His urge to hug her the second he walked in the house or kiss her when she was within reach lingered in his thoughts. Being technically separated but literally—physically—together left him agitated. If only the judge really were a fairy godmother. Then she could fix their shortcomings and stop the divorce.

"Elizabeth said not to bring anything, but I thought it would be good to make my coconut chip cookies."

"You've not made those in months. Hopefully, you won't gift her with the *entire* batch." Camden smirked and reached out for her hand. "Sorry, old habit." He pulled his hand back.

Trinity's gaze went to Camden's hand, no longer on the top of hers. "We should finish up and get to Hammer and Nail. It would be nice to have running water. We can start working on a few things before the extra paychecks come in." When she glanced back up, Camden saw tears resting on the bottom of her lashes. He reached his hand back out and grabbed ahold of hers. When their fingers locked together, they each squeezed, neither wanting to let go.

"Sorry, I'm being ridiculous." Trinity wiped at her eyes.

"No, you're not."

"Let's finish and have you change out of that." She pointed at him with her free hand.

"What's wrong with what I'm wearing? I technically had an interview today."

Trinity snorted as she laughed. "Yeah. You know no one here dresses like that, even for an interview. *This* isn't Chicago."

Camden loosened his tie, squinted, and shook his head before they shared a laugh.

Chapter 6

Trinity

Trinity gathered a shopping cart from the corral outside of Hammer and Nail. Camden held the knotted alder door open for her as they headed inside. The store had remained the same since her first of many childhood trips with her mom.

Low stacked shelves allowed for R. J. to see every customer from behind the front counter. Not that he needed to keep an eye on them. It did, however, allow him to read their faces, assessing for confusion so he could easily step in and offer his advice if needed. While the store was not wide, it made up for it in length. The front area carried the smaller items such as screws and nails, paintbrushes, and batteries. In the back half were stacks of lumber, plumbing, planting pots, and fans. Hammer and Nail didn't have everything they needed, but it would be a good start. They would have to travel into Cactus City to get big-ticket items such as cabinets and flooring.

R. J. glanced up from his wood carving as the bell chimed over the door. "Welcome, Mr. and Mrs. Moore." He set his wood and carver on the counter and stood from the stool. Making his way over, he hugged Trinity.

R. J. wore his standard white T-shirt and jean overalls. A toothpick rested on the side of his lip, and his face was unshaven, his hair gray to the point of near-white. In December, he was the perfect match for Santa and brought out a velvet ruby-red chair for the annual Woolsey visit with St. Nick. "Delighted to see you both together."

"R. J., how's your week treating you?" Trinity asked.

"As fine as can be. I can get out of bed on my own each morning. Can't complain."

"How's your project coming along from a few hours ago?" Camden asked, pointing towards the counter.

R. J. lumbered back to his stool, sat, and held up his block of wood. "My saguaro is coming along nicely."

"Lucky us," Trinity smiled warmly. "We'll be stopping by a lot this summer, so we'll get to see the progression."

Trinity caught the words after they had left her lips. *We. We'll be stopping by*. Why were things she'd said for years sounding so foreign now? They were indeed still we, at least for a few more months.

The toothpick in R. J.'s mouth twitched and moved to the other side of his lips. "I was telling Camden a bit ago I heard about Judge Dunn's ruling." He held up both hands. "I know it's not my place to say, but I more than support her decision. This community doesn't want to see you two separate. You both belong here in Woolsey."

Trinity and Camden looked at each other, both unsure what to say, their faces aware and lost at the same time.

"I've said my peace." R. J. took a sip of his coffee from the brown diner mug he borrowed from Breakfast, Lunch, Dinner & Everything in Between years ago. Only in Woolsey will you see a waitress carry a coffee carafe across a parking lot several times a day.

How should she reply to yet another resident praising the ruling of Judge Dunn? A part of her agreed because she didn't want a divorce either. Trinity started to fear that come September, the townspeople might be locking her and Camden in their house.

"The plumbing pipe you need will be on the third shelf on your left." R. J. picked up his knife and wood block.

Trinity pushed the cart while Camden manned the list. She removed the tape measure from her belt clip and checked for the correct pipe dimensions because Hammer and Nail didn't specifically label bins for items. For pipes, there was a bin of all sizes, and the buyer needed to measure accordingly. It allowed for easier returns because R. J. didn't have to find the correct spot to restock it. If a customer bought the wrong piece, they would walk it back to the bin and swap it out for the correct size.

Camden read from the list as they added items to the cart. Trinity enjoyed the peace she found at Hammer and Nail. To her, it felt like a church might to a worshiper. The smell of lumber lingered in the air, along with the sharpness of metal and new plastic. It smelled like progress.

She and her mom had made weekend trips to Hammer and Nail since she could walk. R. J. and Lillian would chat about all things in life while she chew-tested whatever her toddler hands came upon. Trinity knew her mom still visited with R. J. between the lunch and dinner rush, sharing gossip over coffee. Although there was a fifteen-year age gap between Lillian and R. J., they'd bonded like best friends in elementary school, always trying to one-up the other in their knowledge of desert life or home repairs.

"I thought we could build a nice entertainment shelf system in the living room. It would be a great addition," Trinity stated, pushing the cart towards the stacks of lumber. "You know R. J.'s selection will be way better than the huge stores in Cactus City."

Hammer and Nail didn't carry the standard two-by-four lumber. R. J. had reclaimed wood from around town. She pulled the work gloves from her back pocket, threaded them on, and lifted pieces of wood around, trying to find a few that would match.

"I think that would be a great idea. I know we've talked about building something to hold our books."

"Yes, I don't think non-cookbooks are meant to be stacked in the kitchen pantry," Trinity smirked, holding up a piece of wood to examine it better. "I like the grain in this one."

"Me too. I'm guessing you already have a sketch?"

"Of course." Trinity loaded the board haphazardly into the cart and then added four others after a quick debate. "Camden, look." Trinity's body flooded with the warmth of memories. "I can't believe this is still here!" She pointed at the wall near the back exit of the store. "Did I ever show you this?" Taking a few steps, she reached out and ran her hand over the markings on the wall.

"Are those your height measurements?" Camden drew closer, his eyes squinted.

"Yes, they're mine." Trinity's face lit up.

"How come I never knew about this?" His face twisted in confusion. "And why are your height measurements in a hardware store?"

"When my mom and I moved here, we . . ." Trinity pressed her lips together. While she'd told Camden about her childhood, she left out the first few months of growing up in Woolsey.

"When we first moved to Woolsey, Mom and I lived out of her car. She had an empty bank account, and for a little bit, we stayed with different residents after they discovered we were homeless. We spent a couple of weeks with one resident before staying with another. Once she landed the chef job at the restaurant, she started paying rent for the house. But she didn't know how she would juggle being a single mom, handling land upkeep, and full-time work." Before Trinity could continue with the story, R. J.'s footsteps approached.

"Ahh, your growth chart." R. J. slid his hands into the pockets of his overalls. "When I offered to give Lillian a piece of wood, so she could take it with her if she had to move, she flat out refused because she couldn't pay for it. It was probably a few bucks, but it was Christmastime, and she was saving every penny for gifts."

Camden continued to look at the markings while Trinity leaned over the cart, resting her elbows on the handle. His eyes fell upon her, and she noticed his lips parted with solemn. His expression was a reminder of why she left that part of the story out from her childhood.

"If she wouldn't agree to take a piece of wood," Camden questioned, "why did she agree to mark up your store's wall?"

"Because for over two years, Lil didn't know these markings were here." R. J. winked at Trinity.

"R. J. would tell my mom to sit and relax upfront while he would walk around with me, teaching about this and that. He scooped me up in his arms, allowing me to see the entire store from an adult height. He taught me so much of what I know—and what my mom knows too."

"I'd bring her back here and make a height mark once a month."

Trinity straightened up, laughing. "Until I ratted him out one day at the doctor's office by telling my pediatrician how tall I was."

R. J. chuckled. "Lillian came in here the same day, saying she needed some lumber, and I didn't think anything of it. When she came walking back up front, she had tears in her eyes. She hugged me and walked right out of the store. To this day, we have not mentioned it."

"So what if you'd had to move?" Camden inquired.

"We knew Lillian and Trinity were here to stay. No matter what, Woolsey would keep them here." R. J. gave Trinity a sideways hug.

"It seems as though I continue to learn about all of Woolsey's wonderment." Camden squeezed the list in his hand, wrinkling the edges.

Trinity caught him and knew what he was thinking, the same thing as her. She gazed down at the cart full of items to make the home—their home—better.

"I heard you've been invited to Elizabeth's house for dinner tomorrow." R. J.'s voice broke Trinity's thoughts apart.

"Yes, I'm not sure what to expect. But I'm hoping for some real Southern cooking. Have you visited with her before?" Trinity asked.

"Yes, we've had a few . . . meals. Elizabeth's a Southern belle and a wonderful cook." R. J.'s cheeks flushed above his beard.

"R. J., do you have a crush on the judge?" Trinity pushed the cart towards the front of the store. She turned back to Camden as they shared a grin.

"All I said was that I enjoyed a meal with her. I guarantee she would not entertain such an idea."

Trinity had never thought about R. J. and Elizabeth, but they were the same age. *Have I missed some gossip?* She unloaded the smaller items from the cart, so R. J. could tally up the bill. "Camden, I forgot the bags. Would you mind?"

He nodded. The bell chimed as he opened the door and headed to the truck to get the reusable bags.

"Do you want me to put in a good word for you tomorrow?" Trinity winked.

"No, someone as classy as she would never want to indulge a rusty old farm boy such as myself." R. J. firmly tapped the prices from memory into a tablet that sat in a holder on the counter. He'd never supported getting rid of the antique register, and the way he punched the numbers into the tablet, one could tell he didn't much care for using it.

"Well, I must be the only person you've confided in about your crush. I know if you had told my mom, the whole town would know by now, including my horses."

"Last I heard, you and Lillian aren't speaking to each other." R. J. punched in another price.

"Correct, and I'm still not ready to apologize. She wants me to, I can feel it, but I don't think I need to. I think we're both waiting to see who gives in first."

"You're as stubborn as always, and while Woolsey isn't the best at keeping secrets, maybe one day, it will surprise you."

Trinity removed the bank card from her pocket and handed it over to R. J. "Maybe."

Chapter 7

Camden

Camden had no idea what he was doing. "Righty tighty, lefty loosey," he mumbled as he laid on his back under the sink. Anderson rested his head on Camden's chest, supervising.

"Are you sure I can't help you?" Trinity hovered over his legs sticking out from under the sink as she crossed her arms.

Camden peered around the plumbing. "I can't believe you didn't tell me you lived in a car."

"Do you think that would've helped our relationship with your parents? They already hated me. I didn't want you feeling sorry for me either. My mom did what she had to do to get us away from my father." Trinity opened the refrigerator and poured herself an icy glass of tea. Instantly, the glass began to sweat between her fingers.

"I thought your father walked out on you, and that was why you wanted to find him. However, I can now see why your mom is waiting for an apology, but I can't believe you reached out to him and spent time finding him. Doesn't seem safe."

"It sounds better when you tell others your father walked out versus 'we left because we weren't safe.' And I blocked my number when I called. I needed to talk to him. You know that. I had to put that part of my childhood behind me and move on. I needed to express my feelings toward him."

"I always knew you and your mom were strong, but . . ." He sighed.

"Don't feel sorry for us. It made us who we are, and I wouldn't swap my childhood for yours in a million years."

"How long . . . how long did you . . .?"

"Okay, if I tell you the story, can we move on?" She went to the kitchen table, sat in a chair facing the sink, and propped her bare feet up on a nearby chair.

Camden wiggled himself out from under the sink and sat up.

"I remember leaving in the dark, my mom crying, not another car on the road. I don't know how long she drove for, but the sun came up and went back down again before we stopped. Mom told me later she didn't have a plan, only that she'd stop when she knew we were safe. Shortly after arriving here, Dolores and Barrett found out about our living arrangements and insisted that my mom stop running. We moved in with them for a few weeks, then we lived with R. J. and Aurora's parents as well, for a couple of weeks at a time. Then the house my mom has now happened to come up for rent, and Luis gave her a job as a cook. Everything fell into place. It was as if Woolsey had a plan for us all along."

"Lillian isn't still renting her house after all these years, is she?" Camden rubbed his hands across the wrench.

"No, she saved up enough and bought it when I went into high school."

"You and your mom never cease to amaze me. I know you can do everything—"

"Not *everything*." Trinity raised an eyebrow.

Camden lowered himself back under the sink and wrapped the wrench around the sink's pipes. "Okay, *almost* everything. It's time I learn a few tricks of the trade." His wife's story gave him strength and encouragement—things he'd never felt from his childhood memories.

"But if I did it, we could turn our water back on, and then I could bathe Anderson."

Anderson's head popped up at the alert of the B-word. He shimmied out from under the sink and headed down the hall in search of a hiding spot to avoid his impending bath.

"See, Anderson doesn't mind waiting for me to learn some skills." Camden yanked the wrench to the left.

He heard Trinity pick up a book from the stack she'd borrowed from the library and flip through it. Her mom had taught her many home-improvement skills, such as electrical, plumbing, and drywall repair. She could hang shelves, sand, and paint. And now he knew why her knowledge was so vast. Oddly enough, he began to understand this town more and more through her stories.

With his thoughts tangled up in Trinity, the wrench slipped from his grip and smacked him on the chest with a thud.

"Sure I can't help?" Trinity's voice came from behind a book.

"Nope." Camden rubbed his chest. He wasn't going to give up on this one. He could fix anything just as well as his wife. His . . . wife. He should not think of her as anything else until September. His wife. Just because they didn't sleep in the same bed didn't mean they weren't still together. Lots of people probably did that for one reason or another. Snoring, hogging the sheets. Heck, Lucy and Ricky Ricardo slept in separate twin beds.

He removed the phone from his pocket and pulled up the YouTube bookmarked video. With it on mute, he tapped play. Watching the plumping repair video for the third time, he was bound to get this pipe fixed.

Camden heard Trinity shift yet again in the kitchen chair. It killed her not to be doing the repairs herself or at least helping with the process. If he couldn't learn handyman skills now, how would he be able to help his ever-handy wife over the months to come? Before he could let the notion settle, the cabinets started to rumble. The sink vibrated. Since earthquakes were as rare as snowstorms in the desert, it could only mean one thing. Trinity's best friend, Aurora Easton, was out having a respite from her two kids.

He shimmied out from under the sink before a loose pipe could fall on him. Dishes in the cabinets chattered, and Anderson came bursting out from the back bedroom to bark at the commotion. As suddenly as it started, it halted. Yet, Camden and Trinity knew there would be another round in a few minutes.

Camden wiped his hands on a rag as Trinity dashed over to the front door. She hopped on one leg, shoving her bare foot into her boot.

"That only eggs her on for next time." Camden took a long gulp of water and welcomed the break from the confines of sink plumbing.

"I know! That's the whole point!" Trinity swung open the door and pulled it shut with a slam. She bolted down the front porch steps like a second grader on a mission.

Camden crossed one arm over his body while his other held the glass. Anderson leaned against him for support. For as long as Camden could remember, she and Aurora couldn't go a week without their game. Even during Aurora's pregnancy, it didn't let up.

Aurora and her husband, Mike, owned a small crop duster. Whenever Mike was home from a work trip, she would get a much-needed break from 24-7 motherhood and go flying. The Easton's had two hundred acres and were able to accommodate an airstrip on the property. On Aurora's way out, she'd buzz the Moores' house, and then on the way back—as though a starting gun in a race—she would buzz the house again. Trinity would climb up on Starla, and whoever made it back to the Eastons' front door first won.

The house rumbled again as Camden laughed.

Of course, the first time Aurora buzzed the house, he had no idea what was going on. He'd screamed, "Earthquake! Duck and cover!" and had rushed under the kitchen table. Memories of Trinity grabbing her stomach, buckled over with laughter, as he shoved the kitchen chairs out of the way and scurried under the table filled his mind. Once his nerves had settled, she explained that Aurora had been buzzing houses since her papa had taught her to fly. With Camden being new in town, he was not aware of such an act.

He went to the hall window that overlooked the horse stalls, his fingers resting on the frame. Trinity could strap a saddle on Starla in less than a minute. It took him about five minutes to strap a saddle on Stella. Even with all his practicing, Trinity was quicker.

Dust kicked up as Starla bolted out of the stall, Trinity holding the reins. Anderson rested his head on the windowsill and whined.

"I know, bud."

Anderson loved to be out by the horses. When they adopted him from the shelter, the veterinarian had gauged him to be about a year old, and so he'd been raised right beside Starla and Stella. Camden didn't think it was a good idea to allow a puppy near such large animals, but Trinity assured him that Anderson would never be harmed. She worked with Starla and Stella, introducing them properly and helped Anderson understand they were nothing more than a bigger dogs. Much, much bigger.

Camden knew nothing about dogs or horses when they married. And he didn't want anything to do with them either, considering them nothing more than unnecessary work. As the weeks went by, he learned to enjoy Anderson's companionship and the beauty of Stella, especially when roaming the desert landscape. Reaching down, he rubbed the fur on Anderson's head. Now, he couldn't see his life without pets.

Making his way back to the kitchen sink project, he pressed his palm on the countertop and stretched out his back. He thought about Anderson and the horses. Obviously, he couldn't bring Stella with him. Would they have shared custody? Not if he moved to Chicago. Again, he gave credit to his wife and mother-in-law. There he was, ready to crawl back home to his parents when life crumbled.

Camden hung his head as the depression swept through him, robbing him of his breath. The memory of the night when he and Trinity sat at the table and decided a divorce would be the only option for them came crashing back like a wave. They'd cried, not knowing what else to do and not wanting to hold each other back from the family they both wanted. Even after they made their decision, doubt continued to pummel their shore.

Camden thought of Trinity, who was probably near Aurora's house by now. Both were racing to see who could arrive first, Starla or the plane. A smile crested on his lips, remembering the first time he was a part of the race. She had already mounted Starla but hopped off, strapped on Stella's saddle, and demanded that he get on. He'd only learned how to ride Stella a month before and was still not completely comfortable going at a trot, much less galloping through the desert at full speed. Stella kept up with Starla, their legs in sync, galloping in unison. Camden had yet to master his grip, and every time he went to call out to Trinity, dust flew in his mouth.

With a sigh, Camden returned to his cell phone and hit play for the fourth time on YouTube. However, by the end of the video, he realized he'd zoned out, his mind lost in memories.

A bark from Anderson interrupted Camden, so he pivoted towards the front door. Coming up the porch steps were Ezra and Wyatt Hackenburg, both firefighters who commuted to Cactus City and helped R. J. out as needed in town. They had their baby girl, Jasmine, strapped into the infant carrier on Ezra's chest.

Anderson jumped for the door. His tail wagged at the onset of friendly faces and pets to come.

"Move, Anderson, or I can't open the door." Camden reached down to nudge the dog out of the way.

"If it isn't our favorite neighbors," cheered Ezra upon the front door swinging open.

"We're your only neighbors," Camden joked. "Come in. How are you doing?"

Camden held Anderson back behind the door as the Hackenburgs wiped their dusty shoes on the welcome mat and stepped inside.

Wyatt, who always wore flip-flops, kept his dark chocolate hair cropped short. Ezra usually had six-month-old Jasmine strapped to him in some fashion or other. It was often hard to see Ezra's eyes due to his long bangs that never stayed tucked behind his ears. Jasmine wore the most stylish outfits one could find in Scottsdale. She must own twenty hats to keep her face out of the sun and looked as chic as any baby could.

"We brought you and Trinity dinner. Figured with your plumbing issue and all . . ." Wyatt handed the Pyrex casserole dish to Camden. "My sweet mother, rest her soul, left me with the best recipes west of the Rio Grande."

"Thank you." Camden set the warm dish on the kitchen counter before returning to the living room.

"We didn't just come by to drop off dinner, let's be honest," Ezra stated, patting Wyatt's back.

"Please, sit." Camden motioned toward the couch.

Ezra raised Jasmine from the baby carrier like a pro and placed her sitting up on the carpet.

"When did she start doing that?" Camden's voice oozed with joy.

"Just the other day." Wyatt beamed, snatching a throw pillow from the couch to place behind Jasmine.

Camden smiled, showing his joy to the Hackenburgs, but his heart twinged with pain. Thankfully, Trinity wasn't here to see Jasmine's joyful milestone.

"We do have to make sure she has something behind her just in case she goes down." Ezra leaned into Wyatt. "Tell him."

"Tell me what?" Camden continued to stare at Jasmine as Anderson army crawled on the floor, closer to the baby, sniffing the air around her. "Anderson, be gentle." The mutt reached the baby, and his nose twitched with glee. Jasmine giggled every time Anderson's whiskers swept by her cheeks.

"We're just so proud of Elizabeth." Wyatt folded his hands. "The judge is saving your marriage, and we're glad she was bold enough, too." The Hackenburgs both nodded their heads in agreement, like two synchronized bobbleheads.

Ezra raised his hands in defense as Camden began a retort. "We know it's not our business but come on. You and Trinity are such an amazing couple, and we don't want to lose you as neighbors or as friends."

"This town doesn't want to lose you either," Wyatt added.

"As a married couple," Ezra clarified, turning to Wyatt, who nodded in agreement.

Jasmine giggled as Anderson licked her arm. The laughter caused her to lean to the side, unable to hold herself upright. Ezra caught her and helped her onto her back. Jasmine protested and rolled over onto her stomach, pushing her chest off the ground with her arms. Anderson's paws outstretched as he yawned before snuggling up next to the baby.

"I appreciate your support, but once this house is updated . . . well, it wouldn't be possible for Trinity or me to afford to keep it on our own." Camden rubbed the back of his neck although it didn't hurt.

"Never give up hope." Wyatt crossed his arms, admiring his daughter's new best friend sharing the living room floor together. "They get along so well. Maybe we should adopt a dog, too."

"Do you think we can just make a copy of our adoption application for Jasmine and send it to the animal shelter?" Ezra joked.

"Might be overkill," Camden remarked, admiring how Jasmine and Anderson were at peace, delighted with each other's company. The three men caught up on the latest happenings at the Hackenberg house as the sun lowered for the afternoon out the window behind Camden's shoulder.

"Want to hold her?" Wyatt asked.

Camden brought his hand to his chest. "Me? No. No, that's alright."

I want to, but it will only remind me how badly I don't want to give up on my marriage. How badly I'd love to have kids of our own. He ran his fingers through his hair. *Trinity and I cannot change what life has dealt us. And I need to get over it, move on.*

"I know it must frustrate you seeing Jasmine appear as if delivered from a stork with the snap of a finger." Wyatt reached down and picked her up, resting her diapered bottom on his knee. "We would be more than happy to write a recommendation."

How quickly the town had discovered their inability for Trinity to get pregnant or be able to afford adoption. He wished that word hadn't spread because it was personal. But once one person finds out, soon everyone knows—good or bad. If you don't want a secret told, you hide it inside and never speak a word.

"Thank you. If that were possible for us . . ." Camden rubbed his hands, now sweating, on the top of his jeans.

"Always good to have a letter ready, just in case." Ezra leaned forward.

Why? Camden continued to run his hands back and forth over his knees.

He didn't want to come right out and explain (for another time) that they couldn't afford the adoption fees. Maybe the house restoration confused people. But it was a few thousand dollars, not tens of thousands. He didn't want to mention that while his parents were millionaires, they'd refused to help.

Ezra and Wyatt glanced at each other before turning back to Camden.

"Trinity and I are open for adoption. I mean, we were open *to* it. But it's not possible. You know how steep fees can be." Camden stood, afraid that if he remained seated he would say more than he wanted.

"We should let you get back to your evening." Wyatt stood, followed by Ezra, who picked up Jasmine and slid her into the baby carrier. "Enjoy the casserole and tell Trinity we said hi. I heard Aurora fly over."

"Thank you again for stopping by. A pleasure to see you both and Jasmine. She is growing up too fast." Camden and Anderson walked them to the door.

As he watched the Hackenburgs cross the yard, a loud buzz approached his ear, and immediately, he ducked. In his squatted position, he was level with Anderson.

"It's one of those dang carpenter bees!" Camden squealed to the dog. He could still hear the buzz but was unable to locate the enemy. As he continued to squat, his eyes darted around the front porch, searching for the gigantic all-black bee the size of a quarter.

"It's over there. Now, Anderson, now!" Camden kept low and reached for the doorknob. He threw the door open, hurried himself and his dog inside, and slammed the door. "I hate those things!"

With his heart racing, Camden made his way past the kitchen table with its stack of library books and the unfixed plumbing under the open cabinet doors. The aroma of the warm casserole on the counter made him hungry.

"She won't mind if we give it a try, right?"

After taking a fork to the casserole, he savored a few bites, tossed Anderson a peanut butter dog treat from the canister on the counter, and took a seat at the kitchen table. "Maybe the old school way of sink repair will work better than the YouTube way."

Chapter 8

Trinity

"I win!" Trinity shouted as she dismounted Starla. "Such a good girl." She rubbed the side of the horse's mane.

Aurora greeted her best friend with a hug. "One of these days, I will win for a second time."

"Auntie T!" Aurora's two girls, Ava and Willa, cheered from the front door. They bolted toward Trinity, wrapping their arms around her, one on each side.

The girls had called Trinity *Auntie T* since they were old enough to form words. Although Aurora and Trinity were not technically related, they were still family. After all, they'd spent kindergarten through senior year together until Trinity moved away to attend college in Tempe. They had a monthly girls' time, though, and made it to her and Mike's wedding and the girls' births. However, she did miss Ava's first birthday due to major flooding downtown during a monsoon. Not only were the streets a mess, but cars had floated down I-10 like sailboats.

"Hi, sweet girls." Trinity lowered to their level.

Willa's hair was the color of sweet corn, while Ava's hair had turned dishwater blonde. Only two years apart, the girls got along well.

"Are you staying for dinner, Auntie T?" Ava, the oldest, asked.

"Depends on what your mom is cooking." Trinity winked.

"Daddy's cooking!" Ava exclaimed, placing her hands on her hips.

"In that case, I'd better stay far away from the kitchen."

Ava and Willa giggled.

"Girls, why don't you go see if Daddy needs help so Auntie and I can chat," Aurora suggested.

"I want to feed Starla a carrot," Willa whined.

"Quickly then, girls." Aurora shooed them with her hands.

The girls raced back inside, yelling, "Daddy! Daddy!"

Trinity and Aurora headed over to the covered gazebo off the side of the house. Time and the weather had aged the wood, and electricity had been run underground, allowing for an outdoor ceiling fan and misting system.

"I was going to text you the ruling from the judge, but . . ." Trinity took a seat and arranged the pillows as an armrest.

"No point in that, as we know." Aurora shook her head. "So tell me something the town doesn't know."

Trinity's eyes lowered, and she sighed. "It's hard being around Camden and having to be distant. There's an awkwardness, as if we're pretending everything—every move, every conversation—is fine."

"Like walking on eggshells."

"A part of me wishes we hated each other. It would make things so much easier. I lost count of how many times I've wanted him to hold me or kiss me, but I can't. Regardless of Elizabeth's ruling, come September, the divorce will be approved, and the house will sell."

"The girls will be crushed if Camden stops visiting. Plus, you have that *thing* going on with your mom, which can't help."

Sweat had formed between Trinity's shirt and the pillow. "I thought you were on my side about reaching out to my father."

"I'm on your side, but I think you need to make up with your mom and move forward. Plus, stay with Camden."

"We can't stay married to please our family and friends." Trinity stretched out on the bench and crossed her legs at her boots. "And I doubt he'll stay in town, let alone Arizona after everything's finalized."

"Not only are we upset, but the entire town, too." Aurora pulled her ash-blonde hair into a ponytail using a band she kept around her wrist.

"Enough of what the town wants!" Trinity snapped. "Everyone is acting like this divorce can be prevented, and some mysterious spark of luck will solve all our problems. It doesn't work that way. I'm well aware that all of Woolsey wants us to stay together, but we want a family. So unless someone can pull a kid out of a top hat, everyone needs to be quiet."

"Do you want one of the girls? I'm sure Mike would be okay sparing one of them." When Trinity didn't laugh, Aurora waved her hand as if to swat away the lousy joke like a fly. "At least you will be my neighbor again. It will be as though we turned back the clock and are young and carefree again."

Trinity glanced in the direction of her mom's house, the edge of her driveway in view. "Please, we're still young ... maybe not carefree. We can set up a lemonade stand just like we used to, then we can drink it all since no one comes down this stretch of road." Trinity laughed, holding onto the memory.

"We made the best lemonade."

"Speaking of lemonade, Elizabeth makes the best lemonade. It put ours to shame for sure." Trinity licked her lips.

"So, why do you think Judge Dunn invited you two to dinner? Ulterior motive?"

"How did you know about it already?"

"Charlie at Shop and Save. He said that Elizabeth picked up a basketful of groceries."

"I think maybe she wants to get to know the people she ruled on a personal level. I'm not sure what her ulterior motive would be. She has nothing to gain but extra time in court."

Aurora rolled her eyes and let out a giggle. "It'll be fun, I'm sure."

"I'm rather excited about dinner. I've never shared a meal with a judge before, let alone a Southern cook. I should probably brush up on which fork is the salad fork."

"Bringing your famous coconut chip cookies, I presume?"

"Indeed."

"And you'll bring me some cookies, too?"

"Of course, I always make extra for you. If everything goes south, those always seem to save the day."

"Speaking of saving," Aurora shifted on the bench, "you're sure you and Camden can't go to his parents? Last-ditch effort?"

Trinity glanced out of the corner of her eye, glaring her best friend down. She knew Aurora meant well, only wanting the best for her and Camden. Trinity had gone to her when the hope of having a baby started to waver. After her fancy-Scottsdale-doctor appointments. After Camden and she had discussed every alternative possible. After she shed enough tears to fill up Anderson's blue kiddie swimming pool.

Camden's parents could easily cover the adoption fees, but they shunned their son more or less due to his marriage to Trinity. She wasn't of elite status, and Camden living life as a teacher in the middle of nowhere proved to be their breaking point.

"Unless I wake tomorrow as the Queen of England, the Moores are not an option. Camden won't hear of us asking them," Trinity snipped.

"If you were the Queen of England, you wouldn't need their money."

Trinity yanked the throw pillow from behind her back and chucked it at Aurora. It bounced off her shoulder and landed on the gazebo deck.

"Do you think you and Camden can get the house renovated by September?" Aurora asked, picking up the pillow and using it to cushion her back a little more.

"I'm hoping so."

"Such a shame to finally get the house the way you want it, only to sell it. I know it's horrible, and I don't know how to be supportive because I disagree with it. I flat-out hate to see you two divorce and sell your home. You were supposed to be together forever. If Mike and I could have helped out in any way, we would have."

Trinity's thoughts drifted back to when she first unleashed the news to her best friend. In return, Aurora offered to be a surrogate. Yet, even if the funding was a possibility, Trinity and Camden's doctors reported infertility issues on both sides, making a surrogate useless without a miracle.

"I hate life!" Trinity crossed her arms.

"Don't hate life."

"Be a decent best friend and let me hate life." Trinity hurled the final pillow on her side at Aurora, who caught it before it smacked her. Frozen in a stare down, the best friends furrowed their brows in concentration.

"Momma! Auntie T! Momma! Auntie T!" The girls came running, waving around a carrot stick each. Dirt kicked up around them as they made their way to the gazebo.

Yet, one couldn't break Trinity and Aurora's concentration. They continued their stare down until the girls shoved themselves in their line of sight.

Trinity willed herself to stand and took the girls' carrot-free hands into hers.

As she walked away, Aurora called out, "You know I'm right! You know the whole town is right!"

Chapter 9

Camden

"I told you not to wear a tie." In her hand, Trinity held a clear Tupperware full of her coconut chip cookies.

"It's important to show up looking well-dressed." Camden wiggled the black-and-gray-diamond-pattern tie around his collar. "Even if it's 102 degrees out."

Camden admired his wife, dressed in cropped jeans, flip-flops, and a gray T-shirt. Approaching the judge's front door, they both took a deep breath. Unsure what either of them would expect on the other side, he formed a fist and knocked on the door.

Footsteps grew closer until the door swung open, Judge Dunn on the other side.

"Welcome." She beamed at the pair, her red-chili curls piled into a loose bun on top of her head. "Come in, please." As she moved aside, Camden and Trinity entered.

The home had whitewash walls with abstract paintings framed in gold. A fireplace of pale-red brick nestled itself on the right wall, while a plush emerald-green velvet couch and two floral wingback chairs filled the middle of the living room. A woven rug of royal and sea blues managed to tie the room together. Wide plank hardwood floors led the way to the kitchen. The sound of music thumped from down the hall, filtering out their way.

"Mama will be so pleased you're on time." Judge Dunn placed her hand on Trinity's back, directing her towards the kitchen. "Don't mind the music. She's back there listening to Dolly. I wish she'd turn it down some, though."

Entering the kitchen was like stepping into a time warp. The cabinet's wood grain circles paired well with canary yellow Formica countertops with zinc bands around the edges. In the center of the room, a butcher block island held cups of fresh herbs. In the corner, there was a table up against a breakfast nook bench.

"That stove is angelic," Trinity nearly shrieked.

"Thank you. It's an original Wedgewood gas stove."

"Your Honor, your home is beautiful. Thank you for inviting us for dinner." Camden elbowed Trinity.

"Yes, and I brought you my famous eggless cookies." Trinity held out the Tupperware.

Judge Dunn took the container. "I've heard about these. You created them for your best friend because she has an egg allergy."

"Yes." Trinity clasped her hands together, unsure of where to put them. Usually, she would grab Camden's hand in such an instance.

"Thank you so much. And remember, please call me Elizabeth."

"Have you done any restoration on this home, Elizabeth?" Camden questioned, taking everything in like an appraiser.

"Nothing more than what a little elbow grease could fix." Barefoot, Elizabeth stirred whatever was in the Dutch oven on the stove.

Camden felt overdressed now and yanked at his tie. His feet sweat in his black dress socks, and Trinity elbowed him again to stop messing with his tie as they stood near the island. The silence was worrisome.

Elizabeth glanced over her shoulder. "Please tell me what you would like to drink? I have wine, beer, lemonade, and sweet tea. Oh, and water. My word, y'all have to drink so much water here to keep from dehydratin'."

"Yes, for every glass of alcohol you drink in the summer, you need to follow it up with a glass of water. I'd love some sweet tea," Trinity oozed. "Homemade?"

The judge spun around and headed towards the vintage white Philco refrigerator. "Honey, everything is homemade. Is there any other way?"

"Of course not," Trinity smirked.

"I'd love some as well, please." Camden's thoughts drifted as he took in the vintage kitchen, marveling at how something old and worn could feel as cozy as it did.

"Please take a seat at the table; no reason to stand in this heat." Elizabeth filled four mason jars with the amber liquid and added ice. "Now, let me go get Mama." She set the refreshments on the table and disappeared through the living room archway.

Camden allowed Trinity to slide along the bench to the farthest place mat with Five Alarm Red mums on them. He squeezed in next to her at the place mat with Pumpkin Igloo mums on them. During college, he took many electives that he hadn't needed to so he could stay away from his family longer. One of those classes was floral identification, and he'd hoped taking it meant he could learn about the perfect flowers to impress women. Then when he met Trinity, who was a year behind him, his desire to draw out graduation intensified. His flower education to impress any woman other than Trinity became a thing of the past. Surprisingly, he remembered more than he thought. He eyed the other two placemats, checking his memory once more. Old Double Pink and Snowy Igloo. Dang, he was good. A smile tweaked up the corner of his mouth.

"Mama, I want you to meet Mr. and Mrs. Moore—Camden and Trinity."

He glanced up from the place mats to find a curly-haired woman whose locks were the color of pearls. She was tiny, standing only four-nine or four-ten, and held onto Elizabeth's hand. Come to think of it, his wife appeared to be the same height.

Camden rose from the bench.

"Sit down, son. No need in fussin' over my arrival," the elderly lady chirped. "I only came from the bedroom, not from the palace." Her Southern accent was sharper than her daughter's.

Without the slightest reason why, Camden half-bowed and sat down. Trinity smacked his arm and raised an eyebrow. He shrugged, a puzzled look across his face.

"It's lovely to meet you, Miss . . ." Trinity wrapped her hand around the dampness of the mason jar.

"Call me Mama. No need to remember my name. I won't be here for long." Mama shuffled to the chair at the head of the table and sat with her daughter's guidance.

"Hush now, Mama, you're not goin' anywhere." The judge removed the Dutch oven from the stovetop.

"I am too. I'm going to my grave." Mama's hand had a slight tremble as she tried to steady it to pick up the half-full glass of sweet tea.

"That's a long ways off, Mama, stop acting like it's happenin' tomorrow," Elizabeth scolded.

"I think you look rather young, if I do say so," Camden added to the conversation.

"Oh, bless your heart, son." Her wrinkled hand reached out and rested over top of his. "You need some spectacles."

Trinity muffled a giggle with her hand. Camden nudged his knee against his wife's.

"Supper is ready, y'all," Elizabeth announced, setting the platters in the middle of the table. "We have fried chicken, collard greens, and cornbread. Mama insisted we treat you two to a real Southern-style supper. For dessert, we have sweet potato pie."

"It looks delicious," Camden stated, but inside he was counting the calories.

"Thank you so much for having us over for dinner." Trinity smiled.

After Elizabeth served up Mama's plate, Camden and Trinity helped themselves, their plates overcrowded as though it were a Thanksgiving feast. The judge cut Mama's chicken up for her while Mama slathered nearly half a stick of butter onto her cornbread.

"Everyone always asks couples how they met, but I want to know how you proposed." Elizabeth took a sip of tea.

Camden couldn't think of the last time he told the proposal story or even thought about it. He set his fork down and folded his hands, careful not to rest his elbows on the table. "I'd planned a horseback riding trip at Saguaro Lake Ranch. The location is stunning on its own, with the river and all, but it was mid-November, and the golden colors scattered on the trees below the towering mountain made it even better."

"The area is gorgeous," Trinity added.

He smiled at his wife, his eyes lingering on her.

"And?" Mama encouraged.

"And," Camden continued, "the guide got us set up on the horses."

"The first time he'd ever been on a horse." Trinity waved her fork at him. "We didn't have Stella or Starla yet."

"Yes, I figured how hard could it be? I've seen kids riding them."

"Took him three tries to get on the horse. That poor horse was about to kneel and help him out." Trinity winked.

"Finally, I got up on the horse." Camden leaned back on the bench seat. "Off we went down the trail, with the guide in front. I'd arranged my plan with the guide, so it was just the two of us with the guide on that specific trail. The sun was starting to set, and wisps of clouds were catching the gold and pink tones. I had the ring tied to dental floss around my belt loop and shoved in my pocket. Fearing I would lose it if it were loose in my pocket, I knew I couldn't conceal a ring box without a jacket, hence the floss."

Everyone leaned forward, eager for Camden to continue.

"The tour guide announced he needed to go check on something, and that was my cue. Trinity and I paused, our horses standing next to each other. We took in the sunset as it inched every minute lower behind the landscape. I was sweating like crazy from nerves, but Trinity didn't seem to notice since I don't handle the heat well, and it was still pretty warm for November to a Chicagoan like me."

Without realizing it, Camden reached out for Trinity's arm and placed his fingers over her wrist.

"The sun was in the perfect spot, so I pulled out the ring, forgetting it was attached to the floss. I had no plan on how to untie it! As I'm trying to free the ring without causing enough of a commotion to make Trinity look over, I accidentally tapped the horse—which he took as a signal for *let's go*. The horse took off. I've got one hand tangled up in the floss, and my other hand gripping the pommel. Trinity and the guide were yelling for me to pull back on the reins, but I couldn't with one hand still stuck around the ring string and the other holding on for dear life."

Everyone at the table had set their utensils down.

"Finally, I freed my hand and got the horse to halt. Trinity and the guide caught up, and I was so elated to see Trinity that I blurted out, 'Marry me, please, marry me.'"

"He was trying to hold the engagement ring out for me, but it was still tied to his belt loop, so he had twisted his body all up trying to present it to me." She covered her hand with his. "It was the most uncomfortable position I've ever seen anyone in."

"It didn't turn out as picture-perfect as I'd planned." Camden lowered his head.

"Quite a story," Elizabeth picked her fork back up.

"Why are you gettin' a divorce?" Mama inquired. "You're young and full of life."

"It's complicated." Trinity lifted her hand from Camden's and returned to eating.

"Ain't everythin' in life complicated? I can't even get my shoes tied correctly no more." Mama's shaky hand reached for her tea.

"Mama, you're in front of teachers." Elizabeth corrected her. "You cannot say *ain't*, and it's *anymore*, not *no more*."

"They don't look uptight to me." Mama grinned. "Now, out with it. Why y'all gettin' divorced? The truth."

Camden focused on his food, making sure he continued chewing so he didn't have to be the one to answer.

"Does it matter? Your daughter denied the divorce until we can fix up our home." Trinity gulped half her sweet tea. "We'll sell it and split any minuscule profits, and we can move on with our new lives."

"It indeed matters, sweetheart." Mama wiped her mouth with a cloth napkin. "There is nothin' you can't work out to save a marriage. Nothin'." Her arthritic pointer finger waved at them. "My daughter was right to rule as she did. You can thank her later."

Camden looked at Elizabeth as she gently nodded her head in agreement.

Trinity picked at her collard greens with the fork.

"We can't have a baby." Camden's words sliced through the room as they did his heart.

Mama's spoon slipped from her hand, crashing on the plate. "Goodness, child, I'm so sorry to hear that."

"We wanted to adopt, but we don't have the funds," Trinity added. "We figured the town had already told you . . . or at least your daughter had."

"Guessin' y'all would be nearly my age by the time you saved up enough, being teachers and all." Mama wiped her mouth yet again with her napkin.

"How about some pie?" Elizabeth slid her chair out, refusing to make eye contact with anyone at the table other than Mama.

"How about some bourbon?" Mama requested.

"Now, Mama, we don't have any bourbon."

"We should," Mama snapped back.

Camden and Trinity glanced at each other, folding their lips inward, holding back laughter over the elderly lady's sharpness. Under the table, Camden's knee touched his wife's knee. He wondered if a shiver ran up her spine as it had his.

Chapter 10

Trinity

Monday morning at eight-thirty on the dot, Trinity parked her truck in front of the tan brick building. It had one glass front door and one solid wood back door. The sign, carved into wood and bolted to the front brick, took up the building's entire front. It read, *United States Post Office, Woolsey, Arizona 85502.*

She climbed from the truck and spotted the only other car in the area parked under a mesquite tree near the back door. The American flag, raised for the day, swayed in the breeze. A small desert garden grew at the bottom of the flagpole. Hardy aloe vera and red yucca added a nice pop of color to the ground.

As Trinity opened the door, a bell chimed. "Sydney?"

A head of bleached blonde hair rose from behind the counter. "Hey-llo, Trinity. I was just looking to see if any letters got stuck in the drop box."

Sydney Hernandez was pushing sixty-five but moved like a ten-year-old and had just as much energy. Her earring loops were bigger than her ears, and she wore more necklaces than most stores sold. Today, Sydney wore a rose-printed dress and a stack of beaded bracelets.

"Let me put on some cappuccinos for us!" Sydney nearly floated around, her feet light and delicate on the floral woven rugs spread around the concrete floor. For as long as Trinity could recall, the rugs were as much a part of the post office as Sydney.

Trinity didn't think a manager came to check on the post office, but if they did, she hoped they didn't cite Sydney for her bare feet and all her personal touches. As the cappuccinos were prepared, Trinity pulled out the solo barstool at the counter and sat at a tiny window on the left side of its five-hundred-square-foot interior. A box fan in the opposite corner, near the bank of two hundred and some PO boxes, hummed and pushed warm air around.

Sydney placed a tiny floral lace cranberry-colored teacup and saucer in front of Trinity. "You're here for my job."

Trinity crossed her arms. "Of course, you already heard."

Sydney took a sip of her cappuccino. "Works out perfectly. I filled out all the forms for you. I need you to sign it so I can send it over to my boss, and then you can start next Monday."

"Thanks, Sydney. I'm hoping you can show me what I need to do?"

"First, don't open the mail unless it's for Margie Woodward. She'll have you open all of her mail. Second, put the letters in the correct PO boxes. Don't be hopped up on espresso and fling the mail all willy-nilly into the boxes. Trust me. It *can* happen. Third, always lock up the office, but don't lock the front door."

"Sounds easy, but why do I need to open Margie's mail?"

"She is deathly afraid of paper cuts." Sydney held her cup with both hands, pinkies out.

Trinity nodded; she understood small fears. She had the worst fear of chalkboards. It was such a horrible fear she purchased the whiteboard for her classroom. Every room in the Woolsey School District had a chalkboard. It was more important for students to have funding for art and music than a whiteboard. Even thinking of it now, the scraping noise made her wince.

Shaking the thought of chalkboards from her mind, Trinity asked, "Tell me about this year's summer trip."

"I'm heading up to Prescott. I'll be staying with my best friend, Sharon. She recently lost her husband of thirty-five years. Not only will it benefit her to have the company, but it allows me to get out of this summer heat."

"I'm sorry to hear about Sharon losing her husband." Trinity sipped the cappuccino. "Have you ever been home for the monsoons?"

"Once many moons ago. I don't care much for the monsoon weather. With my asthma, the dust from the haboobs causes me to reach for my inhalers."

"Oh no, I can see why being up north is better for your health."

"Now, tell me how the house is coming along."

Trinity stretched out her legs and then brought her feet back to rest on the rungs of the stool. "We made a list and gathered a few of the supplies from R. J.'s but haven't started anything. First, we need to head to Cactus City to get the tile and cabinets."

"Did you fix the leak under the sink?"

Trinity rubbed the back of her neck and smirked. "Yes, Camden fixed it. It took him nearly all day. I could have fixed it in ten minutes, but he insisted."

"Repair skills are a good thing for him to learn, especially if he'll be a bachelor soon."

As Trinity pondered Sydney's words, the box fan hummed, making it the only noise in the post office. Camden had gone from his parents' Chicago penthouse to a fraternity house in college before they moved in together and were married. He'd never lived on his own. Come to think of it, neither had she. Trinity had gone from living with her mom to a shared college dorm to the house with Camden. All in all, she was still young and could start over, even if the process was a bit daunting. Not that she wanted to, she wanted Camden. She didn't want to live without him. Life could be cruel.

"Trinity? I asked if you could work through to the last week of August?"

"No, school starts back up again on the eighteenth of August."

"Well, then I'll be back the week before, then. I mean, you're staying in Woolsey after the divorce?"

Trinity set her cup down, and the china clanged slightly. "The plan is to move in with my mom. Hopefully, I can start to save up a little for a place of my own."

Woolsey didn't have low-cost apartments or apartments in general. And houses up for sale were few and far between.

"I'm sure your little argument will mend itself soon, too."

Can one thing in this town be a secret? "I guess I could throw a trailer on her property if nothing comes up for sale once I can afford it."

"She doesn't want you two getting divorced. Nor do I . . . nor anyone else in town."

Trinity muffled a grunt. *Please leave us alone about this. We agree, okay, but cannot do a thing about it.* Living someplace where everyone knew your name could be a bit overwhelming. Even a private conversation with her mom found its way around town. Though she'd admit everyone had been kind about the baby news. They gave their condolences upon the information that she and Camden couldn't have children of their own.

Wanting to move past the discussion of divorce, Trinity changed the subject back to the weather. "You do miss out on some amazing weather during the summer. Especially out here, where we can see the storms building for miles in any direction."

"I'll think of you all when I'm up north sipping my margarita on the patio in the ninety-degree weather." Sydney stood. "Another cup?"

"No, thank you. I should get over to Shop and Save before all the good produce is picked over. I wished more garden veggies grew here in the summer."

Sydney made her way to the Dutch door next to the countertop.

"I'll leave the key with Luis over at the diner. You can pick it up on Monday on your way in." Sydney squeezed Trinity in a hug that smelled of lilies.

She pulled out of the hug and held tight to Trinity's arms. Trinity stood there, feeling like a five-year-old waiting to be told that everything was going to be all right.

"Find a way to make it work between you and Camden. Please, you don't want to be old and single like me." Sydney tilted her head, her lips pouted.

"You love being single, or at least you make it seem as though you do." Trinity moved her hands up, cupping the underside of Sydney's arms.

"I do, but you and Camden are supposed to be together, not apart. The town needs you." Sydney smiled and let go of Trinity.

"Needs us?"

"Yes, we need to keep the town flourishing with good folks and families such as yours."

Trinity's heart sank, showing in her weak smile. Even if they stayed married, they couldn't help the town grow with new life. "Have a safe trip."

"Will do, and don't break my cappuccino machine."

At the door, Trinity paused and turned back. "I won't, but if I do, at least you won't hear about it way up north." She slid on her sunglasses and walked out into the brightness of town.

A part of Trinity wished she could pick up and go to Prescott. She wanted a break from everything. Trinity got in her truck, and it started up on the second try, then she drove the half-mile to Shop and Save, the only grocery store in Woolsey.

Shop and Save resembled something one might stumble upon in Texas in the late seventies. The store had a front porch with a wood deck level to the dirt parking lot. Sun-bleached, trim-lined windows decorated the front. The main door was not automated like the typical grocery store in the city. The top half of the French doors were glass, framed in a diamond pattern.

Trinity reached for the doorknob as it swung open. "Excuse me, Mrs. Moore." The man stepped back inside the store, allowing her to enter. "Have a good day." He carried his groceries in an unmarked brown grocery bag.

"You as well, sir."

She'd seen the man before but couldn't remember his name. He was most likely the parent of one of her students.

Shop and Save provided grocery carts, but they were rarely used over the baskets. First, there was no real spot to corral them up. Second, they were a pain to push through the front door. Third, the wheels stuck in between the porch's wooden slats and the dirt of the parking lot.

Trinity grabbed a worn green basket from the stack and headed to pick out some vegetables. The spring run of carrots and lettuce was all but gone from her garden, but the tomatoes remained. She picked out four potatoes, some mushrooms, and two heads of lettuce. Adding a loaf of bread to the basket and a bottle of wine, she headed to the checkout line, the only one in the entire store. They could easily add another check stand to accommodate customers when the store was crowded. But the store owner, Charlie Tow, liked a long line because it gave residents a chance to catch up.

"Trinity Taylor?" A squeaky voice came from behind her.

Trinity pivoted around, her hands holding the basket in front of her.

"Trinity Taylor, it is you, my heavens!" In one hand, the woman had a basket overflowing with items. In her other hand, she held the small hand of a dark-haired boy, who looked to be about three years old. "It's Rhonda. Rhonda McCarthy."

"Oh goodness, it is you, Rhonda." A smile came over Trinity as she remembered. "It's Moore now. I . . . I'm . . . I'm married."

Their senior year of high school, they'd done a science project together and nearly blew up the school building. Trinity attempted to hug Rhonda amongst the groceries. "And who is this little guy?"

She bent down in greeting, but the boy yanked the lollipop from his mouth. "Stranger!"

"I'm so sorry." Trinity shot back up. "I didn't mean to scare him."

"It's okay. Calm down, Aiden. Aiden! This is Mommy's friend from school."

The kid shoved his lollipop back in his mouth. The grocery store customers returned to what they were doing before Aiden's vocal alarm went off.

"I see you taught him stranger danger skills," Trinity chuckled.

"He takes everything to the extreme; guess it's better than the alternative. How have you been? Other than being married. Do you have kids?"

"How have you been?" Trinity ignored Rhonda's questions.

As far as Trinity could remember, she'd not heard anything about Rhonda and her life since they'd finished high school.

"Moved to Missouri after graduation, met a man, got married, had Aiden. Another one on the way." Rhonda looked down at her belly.

"Congratulations. You can't even tell yet. How far along are you?"

"Only four months."

Trinity smiled, and the line finally started to move forward. "Are you living here again?"

"Yeah, just got in last night. We're staying with my parents. My husband's work keeps him away from home. So, with Aiden and the baby on the way, we decided it'd be best if I were with family until his work travel lessens a bit."

"I completely understand. Is Aiden getting ready for preschool in the fall?"

"No, not until next school year. Are you a preschool teacher?"

"Kindergarten. But the preschool teacher is great."

"So, married, but no kids?"

Trinity closed her eyes as if to find the answers she should use. The line moved forward again, and Trinity loaded her stuff onto the counter. "Yes, married for three years, but we're divorcing."

Rhonda nodded her head but looked as though she held back on commenting. "What a shame."

Trinity paid for her groceries, thanked Mr. Tow, and cradled the paper bag in her arms.

"Again, congratulations on the pregnancy."

"Thank you." Rhonda gave a wave now that her hand was free of the basket. "See you around, I hope."

Trinity couldn't respond as the weight of her impending divorce lumped into a ball in her throat. The thought of how Rhonda had not only one kid but another on the way etched in her mind. Hopefully, her future with a new husband would hold the family she desired, either with stepchildren, the chance at a pregnancy miracle, or a bank account to solve the adoption issue.

Chapter 11

Camden

The door from the garage sprung open, startling him. "Hi." Somehow, he'd missed hearing the garage door opening.

Camden felt his wife's sadness the second she walked in the room as though it wafted off her like steam.

"Hey." Trinity tossed her keys on the edge of the kitchen counter and unloaded the single grocery bag. Her shoulders nearly folded over as she sluggishly moved around.

"Want to talk about it?" Camden inquired.

Trinity paused before turning to Camden. Her eyes were red at the edges, a clear indication she'd been crying. "Rhonda from high school is back in town. She has a toddler and another one on the way. It shouldn't bother me so much, but—Never mind." She waved her hand and bent down to pet Anderson whose tail swished with joy. "I thought it would get easier over time."

"I know it's unfair."

Trinity glanced up at Camden. "Life is . . . well, it doesn't matter. We tried, and we can't. All other avenues are closed. Time to move on."

A lump formed in Camden's throat, preventing him from replying immediately. Not that anything he said could fix it. It hadn't helped a year ago, and it sure wouldn't now.

Trinity's hand rubbed at her neck. She did that when a tension headache started to form. "Let's get started on these house projects. It's a lot to do before the first of September."

He used to massage her neck to help them go away. *Can I do it now? Should I?* Camden made his way over to Trinity and reached his hand out. Adrenaline flowed, and his stomach fluttered like a first date. Gently resting his hand on the back of her neck, he used his fingers to massage the tension away. The warmth and softness of her skin under his fingertips comforted him.

Even though he knew the answer, he wanted to ask Trinity why they were getting divorced. He needed to ask because he needed the reminder every minute of the day. Sometimes dreams crush love.

"Thanks." Trinity reached back and touched Camden's hand. "We need to review the list."

As she brushed him off, he felt as though he'd done something inappropriate. "You're the expert with all the knowledge. I'm essentially your tool boy."

Trinity, midway through a sip of water, started to cough. "Tool boy?" She cleared her throat. "Okay, tool boy. Let's start on demolition first. A clean slate, but only one room at a time."

"What about the flooring?"

She tilted her head and observed their home. "We need to rip up the linoleum in the kitchen and bathrooms, remove the kitchen cabinets and all the baseboards."

"Do we have the funds to cover all the flooring right now?"

"Yes and no. If we get tile, we can't get cabinets until at least the end of July. We need to buy it all at once. Different runs come out slightly different."

"Tile? Color?"

She pulled out her phone and scrolled to her Pinterest app. "I would love to use this style." Trinity handed the phone over, and their fingers brushed each other.

Shivers flooded Camden. He could not keep touching her if he couldn't have her.

"I remember you showed me this." He'd seen the faux wood tile during a home improvement show. She insisted they put it in when they could, and now that they could, she wouldn't be enjoying it for long. "They should have that at the big box store in Cactus City, right?" He handed the phone back to his wife, making sure his fingers were as far away as possible when she took it. "Can we fit it all in the truck?"

"Yes, they will. And yes, the truck will be weighed down and get poor gas mileage, but it'll be cheaper than having it delivered."

Trinity went to the junk drawer in the kitchen and removed the measuring tape. "Help me measure so we can get a rough estimate for how much we'll need for each room."

They moved about the house, measuring out the kitchen and both bathrooms. Camden took notes on his cell phone. Anderson, curious about what was going on, joined them until the measuring tape sliding back into the holder sent him running for cover.

"I'd like to go pick this up today before it gets too late and we get stuck in traffic," Trinity suggested.

"We could get lunch in town," Camden offered.

"Probably would be best if we save our money. Plus, I bought stuff to make spaghetti tonight. If we ate lunch in town, it would be a late lunch."

Camden's mouth watered. Trinity's spaghetti rivaled that of a five-star restaurant. She always kicked him out of the kitchen when she made it, saying it was a secret recipe. He would never be able to duplicate her recipe. It seemed petty to think about the effect divorce would have on his dinners when there was so much more he would miss besides a silly meal.

Camden's thoughts drifted to all the things he loved about Trinity: her caring spirit; the way she knelt when she spoke to kids; how she asked her students important questions that made them beam with joy; her gorgeous makeup-free face; the way she hummed when she cooked because she was too nervous about singing aloud when he was around.

He'd caught her once, though he never told her. Late one night, after a long stretch of teacher conferences, she'd cranked up the music and hadn't heard his car pull in. Camden's hand paused on the garage door's knob as he leaned in close. Loosening his tie, he sat on the garage step and listened to his wife belt out "When the Lights Go Down" by Faith Hill. If it hadn't been so hot in there, he would have remained sitting in the darkened garage listening to her beautiful voice for hours.

"Camden, what are you smiling about?"

"You, singing."

Trinity put her hand on her right hip. "You've never heard me sing." She waved her pointer finger in a disregard motion.

"Actually"—he set down his water glass and moved toward Trinity in quick sweeping steps—"I have. On a rare 105-degree night in May." Without thinking, he wrapped his arms around her waist and pulled her gently towards him. Taking her left hand with his right, he swayed slightly. "You had on one of your Faith Hill albums."

Trinity's face flushed, and she buried her head in Camden's shoulder. "Oh, the teacher conference night," she mumbled into his shirt. "When you startled Anderson and me because we didn't hear you come home. Your smile was far too big to be coming home from parent-teacher night."

She pulled back from his gentle grip, their eyes meeting. Camden continued to sway ever so slightly.

"Well," she softly stated, "never again."

Camden moved his lips towards Trinity's. "That's a shame."

The world around him was muffled as though he were underwater. He wanted to take his hands and place them on the side of her face, his fingertips in her hair. Yet, he knew if he did that, he would kiss her. And he could not do that. If he kissed her, he'd be crossing some unspoken line. *Right?*

Camden glanced at her lips. Her delicate, peony fragrance filled his nose. Trinity leaned into him, her body pressed up against his, and her neck stretched toward his face. Like a breeze, her lips feathered his. He couldn't hold back. Squeezing her into him tighter, he returned the kiss, melting his lips into hers. Camden's entire body tingled.

As she exhaled, their lips parted. Trinity licked her lips. "We shouldn't . . ."

With his arms still wrapped around her waist, Camden nodded. "Right, we shouldn't."

"We should get going to the store."

Nodding some more, he released Trinity from his grip. "Let's wait until tomorrow. It's not too hot out. We should enjoy our week of freedom before we have to start work."

Trinity remained close but no longer in his arms. "Take Stella and Starla out?"

Camden stepped forward, his right hand back on her hip, and nodded.

"Good plan." Trinity shifted from his grasp. "Get changed then."

Trinity pivoted and headed to the garage door, snatching her hat off the rack. She turned her head back around over her shoulder. "Well, we can't get going with you checking out my butt."

"I was—" Camden paused. "Alright, I'm going. You're killing me!"

"Tell me about it!"

Chapter 12

Trinity

After lying awake all night thinking about *the kiss*, Trinity poured herself a second cup of coffee. Taking the paw-print-covered mug by the handle, she and Anderson returned to the front porch.

The sunshine had already heated the landscape. A mild breeze came from the west, and the mesquite tree limbs shifted aimlessly in the wind. The sound of the spinning mini windmill out back filled the morning as the birds carried on their conversations.

Last night's kiss drifted into her mind again, and she couldn't help but smile. It had been over a month since their lips last met, and even thinking about it right now caused her heartbeat to race as she sat on the bench swing. Shivers of delight traveled from her shoulders to her toes.

They weren't getting a divorce because they didn't love each other anymore. They were getting a divorce *because* they loved each other. Because they wanted the other to have the family they'd planned for themselves. Trinity knew Camden blamed himself just as much as she blamed herself—their baby-making areas hated each other. Between her hostile uterus and his low sperm count, in vitro fertilization would not be possible. Even if they had a million dollars in the bank, they could spend ten years trying.

If only Camden's parents didn't hate Trinity and his decision to live "in the country," then they could help out financially, providing at least the option of adoption. Trinity shook her head and took another sip of coffee as Anderson stretched out under the fan. As long as Camden married someone who didn't have fertility problems, he had a chance. And she did, too. If he had the option to have children of his own to carry on his bloodline, then he should.

A pain snapped like a rubber band in the middle of her chest. If she didn't know better, she would think it was heartburn from the dark French roast. Every time she thought about babies, her chest burned and tightened from the stress, sadness, and the inevitable loss that came along with it.

Her desire to mother children had been in her since childhood. She and Aurora carried around their dolls, swaddled in blankets, fed them pretend meals, tucked them into their doll beds, and changed their outfits. Both Aurora and Trinity had grown up as only children and didn't have younger siblings to mother. When Aurora had Willa, she insisted on not waiting too long before having another so the siblings could be somewhat close in age. Unlike Trinity, Aurora seemed to become pregnant if her husband so much as looked at her.

Trinity recalled Aurora's hesitation in telling her best friend she was pregnant with her second child because, at the time, the doctor had just informed Camden and Trinity they wouldn't be able to have children of their own.

When Trinity peered up from her coffee mug of memories, she noticed two figures coming toward her. The intense sunlight backlit them, blurring their features. Anderson's head raised, and he stood, letting out a single bark to alert Trinity, just in case.

"Hey, how are you?" Trinity called out.

It was not like the Hackenburgs to be up and about so early. As they grew closer, she could see they had Jasmine with them. Trinity stepped off the porch, meeting them near the queen palms just off the front walk. "Everything okay?"

Overdramatic panic spread across Ezra's and Wyatt's faces. "We have an emergency," they said in unison. Jasmine kicked her bare feet and let out a squeal.

"Oh no, what's wrong?"

Ezra hoisted Jasmine forward as though she had a smelly diaper. "Here, take her."

Thanks to many teenage years of babysitting, Trinity scooped up Jasmine like a pro. In one hand, she held Jasmine, the other her coffee mug. Wyatt removed the floral baby bag from his shoulder and threaded it over her mug and up onto her shoulder.

They set the Pack 'n Play next to Anderson, who sniffed it.

"Wait, what's happening?" Trinity's brow creased in confusion.

Erza and Wyatt glanced at each other, then Wyatt said, "Fire."

"Yes, a f-fores-st fire, up n-orth," Ezra stuttered.

"Oh, no! I didn't hear anything about it on the news. And isn't it your anniversary today, too?"

"We need you to watch Jasmine for us," Ezra added as Wyatt nodded his head.

"Oh, I . . ." Trinity glanced at Jasmine, who had already wrapped her plump fingers around a strand of her hair.

Jasmine squealed as she yanked at the strand. Trinity leaned her head toward the baby to lessen some of the tension.

"Thank you so much!" Ezra grabbed Wyatt's hand. "We so appreciate it."

"When will you be back? Later tonight?" Panic rose in her voice. "What do I feed her? When do I feed her?"

"You're a natural, don't worry." Wyatt kissed Jasmine's cheek. "Bye, pumpkin."

"We love you," Ezra oozed. "We put her feeding schedule and formula in the bag."

"But when will you be back?"

"Not sure!" Wyatt waved, his back already turned around to Trinity. "Have fun!"

Trinity bounced Jasmine on her hip as she held her coffee mug from spilling. Anderson looked up at her as though to say, What's with the baby? I thought I was the baby?

"Okay, then. We can do this," she said to the dog and the baby.

The front door opened, and Camden appeared in the doorway, shirtless and with gym shorts on. *That's it. I'm changing into lingerie if he's going to walk around like that!* She made her way up the porch steps, Jasmine on her hip without caring that her parents left her with the neighbor lady.

"Why do you have Jasmine?" Camden questioned, his T-shirt in hand.

Yes, please put on your shirt. Those abs are smiling at me.

"Because the Hackenburgs both got called to a forest fire up north. Can you grab that playpen?" She motioned with her head to the item out in the front yard.

Once inside, Trinity set the coffee mug on the kitchen table and slid the baby bag off her shoulder, depositing it onto the kitchen floor. Switching Jasmine to her other hip, Trinity exhaled her mixed emotions. Joy and hurt filled her. How she loved holding a baby, but she wanted to keep her heart in one piece, too.

"So, we're . . . babysitting?" Camden threaded his shirt over his head and set the playpen on the carpet. "For a few hours?"

"For at least a few days, I think."

"Days?" Camden's eyes widened. "Can they do that? Can we do that?"

"It's a baby, of course, we can. We handle Anderson and the horses. We're both teachers, for goodness' sake. In case you forgot, this is why we're getting divorced. If we can't do this, then we don't have to get divorced."

As the words left her mouth, her heart sank to her feet, and Trinity placed her free hand on her chest. The realization of Jasmine filling their broken dreams traveled into their minds, leaving the room silent.

Trinity went to the couch and sat, resting Jasmine in her lap, propping her back up with her legs. After a hilarious round of peek-a-boo, Camden joined them on the couch.

Jasmine squeezed her hand around Trinity's pointer fingers and tried to pull it to her mouth to chew on. "Would you see if they put a teething ring in the diaper bag?"

Camden went to the bag and rifled through the pockets. "I don't know what I'm looking for."

Trinity craned her neck. "Usually, it's a circle shape of some kind. However, it's been years since I last babysat. Probably some fancy tech thing now. Maybe the cell phone has some teething app on it."

"This?" Camden held up a ring-shaped toy.

"Yes, but it needs to go into the freezer."

He placed it in the freezer and returned to the couch. The perfect life surrounded them as she thought about them as though in a snow globe of happiness. Trinity's heart had never felt so at peace as it did at that moment.

"I don't remember hearing anything about a fire up north. Did they say where?" Camden reached out and tickled Jasmine's belly with his pointer finger. Jasmine went into a fit of laughter as she leaned forward.

"Nope."

Ezra and Wyatt were both firefighters with the Cactus City Fire Department. Being such a small town, Woolsey didn't have the funds to support its own fire department. But the town was fine with R. J. coming to the rescue if needed, and the Hackenburgs were always willing to help, as well. However, in all her years living here, she could recall only one house fire. Most fires were from lightning strikes. And in all the years she knew the Hackenburgs, they'd never been called to fight the same fire.

"I'm grateful that although we have the same job, it doesn't hold the dangers of firefighters. It's like getting on the same plane and leaving your baby behind." Trinity ran her thumb over the bottom of Jasmine's bare foot. "And on their anniversary."

"I'm sure everything will be fine." Camden reached out to tickle Jasmine again.

"Do you want to hold her?"

Camden froze. For as long as Trinity had known Camden, she'd never seen him hold a baby before.

"No, you look like you have it handled."

Trinity sat up and lifted Jasmine under her arms. She twisted and hoisted the baby at Camden's chest. "Here, hold her."

Camden resituated himself on the couch and held out his hands as if taking a turkey from a hot oven. Trinity giggled as she placed Jasmine into his arms. He had her sit in his lap, his hands still under her arms supporting her body. "I guess we won't be getting the tile or any demolition done today."

Trinity leaned back into the couch, viewing the sweetness in front of her. "Probably not."

Camden made faces at Jasmine as she took each one in with great wonderment. Trinity's heartbeat was loud in her ears as she watched him with Jasmine. Why couldn't they figure out a way to stay together and have a family? Maybe she could reach out to his parents behind his back and show them that she was worthy of her son's love by becoming more refined. What's a little sneaking around if it saves a marriage versus ends a marriage? If it worked, then Camden could have his parents back in his life, too. Desperate times called for doing the forbidden. Determination grew inside her, like the smile forming on her face.

Chapter 13

Camden

"How are we supposed to know when Jasmine is hungry?" Camden wiped his hand on the dish towel.

"Ezra left a feeding schedule. He taped it to the rice cereal box." Trinity balanced Jasmine on her right hip and held Anderson's tug rope in her left hand as he attempted to pull Trinity over. "I'm starving. Do you want me to cook dinner or feed Jasmine?"

"I can't feed her." Camden shook his head.

Feeding and diaper changes were both beyond his knowledge and potentially dangerous. He'd seen home videos online.

"You can feed her and change her," Trinity offered.

"I have no idea what I'm doing; I'm only a part of this because we're married. Otherwise, the Hackenburgs would never have left Jasmine alone with me."

Trinity let go of Anderson's tug rope as he skittered backward, surprised that the tension on the rope had suddenly been abandoned.

"Then you should do both. You'll need it . . . someday." Trinity kissed Jasmine's cheek.

Camden hoped she was right. He also hoped she could use all her knowledge of parenting long past this brief stint with Jasmine.

"Alright." Camden held his hands out and approached Trinity.

As she handed Jasmine over, Jasmine squealed in laughter.

"Are all babies this happy?" Camden quickly wrapped Jasmine into his arms. He was pleased so far that everything came quickly to him with the baby.

"Not all babies."

"What's that smell?" Camden's nose tried to hide up inside itself.

"Yeah, she pooped." Trinity laughed.

"Are all babies this stinky?"

"Yes." Trinity smacked a new diaper on Camden's arm. "Come on, you big baby."

Camden laid Jasmine on the makeshift changing area—a blanket on the living room floor—as he sat back on his knees.

"You saw me change the wet one; this is the same thing, only stinky." Trinity flopped onto the couch and placed her feet on the coffee table.

"Easy, minus the smell." Camden undid the diaper and winced. "Fast and easy."

As Camden held onto Jasmine's ankles, he pulled wipe after wipe from the container. With neither of them paying attention to Anderson, the dog no longer understood why he was not the center of attention and approached Jasmine's changing area with the rope in his mouth. Then, he dropped the rope so he could smell out the competition.

"No!" Camden shouted.

Trinity sat up as Jasmine started to cry, and Anderson laid down on the edge of the baby's changing blanket.

"Anderson just dropped his rope on Jasmine's dirty diaper." Trinity's surprise switched to giggles as she fell back onto the couch.

"Stop laughing and help me," Camden stated over Jasmine's crying.

By the time Trinity got up from the couch, Camden had placed a clean diaper on Jasmine and picked her up. He rocked her, and her crying calmed. As Trinity bent down to get the rope off the dirty diaper, Anderson jumped up and grabbed hold of the other end of the rope.

"Drop it," Trinity demanded.

Camden's eyes widened, and his mouth fell open. He watched as Trinity attempted to get Anderson to stop tugging on the poop-covered rope.

"Anderson, you drop it right now," Trinity growled. "We love you all the same. You're not being replaced. Now, you listen to me."

Anderson crouched down on his front legs and shook the rope, ripping it from Trinity's hand.

"Drop it." Trinity hunched over, attempting to snatch the rope back up.

But Anderson had other plans. He dead shook the rope before he finally dropped it on the floor. Anderson sniffed the air, recognizing the odor on his toy, and backed off.

"You need to learn to listen," Trinity scolded Anderson as she slowly inched closer to the rope and picked it up in a pincer grasp. "Good thing I love you, Anderson."

"Poop flew off the rope when he shook it." Camden swayed Jasmine in his arms.

Trinity glared at Camden. "Don't worry, I'll put Jasmine in her playpen, let Anderson outside, and we can clean it up."

Trinity dropped the poop-covered rope in the kitchen trash along with the dirty diaper and took the bag outside to the trash can, letting Anderson out with her. When she returned, Camden wrapped his arms around her, but her body stayed rigid in his embrace.

"Come on," Camden whined, "you have to admit that was funny."

Trinity relaxed in his arms. "That was a nightmare." She continued to melt into Camden's embrace, her chest rising and falling against him.

Jasmine's babbling turned into crying, so Trinity went to her and picked her up.

"How about I clean up the poop, and then you get started on dinner. We can feed Jasmine together. Sound good to you?" Camden asked as he let Anderson in and directed him to his dog bed.

"Sounds perfect, thank you, Camden." Trinity removed the rice cereal from the diaper bag along with the tiny bowl and tiny spoon. "Oh no, we don't have a high chair or car seat to feed her in."

"Why would they not leave a car seat?" Camden searched for more little spots to clean up.

"Because they don't want us to leave the other in charge?" Trinity smirked. "Honestly, they probably forgot. They were frazzled, to say the least."

"That makes sense. Yet, also cruel." Camden chuckled. "Not that I would leave all the responsibilities to you with Jasmine. We're partners until September."

As the words left Camden's mouth, his heart twisted. Out of the corner of his eye, he watched his wife prepare dinner with Jasmine on her hip. After he found and cleaned the last of the diaper-meets-rope mess, he released Anderson from his spot and scoured his hands as though preparing for surgery.

"Can you prop up some pillows so we can feed Jasmine on the couch?" Trinity held the baby in one arm as Jasmine reached and squealed for the bowl of her cereal in Trinity's other hand.

"Great idea, look at you with all your parenting knowledge." Camden winked.

Camden fluffed and situated the pillows creating a perfect couch high chair. Then he lifted Jasmine from Trinity's arm and nestled her upright on the couch. Trinity handed Camden the bowl and spoon. He took it with pride, laced in fear.

"She's not going to spit this back up or anything, is she?" Camden sat it at the edge of the coffee table.

"Not sure, let's find out." Trinity backed away with overdramatic steps.

"Let's show her who's boss." He prepared a bite of cereal and placed the spoon in the baby's mouth. She happily accepted it.

Every time Camden approached Jasmine's mouth with a spoon of rice cereal, the baby leaned forward and wiggled her arms in delight.

"She loves this stuff," he called out to Trinity, who returned to preparing dinner in the kitchen. "She gums it up so fast. She doesn't even need a bib."

Anderson rested his head on the edge of the couch. His eyes rose and fell as he glanced at Camden, the bowl, and the baby. The dog inched closer to Camden and let out a whimper.

"You can't have the baby's rice cereal." He petted Anderson's head. "Besides, it's all gone." He showed his dog the empty bowl.

Anderson lunged forward and shoved his muzzle into the bowl, licking the remaining smidge of rice cereal.

"Anderson," Camden scowled but allowed him to finish licking the bowl as Jasmine belly laughed at the dog.

"What's going on in there? It sounds like I'm missing a party." Trinity strolled into the living room, wiping her hands on a blue dish towel.

The smile on Trinity's face sent a shock wave through Camden—a perfect moment that was a reminder of the end to come. The death of their marriage, so that moments like this one could be real. Yet, as he took in the baby, Anderson, and his wife, he questioned the biggest issue of all. *Even if I'm able to have kids in the future, will I feel this way with someone else?*

Chapter 14

Trinity

Camden paced the living room floor with his coffee mug in hand. The house echoed with emptiness without Jasmine there anymore. Her dads came and got her a mere forty-eight hours after dropping her off.

"Did it seem as though Ezra and Wyatt were well-rested upon their return?"

Trinity sat on her knees, scraper in hand at the edge of the kitchen's linoleum floor. "They looked remarkably revitalized after fighting flames for two days." She sat back on her heels. "What are you thinking?"

"Something seems off about the whole thing. We never saw anything about a fire up north on the news."

"Maybe we missed the report. If they were keeping a secret, this town would be whispering it through our windows right this instant."

Camden placed his mug in the sink. "You're right." Then, leaning against the cabinet, he fixed his vision off into the distance.

"I know you're not all that handy, but could you please help me anyway?" Trinity had braided her long hair at the base and twisted it up into a bun. "Camden?"

Camden glanced down at her, his stare blank.

Trinity set the scraper down and moved her legs forward, sitting her bottom on the floor. Ever since Jasmine left, she'd noticed Camden stared off often, clearly lost in thought.

"Yes, Trinity? Did you say something?" he asked.

Trinity sighed, missing the joy which filled the house when Jasmine was theirs. "The weather moving from spring to summer always takes me back to childhood. The box fans humming in every room of Mom's house. The front door open, allowing the last of the spring breeze to sneak through the screen door. Aurora and I had cherry-stained lips from too many midday popsicles while we played Barbies on the living room floor. Our bare feet and poorly painted pink toenails covered in the dirt of the desert."

Trinity would give anything to raise a child here in Woolsey. It would have the same upbringing as she'd had in a town full of community and love; even if it was overbearing at times. The deepest weight crushed her at not being able to picture having a family with anyone other than Camden. Especially now, after the time they'd shared with Jasmine.

"What about your childhood in Chicago? When spring turned into summer."

Camden went to his knees with another scraper and jammed it at the edge of the flooring, and started to move forward, wigging it sideways until it became stuck. Anderson rested on the couch as John Mellencamp played softly on Pandora.

"Depends on which nanny was working. Some years I had a fun nanny, other years, I had a stiff-as-a-stick one. I must have been through about four or five by the time Nanny Eliza started. She lasted the longest until I got her fired."

The kitchen filled with the mild scent of age from the removed linoleum as it exposed the concrete. Trinity watched him from the corner of her eye as she continued to scrape.

"I desperately wished to go swimming in one of those tiny blue pools, like Anderson has outside. I'd seen it in a movie or television show. But we had our ginormous pool inside the penthouse. When I asked my mother for one, she scoffed at the idea. However, I kept bugging Nanny Eliza to get me one without my mom knowing. Eventually, she caved and surprised me with one while my parents were out of town. Nanny Eliza carried it up to the rooftop patio and filled it up with gallons of water she'd lugged up there. I sat, covered in sunscreen, splashing around in this tiny pool as though it was the best thing in the entire world. I jumped and spun around and around as Nanny Eliza laughed so hard she started to snort. She had a cooler next to the lawn chair she'd brought and opened it, handing me one of those ice cream drumsticks. I sat in a pool way too small for me as I licked the ice cream cone and those little chopped peanuts fell into the pool water around me."

"How come I never heard that story before? It didn't even come up when we bought Anderson his pool." Trinity tucked a strand of hair behind her ear, which had fallen out of the bun.

"You know I don't like to linger in my past, especially when I can live vicariously through your *Andy Griffith* childhood."

Another reminder of why she desperately wanted to raise a child in Woolsey.

"Speaking of ice cream, why don't we have a Dairy Queen?"

Trinity's head shot up, her forehead creased. "Dairy Queen?" she laughed.

"After three years, you never cease to throw me with your random questions."

"Yes, every small town in every show or movie has a Dairy Queen."

"There's one over in Cactus City."

"That's forty miles west. And it's not a random question. A random question would be why is football not played from January to June?"

"Because NASCAR starts in February."

"Of course!" Camden threw his hands in the air and rolled his eyes.

"So dramatic," Trinity joked.

Camden placed his hands on his legs. "Seriously, why don't we just tile over the linoleum instead of this tedious process?"

"Because it's not the correct way to do it, it would be a shortcut." She dug the scraper into the floor, the glue still tacky as it gave way, peeling up in one nice long strip. "Are you craving ice cream at nine in the morning?"

"Possibly." He smirked.

"We need to get some of this demo done first, or we'll never be ready in time." She shoved the scraper under another section and lifted the linoleum, running its blade along the concrete foundation until she reached a spot where the glue was dried, snapping the linoleum strip, thinking all the while, *And that may not be a bad thing.*

They loaded their demolished flooring into the empty cardboard boxes in the back of Trinity's truck. There would be many trips to the Shop and Save's dumpster. Trinity had cleared it with Charlie and offered to pay him, but he waved her off, reporting that most of the time, the dumpster didn't get too full anyway.

Once the linoleum floor had been removed, Trinity instructed Anderson to stay in his bed. It was well over 105 degrees, and she didn't want him outside in the heat for too long. With the windows open and the fans spinning, she poured the adhesive remover over the remaining glue left on the concrete. Together, she and Camden scraped up the glue and cleaned the foundation, making the floor smooth and free of debris.

"It will be pretty stinky in here for a while, probably not too safe for Anderson or us." Camden wiped the sweat from his forehead. "It did say pet safe, but still. Dairy Queen?" he winked.

Trinity chuckled and shook her head. "Okay, ice cream cones all around."

They piled into the truck and backed out of the garage.

"Giving up the Mayberry life is going to be more challenging than I ever thought," Camden remarked. "I don't know many places we can leave the house all open like this."

"Giving up on us is going to be harder than I ever imagined," Trinity added.

Dust from the road swirled up behind the truck's tires as they passed the Hackenburgs' home. Wyatt waved at them from the open garage and jogged out to Trinity's truck as she slowed to a stop. Camden cranked the window down.

"Thanks again for taking care of Jasmine." Wyatt rested his fist on the window frame.

"We enjoyed our time with her." Trinity beamed as she leaned across Anderson, sitting in the middle of the bench seat.

"Ezra and I brought you back some wine; we forgot to give it to you."

"You didn't need to get us anything." Camden smiled.

"Indeed, we did. I'll bring it over once you return." Wyatt tapped the door frame with his hand. "Gonna be gone long?"

"Not sure, heading into Cactus City after we drop off the old linoleum in the back. The house is airing out right now from the glue remover." Trinity pushed in the clutch and shifted into first.

"I'll drop it by later tonight, then. Have fun, you three."

Wyatt stepped backwards and Camden half-waved, then rolled up the window. Once they were farther down the road, Camden turned to Trinity. "Who stops to get wine for their neighbors when they're out fighting a fire?"

Trinity glanced at Camden before focusing back on the road. "Something definitely feels off."

"They brought us back wine but didn't remember to bring Jasmine's car seat over?"

"Maybe the fumes from the glue remover are getting to us."

Trinity turned onto State Route 287, but her thoughts were far from focused on the road in front of her. Trinity glanced at their town, shrinking in her rearview mirror. Her little piece of Mayberry.

Chapter 15

Trinity

Trinity licked the chocolate ice cream, rotating the cone. Anderson continued to drool, hoping to get some of their ice cream, too. He'd already gobbled up his tiny vanilla cone in two bites. Camden shoved his long red plastic spoon into his ice cream cup.

The midday sun beat through the truck's side windows. The Dairy Queen needed a face-lift, as it had been unchanged since Trinity's childhood. The sign atop the red-and-white building had neon lights outlining the letters, and a vanilla ice cream cone jetted off the end. It didn't have a drive-through or inside seating, only two walk-up windows and a couple of sun-bleached picnic benches near four parking spots. Cactus City had a population of about twenty thousand, allowing for lines to form relatively quickly at the Dairy Queen on summer days.

"Maybe we could foster a child?" Camden's vision remained on his cup of blended chocolate and vanilla ice cream.

"We discussed this; it would be too hard for me knowing the child could leave at any point."

Camden pivoted his upper body and faced her. "I heard that sometimes the foster parents adopt them if the Department of Child Safety can't find a permanent home."

"The chances of that are far too great to risk. It sounds petty, I know. There are so many kids in the foster system, but I'm even missing Jasmine." Trinity licked more of her cone.

"I am too."

Trinity pet Anderson as drool continued to bubble and fall from the sides of his mouth. The air conditioner ran on medium, keeping them cool. "Do you think if we worked jobs every summer, and on the weekends, we could save up enough to adopt?"

"After the numbers the adoption agency gave us, it would take us about"—Trinity used her thumb, tapping it on her fingers as she counted on one hand—"four, maybe five years. And we would be so busy working we'd never see each other or have time to spend with Anderson."

"Yes, I guess you're right. Plus, we have to add the time it takes to save the funds to the wait for an available adoption."

Trinity's heart collapsed with disappointment. But she wouldn't lose hope just yet. She still needed to place a phone call to Mr. and Mrs. Moore. Over the last several days, she'd rehearsed what she would say and felt more than prepared. The only thing was she couldn't let Camden know she planned to call them. If it went well, she would have no choice, but it wouldn't matter at that point. How could he be upset if it saved their marriage?

"Remember when we came here after our wedding?" Camden asked.

How could I ever forget! "Of course I remember."

"We looked like we skipped out on the country prom." He scooped the final bit of ice cream onto his spoon and into his mouth.

"I loved my dress. I wouldn't have changed a thing."

Camden reached out and took her hand. Trinity's heart skipped a beat like a rock skimming over the lake. "You were beyond beautiful, and I wouldn't have changed a thing either. Well, maybe not getting soft serve all over my tux."

"You started that food fight!" Trinity shrieked and laughed.

"I was trying to help you not drip ice cream on your dress." Camden squeezed her hand.

"So much for that. By the time we finished, both of us were covered in ice cream from head to toe."

"All I remember is that my bride was craving an ice cream cone, and the Shop and Save was closed for the night, and we didn't have any at the house."

"You've been an amazing husband from the start."

"I'm still your husband . . . so we should probably kiss."

"Camden." Trinity's face turned rose pink. The memory of the kiss they'd shared only a few days ago lingered in her mind as though it'd happened moments ago. Her toes tingled, and her fingers went numb in anticipation.

"I'm sorry, I really shouldn't be so forward. Sometimes I try to forget about our future."

As if hoping she could save their marriage by doing the one thing she shouldn't, she grabbed Camden's chin and pushed her lips against his. The cold of the ice cream lingered on their lips.

When they parted, Trinity breathlessly whispered, "We need to stop doing this."

Camden nodded as he pulled her in for another kiss while Anderson lay on the bench seat between them, still pouting about not getting more ice cream.

With the truck bed stacked full of tile boxes, Trinity backed into the garage.

"Trinity!" Wyatt called out as the sun's remaining glow of tangerine and fuchsia faded on the horizon. "Here's the wine. Thanks again for caring for Jasmine."

Trinity took the tanned bottle of wine from Wyatt's hand as Anderson dashed off to potty. "Thank you, but you really didn't need to."

Wyatt held out a box for Camden, which he took. "What's this?"

"Need something to go with the wine, right?" Wyatt grinned. "Again, thank you for helping us out. Can I give you a hand bringing anything in?"

"No thank you, Wyatt, we can handle it." Camden examined the box of cheese and crackers.

Wyatt turned and headed back to his house, lifting his hand in the air in a wave. "Have a great night, you two."

Trinity tilted the bottle so she could read the label in the light of the garage door. "Wow, this is some bottle. A 2010 cabernet . . . from Utah. How far north did they go?"

Chapter 16

Camden

Camden had no idea what to do next. His thoughts were full of Trinity's lips on his.

"It works best if you take the plate to the table instead of staring at it." Lillian patted Camden on the back as she snorted a laugh, letting her hand linger on his shoulder. "So, do you want to talk about it?"

He pulled his eyes from the plate and turned his head to his mother-in-law. "Nothing to discuss. It won't change anything. It is how it is, Lillian." Camden shrugged his shoulders and carried the plates to the customers who waited eagerly to eat.

The restaurant's front door opened, and Alexander glided inside, sunlight wrapping around him as though he'd stepped down from heaven.

"Welcome! Grab any seat you'd like, Alexander," Luis instructed from a nearby table where he sat reminiscing with some friends who'd come in for lunch.

"Thank you kindly. However, I do not have the time to linger. I came to deliver a message to Mr. Moore." Alexander placed his hands behind his back and remained standing near the door.

Lillian came out from the kitchen yet again. In such a small town, she spent as much time cooking as she did chatting.

"No, you must stay for lunch." Lillian pulled out a chair at an empty table near the window. "Now tell me what you're hungry for, and I'll make it. You don't even need to waste time with a menu." She placed her hands on her hips.

Alexander sat, folded his hands, and placed them on the table. "An egg salad sandwich would be rather enjoyable."

"Sure thing, sweetie." Lillian turned toward the kitchen.

Alexander raised his hand. "Ms. Taylor, if I may possibly add some fries on the side?"

"You got it!"

Alexander's face hinted at a smile as Camden approached. "Mr. Moore. Judge Dunn's mother has requested you stop by and see her."

"She did?" Camden crossed his arms. "By chance, do you know Mama's name?"

"I'm afraid I don't. Father and I have been instructed to call her Mama, although it seems improper to me."

"Did she say when she wanted to see me?"

"Yes, immediately. For lunch." He turned his attention to historic town photos placed under the table's laminate top.

"Does she know I'm working?" Camden glanced around the diner.

"She does. That's precisely why she sent me here. She informed me that Luis would understand the importance."

Camden huffed and went to Luis as though he needed to ask a teacher's permission. "Luis, sorry to interrupt, but it seems the judge's mama has summoned me." Camden chuckled. "I clearly cannot leave in the middle of my—"

Luis waved a hand. "No, go on. It's not too busy."

"Are you sure?" Camden slipped his hands into his pressed dress slack pockets.

Waving him off again, Luis returned to the conversation at the table.

Leaving the restaurant with his server apron on, Camden started up his car and drove the two minutes to the judge's house. Upon parking, he untied the apron, tossed it on the seat, and straightened out his button-down shirt and tie. He didn't like pairing his tennis shoes with dress pants, but Luis insisted that he wear them instead of dress shoes.

"Camden." Judge Dunn stood at the opened front door wearing a skirt, flip-flops, and a blouse.

"Hi, Judge . . . Elizabeth. I heard your mama wanted to see me?"

"Yes." Elizabeth held the front door open. "I just set lunch out for you both. I have to be back at the courthouse soon. If you need anything, let me know."

"Thank you." Camden took hold of the doorknob and walked inside before closing it. "Mama?"

"In here, young man. You're late."

As Camden entered the kitchen, he checked his watch—11:32. Mama sat at the end of the table with a napkin in her lap, so he pulled out a chair and joined her. "I didn't know we had a lunch meeting. I surely can't be late."

Mama cleared her throat. "I'll let it be. Please serve us up some lunch, son."

In front of them were two containers, one with a macaroni salad and the other with pulled pork. He assumed iced tea filled the clear pitcher that sat next to a bowl of rolls and a jar of barbecue sauce.

"Grab yourself plenty of napkins. We'll need them for those sandwiches," Mama instructed.

Once their plates were full, Camden asked, "To what do I owe the pleasure of this lunch?"

Mama's trembling hand reached for her tea. "I wanted to discuss savin' your marriage."

"Now, Mama." Camden took a bite from his pulled pork sandwich.

"Hush. I can tell someone dressin' like you, in this heat, comes from money. So, where are your parents? Why ain't they steppin' up?"

"They didn't approve of my marriage." Camden wiped sauce from his fingers with his napkin.

"And why the heck not?" Barbecue sauce rested in the corners of Mama's mouth. Her fingers looked as though she had dipped them directly into the sauce.

"As you mentioned, yes, my parents are well off. However, I *did* come from money. While Trinity is perfect for me, she didn't meet their high standards, and now I *don't*." Camden took a bite of macaroni salad. "Plus, medically speaking, money won't help."

"But adoption?"

"Yes, Trinity and I have discussed adoption."

Mama glared at him, her mouth moving as she chewed.

He continued, "Financially, it's beyond our means to afford adoption."

"It's good seeing a smart young man like yourself wantin' to adopt. There are many children in need of families."

Camden nodded his head in a *maybe* fashion, unable to commit to a full yes or no. *This* was a conversation he didn't want to have. While he enjoyed the company and the food, the conversation only reminded him of his future, yet again. The sadness weighed on him daily, he didn't need this too.

"You would accept any child?" Mama wiped her mouth with the napkin and then folded it, sliding it under the lip of her plate.

"Yes, Trinity and I have discussed it at length. Honestly, Mama, I'm not sure why we must hash this out. It's a moot point." Camden topped off Mama's glass with more tea.

"I'm an elderly lady tryin' to converse with a bright young man about his options to prevent divorce."

Camden set the pitcher down and grabbed himself another helping of macaroni salad. "I'm guessing your daughter didn't make lunch?"

"You're correct. I love her with all I have, and she can cook, but her macaroni salad is horrid, and she didn't have time to properly cook pork today. She picked it up from the grocer."

The "grocer" would have to be Shop and Save. They did a cookout every Saturday, then boxed up any leftovers to sell the remainder of the week. You could smell them smoking on the barbecue all around town. Many residents could be found outside at the picnic tables on the grocery store's porch between eleven and one on Saturday afternoons.

After he and Trinity had bought the house, she'd introduced him to a good deal of the locals during those cookouts. At first, he'd found it incredibly odd that anyone would sit outside a grocery store as though it were a church gathering. For a reasonable price, folks ate buffet-style, moving down the line to collect a meat entree, sides, and drinks. Each Saturday cookout meant sitting with a different resident, everyone feeling neighborly, even if they lived on the other side of State Route 287. Not that the 287 was some big road, but it was the only road in town with a speed limit over twenty-five miles per hour.

Camden missed attending the Saturday cookouts with Trinity. When they'd decided to divorce, they also knew it was best to lay low and avoid major town gatherings. But maybe they could go a few more times before summer was over, for old times' sake.

"Cat got your tongue, son?" Mama's voice broke through his thoughts.

"Forgive me, Mama." Camden wiped the sauce from his fingers.

"Even if your folks don't like Trinity, it might behoove you to speak with them about helpin' out with the adoption fees. You're still their son. Nothin' goin' to change that."

"I did. A while back, when we found out we couldn't have kids and Trinity and I were discussing options. My mother hung up on me. Trinity doesn't know about that."

Mama's spoon fell from her hand, clattering onto the plate. She reached out to Camden's arm and took hold of it. "Well, now. That just won't do, will it? Not on my watch."

"I'm not sure what you mean."

"Never mind, now. My mind is fumin'. My thoughts are on fire. I will hush up about this, as I dare not speak ill of others. Please escort me to the sittin' room. This chair is hurtin' my back."

He assisted Mama from the chair and guided her to the living room. Then he went back and grabbed their drinks, placing them on the end table's coasters.

"My sweet daughter, she never married nor had children. How I always wanted grandchildren. Oh, how my mind is wanderin' off in dislike of your parents." Mama reached for her tea and took a long sip before setting it back down.

Camden glanced around the room, trying to locate any family photos. "I take it Elizabeth is your only child?" The room only held landscape paintings and several small black-and-white photos.

"I came from a family of eleven brothers and sisters. I'm the only one who bore only one child. My siblings all have grandchildren and great-grandchildren. However, Elizabeth always focused on her schoolin' and career. She could've adopted if she wanted to."

"The Hackenburgs adopted their baby girl, Jasmine."

"Yes, they are a delight. They came over and introduced themselves when I first moved here. We have a standin' supper with them every Thursday. My daughter, however, regardless of funds, doesn't want to be a mom. I learned to bite my tongue on the matter many, many years ago. She's happy, and that's all that matters."

Camden smiled weakly. First, he wished Trinity and him were in the same boat as Elizabeth. Second, he hated the reminder of how amazing Woolsey was and how much he would miss it come September.

"You and Trinity have a dog, right?" Mama reached for her tea again.

"Yes. Anderson. We adopted him as a pup from a shelter. Sometimes, I miss those puppy days. We were these new dog parents, unsure how to do anything, and questioning everything. Trinity and I bonded in a whole new way once Anderson came into our lives."

Mama took a tissue from her pocket and wiped her nose. "Puppies are such a joy. I do so miss havin' animals, but my own two feet are enough of a fall risk."

"Mama, I want you to know that regardless of what you might assume with the divorce, I do love Trinity and—"

She raised her hand to silence him. "Hush now. I never doubted that. I saw it when I first met y'all over supper. Listen here, son, life has a way of bringin' what you need without explanation when you least expect it. If it's supposed to happen in our life, it always finds a way. You and the missus work on gettin' your house ready this summer. I have a feelin' your fall will be rather busy."

Camden processed Mama's words. Of course they would have a busy fall. They would be divorced and trying to start over. His heartbeat raced as frustration welled up inside him.

Why did Mama have to repetitively hammer home the obvious?

"If life is as you say, then why are you not a grandma?"

"Liz had her reasons. Even her mother can't argue with a judge."

Camden stood and straightened his tie. "Thank you for lunch, Mama. I should get back to work."

"Thank you for your company."

"My pleasure." Camden stepped forward, then paused and pivoted. He didn't know if he should shake her hand or hug her. *What's proper etiquette?*

"Hug this old lady before you leave, please. I might be dead before I see you again." Mama raised her hands like a toddler wanting to be picked up by their parent. "And have your wife bake me some more of those coconut chip cookies."

"I'll see to it that Trinity makes you some more cookies. And you're not dying any time soon with all your spunk, Mama." Camden leaned down and hugged her.

"You might be right, son. I would cause too much trouble north or south of the Earth for sure."

Just as Camden pulled the front door shut to the judge's house, he swore he saw Mama pick up the landline phone that rested on the end table next to her. The only reason it stood out in Camden's mind was because he didn't know anyone who still owned a landline, let alone someone who needed to jump on it and make a sudden call. Then again, he never called anyone Mama, either—not even his own mother.

Chapter 17

Trinity

"I had lunch with Mama." Camden entered the kitchen from the garage. "She wants another batch of your cookies."

Trinity's right hand gripped a cordless drill as she removed another screw from the kitchen cabinet door. "Doesn't she know we ripped apart our kitchen?" Trinity extracted the door from the hinges and added it to the stack against the wall.

"How come you aren't smashing and ripping the cabinets off? Like on the shows we watch. You know"—Camden raised his hand into the air—"demolition!"

Trinity laughed as she climbed off the counter, ready to power the drill in reverse. "First, because we have Anderson, and he isn't big on wearing safety glasses or staying out of the way." She moved to the next cabinet door. "Second, because I don't want to clean up a huge mess of flying cabinet shrapnel."

Camden loosened his tie. "This is why I think your mom should be helping us out. You should make up with her quickly, please. I have zero knowledge about any of this." He wrapped his now removed tie around his hand. "I'm not a green hammer."

Trinity peered at Camden. "You're *not* a green hammer?"

"You know an expert gardener has a green thumb. I figured since you're excellent at restoration and home repairs, you would have a green hammer. Thus, I'm not a green hammer."

"Green . . ." Laughter shook Trinity's body. "Hammer." Tears formed in her eyes as the laughter turned to uncontrollable giggling.

"It wasn't that funny."

Trinity shook her head as the laughter faded. "Of course not."

Camden headed to the bedroom to change while Trinity continued to work on the cabinet doors. He returned in black basketball shorts, pulling a worn T-shirt over his head.

"What did Mama want? Besides another batch of my cookies." Trinity attempted to look away, lowering her head, but her eyes lingered while they could, ogling his muscular bare chest until the fabric hid it.

"To grill me about my parents."

He could have finished dressing in the bedroom. For a man who didn't know the difference between a crowbar and rebar, he sure knew his way around a barbell. Trinity took a drink of water as she moved her focus to the doorless cabinets.

"She wanted to know if we'd considered adoption." He paused, locking eyes with her.

Trinity's vision was lost in the foreground as her chest tightened with disappointment. Of course, they'd considered it. They'd considered every option short of robbing a bank or stealing a baby.

"Does she know your parents have money?" Trinity set the drill on the kitchen table.

"I'm sure her daughter researched us when we filed the divorce paperwork. It's not like she's swamped with murder trials. And my parents are easy to find on the Internet with a quick search. Plus, Mama said the way I dress gave it away . . . that I came from money."

"Can we not talk about this?" Trinity stared at her gloves. "Not about your parents, my mom, or adoption."

"Right, let me help you with the cabinets." Camden grabbed his work gloves off the kitchen table. They were like a new catcher's mitt. She watched him flex his hands a few times, attempting to stretch them out a bit. "What shall I do?"

"I need you to support the cabinet as I try and get it loose with the crowbar. We'll do the uppers first." Trinity swapped her drill for the crowbar. "Anderson, couch."

Reluctantly, Anderson eased up from the concrete but only made it to the edge of the carpet before flopping down.

Standing on top of the counter, Trinity jabbed the crowbar behind the upper cabinet and pushed it toward the wall. After two more jabs, the wood snapped free from its hold of nails. "I'm trying not to damage the drywall, but we might need a few repairs here and there." Wood continued to splinter and crack as the cabinet snapped off the wall. "The new cabinets will be installed properly. I'm surprised these things held as long as they did with only nails. Maybe all the layers of paint and the grease from cooking adhered them to the wall."

Half on the countertop, half on the floor, Camden took the full weight of the cabinet and lowered it near the pile of doors. "That's one down. I really think I should veto this process. Not only does demolition look more fun, but it would speed up the outcome."

"There're only five cabinets up here. Calm down, Mr. *Not* Green Hammer."

"Alright, Mrs. Green Hammer."

As Camden took the final cabinet to set near the others, something wiggled in a darting motion across the top.

Camden let out a shriek of a nine-year-old girl. His hands released the cabinet, sending it crashing onto the concrete. As he scampered back to the safety of the nearby wall, Camden's hands clenched his chest. "What was that? It was huge!" His voice cracked.

Trinity searched the wreckage to find a tiny gecko hovering in the corner of the cabinet's top. Cupping her hands, she scooped it up. "It's a baby gecko. Open the door. I'll put it outside," Trinity insisted.

"Unless you're taking it over to the Hackenburgs, it's not far enough." Camden shook off his shivers as he made his way to the door.

"We go through this every time you see a gecko. They can't hurt you. They eat spiders, which *can* hurt you. Maybe if you hold it, you can overcome your fear."

Camden's head shook rapidly. "I think Anderson is supposed to chase those." He held the door open, leaning away from Trinity and the beast she had cupped in her fingers.

"No, Anderson loves geckos because they're friendly critters."

"At least put it past the mesquite." Camden pointed at the tree farthest from the house.

"Yes, ya big baby," Trinity called as she stepped off the front porch.

The sun had set but the light held on a bit longer in the sky as the pale blue slipped into deep indigo. As she kneeled, she opened her hands and freed the gecko. It scurried away as Trinity pouted. "Sorry, he's afraid of you."

Standing, she took in the nighttime atmosphere. The crickets started, their stridulations drifting across the yard. Chirping crickets meant there were not any scorpions nearby, a bug she didn't like. Approaching the house, the drawn-open curtains allowed her to see Camden petting Anderson as they sat together on the couch. She chuckled, thinking about his reaction to the gecko. The wild, wild west was not his thing, and she'd learned that rather quickly during their date nights.

Drawing closer to the porch, Trinity reminisced on date memories with Camden. How he'd awkwardly sprung from his chair on the patio of Rock Bottom Brewery when a shiny black bee the size of a quarter had buzzed his head as he forked his bowl of mac and cheese. The scrape of his chair legs slid backward before it crashed to the ground. Did you see that? he'd bellowed, terror across his face. But she'd been too busy trying to keep her drink from spraying out of her mouth to answer him.

Ascending the porch steps, she paused and sighed. She hoped this summer would drag on forever. Trinity's final attempt, a phone call to his parents, was hidden up her sleeve. Although she could pretty much guarantee the outcome, Trinity had to give it a try. She would never get over the regret if she didn't.

Opening the door, the soft sounds of a guitar and piano filtered from the television. Camden stood. "Figure the music would be nice while we work."

Trinity nodded. "Are you sure you can help me?"

"As long as you check for geckos. I don't want any more surprises." Camden shuttered.

She patted him on the back as they made their way to the kitchen. "Come on, you big brave man."

"Don't make fun of me," Camden declared. "When you need a big strong man to . . . to do something . . . strong, then who will be laughing?"

"Me, I'll still be laughing." Trinity picked up the sledgehammer. "We need to free this faux wood laminate countertop from the lower cabinets."

"Now it's all right to make a mess?"

"No, I'm going to carefully hit this upwards, from underneath, no mess, hopefully. It'll make it easier to pry the lower cabinets from the wall. Unless you had another plan?"

He crossed his arms and leaned back against the edge of the kitchen table. "No, you know what you're doing."

With Anderson asleep on the couch, she lowered her safety glasses from the top of her head and took a swing. Since the sledgehammer was heavy in general, it made it difficult to swing in an upward motion. She stood as though she were trying to make an underhanded "granny" basketball shot.

"Looks like all those times you mocked my kettlebell workouts are coming back to haunt you," Camden smirked.

She glanced at her form. It did indeed appear to be the same stance and motion he used with the kettlebell. "I get my workouts the way nature intended, climbing mountains, handling the horses' care, and home repairs." Staring at a workout on television or using a stationary bike bored Trinity. She loved to be out in nature and managed to keep fit doing that. "Some of us don't melt in the sun."

"I don't melt in the sun. I enjoy being out with you, but it's rather warm sometimes when you go."

"It's the desert, of course, it is." Trinity swung up. The front section of the counter popped up. She worked her way around until the entire counter was free.

With Camden's help, they carried sections out to the garage. Earlier, Trinity had taken a Sawzall to the section around the sink so they could keep it operational until the very last moment possible.

She wedged the crowbar between the wall and the lower cabinet's back, working it free. Camden helped by attempting to pull the cabinet forward. As they freed each section of lower cabinets, they moved them to the garage and set them in a line to dispose of later. Then they took the cabinet doors and stacked them off to the side.

"One left, besides the sink section—that's staying for now. Do you want to do the honors?" Trinity handed the crowbar to Camden.

"Thank you." He took it, bowing his head in gratitude. Cracking his knuckles and loosening his neck, he approached the final cabinet to demo. Camden shoved the crowbar behind the cabinet's frame and then pushed it toward the wall to leverage the cabinet free. It popped off the wall in one clean snap. As his lips began to turn up in a smile, something beige with chestnut spots jetted up the wall. With the crowbar clutched in his grip, Camden practically moonwalked twice the speed of light out of the kitchen.

Trinity lunged forward and cupped the three-inch-long gecko in her hand against the wall. By the time she turned around with it secured in her hands, the bedroom door slammed shut, followed by a loud shrieking moan. As Trinity made her way past Anderson on the couch, she snickered. "Maybe this one should go in the Hackenburgs' yard, just to be safe."

Chapter 18

Camden

"There's no way this is going to be an easy process." Camden sighed as he took in the triton pattern of three different brown shades. "How have we lived with this so long?"

They'd moved the bed, dresser, and both nightstands into the middle of the room.

"To be fair, we don't spend a lot of time in here. Nine months out of the year, we're outside. It doesn't leave much time for staring at bedroom walls." Trinity placed her hands on her hips. "I'm not looking forward to this either; I've never removed wallpaper before."

"Remind me why we can't paint over it?" Camden studied the circular scoring tool in his hand.

"The moisture in the paint can cause the wallpaper to loosen and bubble." Determination shined in her eyes.

Camden stepped onto the stepladder facing the wall.

"Exactly. Plus, this house has a swamp cooler, and if the last owner didn't crack a window when they ran it like we do, then we could have mold behind it, and we'd need to replace the drywall."

Trinity took her circular scoring tool and held it against the wall. "Okay, let's get this done. The instructions say to gently push the tool in circles over the paper to score it so that when we spray it, the moisture can get under it."

"Moisture is bad and good. Alright, makes sense." Camden worked his way over the wall, moving the ladder as he went. "At least there aren't any geckos hiding under the wallpaper."

Trinity worked the lower section of the wall as Anderson gnawed his marrow bone on the bed.

"Remember how happy we were when we bought this house?" Trinity paused in her swirling motion.

"We even loved this wallpaper," Camden confessed.

Trinity stood back and observed. "Clearly, we were blinded by love. House love."

They returned to work, slicing the wallpaper section by section.

"Now what?" Camden stepped down from the ladder. "That was easy."

"We need to see if we can peel any of it." Trinity sat on her knees, focused on the bottom of the walls.

Camden kneeled next to her, using his pincer grasp to pull a piece off. "This is worse than trying to take a label off a glass!" he huffed.

"Let's move on to spraying it with warm water." She pushed up off the carpet and went to the kitchen to fill up the spray bottles.

They sprayed a fine mist of warm water on the walls, Camden sticking to the top and Trinity to the lower half.

"Now." Trinity handed him a scraper.

Camden took the scraper to the wallpaper. But it seemed like all he was doing was re-adhering it to the wall. "Why is it not scraping it off?"

"Take your spray bottle and add a little more water and then scrap the area," Trinity instructed with a few strips of wallpaper at her feet.

He sprayed the area again and then dug the scraper in, a little too hard. Not only did the wallpaper come off, but so did some drywall. *Oops!* He was scraping too hard. *It needs to be softer.* He wiggled his shoulders as though the wall was an opponent to be challenged. Camden sprayed another area and gently took the scraper to it, but his effort yielded no results.

"What do we do if this doesn't work? I've seen some kind of steamer used on television."

Trinity had several more piles of wallpaper on the floor. "There wasn't anything for rent within a hundred miles. I looked online, they sell them for about eighty bucks, but I didn't feel we needed to spend money on that unless scraping didn't work. Are you having trouble? It's hard to get the scraper in there without pushing too hard or soft."

"Speaking of." Camden pointed to the gouge he'd created.

"It's okay. We can spackle that up." Trinity's lovely smile lit up her face.

The fact that she went with the flow of anything, like the perfect stream, made him more aware of how much he loved her. He needed to get his mind off the divorce and his poor scraping skills.

"Do you want to talk about your mom?" Camden returned to his attempts at scraping.

"Are you only asking because you want her help around here?" Trinity peeled back a decent-size strip of wallpaper.

"That would be a plus, but no. I miss having her over, and I miss going to see her."

"You can hang out with her. She doesn't hate *you*." Trinity winked.

"She doesn't hate you, either." He waved the scraper at her.

Camden's thoughts went to the day Lillian had shown up at the house for dinner. Trinity had unintentionally left out a sticky note with her father's name and phone number. For as long as he had known Trinity, she'd wanted to find her father, talk to him, and obtain some form of closure. She had no desire to see him face-to-face; she didn't think she could ever do that. But Trinity needed to talk to him, if, for no other reason than to tell him he was a horrible person. And he, hopefully, had bettered himself. Camden had been there for the phone call, which Trinity finally got up the courage to make a week after Lillian had seen the sticky note and stormed out of their house. Her mom had been very adamant about Trinity never searching for him for her and her daughter's safety.

With a trembling hand holding onto his, Trinity had dialed her father's number after blocking their number. In Camden's mind, she was safe. Plus, if her father hadn't come after them when she was a child and first moved to Woolsey, he had no reason to now.

The phone call hadn't lasted but five minutes, and he held her hand the entire time. Trinity's grip turned sweaty from anxiety. She spoke her mind and let her anger, which she held since childhood, go—finally gaining the closure she needed. After the call ended, she took the sticky note and a lighter and set it ablaze before dropping it into the kitchen sink.

"Camden?" Trinity placed her hand on his shoulder. "You zoned out. Is the 1970s glue getting to you?"

"No, just lost in thought." He didn't want Lillian and Trinity to become like his parents and him. "Let's invite your mom over for dinner. I agree one hundred percent with you calling your father, but maybe if you tell your mom sorry, she'll allow you to explain why you went against her wishes."

"Maybe I should say sorry. I hate this separation between us, especially now."

"You need her."

Trinity nodded. "Okay, but you invite her over next time you're at work. She'll be more likely to say yes if it comes from you."

"Deal, but only if you show me why I'm unable to remove this wallpaper like you." Camden clenched his teeth, fearful of his subpar handiwork.

Chapter 19

Trinity

"May I please speak with Mrs. or Mr. Moore?" Trinity's voice quaked.

She sat upon the swiveling barstool, drumming her fingers on the counter of the minuscule post office. Anderson had made himself at home, stretched out, half on the floor, the other half on the rug near the box fan. She loved being able to bring her dog to work every day. It made him less hyper when she got home and wanted to unwind. Thankfully, Anderson had calmed down a great deal from his rambunctious puppy days, which had lasted for years after his adoption. He could play fetch for hours upon hours in the yard, requiring a nightly bath to rid him of all the dust.

"Hello, this is Mrs. Moore speaking. How may I help you?" Mrs. Moore's voice was sharp and stern through the line.

Trinity nearly dropped the phone attempting to switch hands. "This is Trinity, your son's wife."

"Why yes, I assumed it was someone from that dreaded town by the area code on my caller ID. My secretary usually asks who's calling. However, it slipped her mind. Now, how may I help you?"

"I wouldn't call you about this if I didn't absolutely need to. And I don't like asking for a handout, so I want to make sure you know that." Trinity took a deep breath. "I hoped you could find it in your heart to assist us with adoption fees so your son and I can have a chance at being parents. We're filing for divorce because we can't have children of our own and we can't afford the adoption fees."

Silence.

Trinity swallowed her pride. "I know you love your son, even if you don't like me. And he wants children . . . with me."

"Ms. Taylor," Mrs. Moore interjected, making it known that she didn't want to associate Trinity with her married name. "While we love our son, we did not support him in his decision to marry you and throw away his life in favor of some dusty, disheveled community. We would much rather he be a single father and adopt a child on his own than be married to you with one. He's more than welcome to come home and return to being a part of this family. We have already discussed this with Camden. Why don't you give him the life he deserves and free him of your marriage? You say you love him. Do the right thing."

Trinity held back tears, but the lump in her throat caused her voice to weaken and crack. "Because I want a family with *him*."

The hate she harbored for Camden's parents was similar to how she felt when she watched those news reports of a mistreated dog. While his parents could give the world to her wonderful husband, they chose to ruin his life from afar. Maybe this whole thing was supposed to happen. Camden would be better off without her.

"Mrs. Moore, looks like you'll get your wish."

"Perfect, it's about time. Goodbye, Ms. Taylor."

The call ended, and Trinity set her phone down. So, Camden had already reached out and asked them. If she had known, she never would've made the heartbreaking call. Not only was their last hope officially dead, but his mother hated her for no good reason at all. Trinity felt as small as the dust in the desert air. The words of Camden's mother echoed in her mind, spreading doubt within her. There had been a few moments each day where Trinity had a seed of hope that some way, somehow September 1 would be the day they went to Judge Dunn and told her to rip up the divorce paperwork. Never having wished harm to anyone before, she sure wished it on Mrs. Moore right then. A broken foot or arm or losing their fortune sounded good.

Before Trinity's mind grew any darker with the thoughts, the bell chimed above the door. Anderson sprung from a deep sleep and placed his paws on the counter to see who entered. She shook her head as if doing so would release the hurt she had endured moments ago and re-centered herself.

"Oh my, are you alright, Trinity? All the color has gone from your cheeks." Margie Woodward, the resident who needed all of her mail opened, breezed up to the counter. She appeared in an outfit that one would wear on a safari deep in the heart of Africa.

"I'm fine. How about I make us a cappuccino?" Trinity suggested, standing from the stool. She pet Anderson on the head, his paws still poised on the counter.

"Even though it's only nine in the morning, and already ninety outside, I think I shall take one." She sat on the barstool on the other side of the counter. "Anderson, should you be up there?"

Anderson whined and placed his paws back on the ground.

"Good boy." Margie set her sunglasses on the counter. "Oh, are these your famous eggless cookies?" She gestured to a plate of cookies near the cappuccino machine.

Trinity placed Margie's periwinkle lace cappuccino cup on a saucer in front of her. "Yes, please have one. It was difficult without the counters, yet, I made a batch for the judge's mom, so I made an extra batch for anyone stopping by for their mail."

Margie took one from the stack and bit off a piece. "You need to talk to Luis about putting these on the menu and also over at Shop and Save. Charlie should give you a little basket in the checkout lanes. There are lots of folks with egg allergies, not to mention they're scrumptious."

"Thank you, but I don't want to step on my mom's toes over at the restaurant. Especially right now." Trinity took a sip of her cappuccino, reminding herself not to let her pinky finger raise in the air. She didn't know why—she wasn't classy in any way, shape, or form—but it went straight up as though an old habit when holding such a dainty cup.

"I don't think your mom would feel that way. I know you two need to make amends, but now that the color is coming back to your cheeks, tell me—what's wrong? I think this is beyond Lillian."

Trinity shook her head. "My last hope."

Margie took a double sip of cappuccino and finished off the cookie. "Don't ever lose hope, dear, never." She took her hand and placed it over Trinity's. "There is always hope to be had."

A smile, though weak, warmed across Trinity's face. "Unless a baby falls from the sky in a monsoon, I think this one is done."

"Now, now." Margie shook her finger. "I won't hear of this negative talk. You've opened my mail, I presume?"

Trinity placed a stack of mail wrapped up with a rubber band on the counter. She'd used the metal mail opener and sliced the envelopes first thing in the morning. Margie removed the junk mail and stacked the magazines in a pile next to the opened letters. Trinity had not seen anyone receive this many letters since she could remember. They weren't bills but letters with stickers on the closures and animals on the return address labels. Trinity didn't think the post office had much use anymore outside of Christmas cards and presents.

"Margie, do you have a birthday coming up?" Trinity took a long sip.

"No, not at all."

"You always get this many letters?"

"Oh, yes, of course. How else will I know what's going on with all the family members?"

"Email? Phone? Social media?"

Margie shook her head. "Oh, dear. Heavens no. An occasional phone call, yes, but none of that internet stuff. That's how they track you. No thank you."

Trinity's eyebrows rose. *What could "they" be tracking? Margie's horses?*

"We don't discuss anything important over the phone. That's what the letters are for."

Margie pulled the letters and cards from their envelopes. Seeing all the cards caused Trinity to miss the connection of receiving a handwritten letter on paper. The way the ink soaked into the page. The way it grabbed hold as though a branch of life was etched on it. She thought of the letters and notes she had saved in a cedar chest where she kept all her important treasures. Inside, a collection of items she'd gathered over the years with Camden were safely stowed away. He had a way of putting things in writing that he could never manage to perfect in speech. Thinking of her most favorite note from him—a scrap piece of paper declaring how much he loved her—she beamed. Camden had covered it in tape and hid it under a bar of soap for her to find when she showered.

"Trinity?"

Trinity looked up from the cappuccino cup clutched in her hand. "Yes, sorry. Did you say something?"

"Nothing important. Thank you for the cappuccino." Margie stacked the cards and letters with her magazines. "I'd best be getting back home before the sun bakes me through my car windows. I'll see you next Monday."

The bell chimed, pulling Trinity from a fog of memories, announcing Margie's departure. A burst of heat from outside traveled towards the counter, reminding her that summer had most definitely arrived.

June was usually the most challenging. Residents hid from spiking temperatures and dry air, waiting for the summer rains. Last summer, there had been only a few monsoons, and every resident hoped this year would be different. While flooding caused issues, and lightning presented the possibility of wildfires, there was nothing like the sweet smell of rain in the air, bringing the land to life with the downpour. A town of brown suddenly transformed into a forest of greenery. Yellow and purple flowers blossomed, causing dragonflies to fill the air and butterflies to dance upon the bushes.

The door chimed as more residents filtered through with hellos and pets for Anderson, munching cookies and gathering their mail. After two hours, the plate of cookies sat empty and the trash can had filled with junk mail tossed by residents on the way out. Trinity emptied the trash into the larger container and sorted the mail that had come in an hour ago.

Glancing at the empty cookie plate, she rested her head into her palms as her elbows pressed firmly on the counter. Maybe Margie had been onto something about the coconut chip cookies. If Shop and Save carried them, as well as Luis's restaurant, it might bring in extra money. She would need to buy supplies in bulk, though, and that would require a trip to Cactus City. Then again, her kitchen currently wouldn't have the capabilities to handle all those batches. Trinity thought of her mom's large kitchen with ample counter space and a double oven. *I wouldn't be taking away anything Mom cooks or bakes at the restaurant, simply adding to it.*

Trinity pulled out a notepad and started to add up costs. Joy and hope returned to her heart all because of Margie. Maybe she and Camden were not entirely out of options after all.

Chapter 20

Trinity

Grateful for the steady pace and calmness of sorting mail and putting it in the boxes, Trinity hoped her mind would forget Mrs. Moore's harsh words from that morning. As though she'd sent out a mental distress signal to her husband, Camden entered the post office.

"Trinity?" Camden called out.

She popped her head around the corner. "You brought me lunch?"

In his hands, he held a dinner plate with a sandwich, fries, and a bottle of water. "Yes. I didn't see you pack anything when you left this morning." Camden set the plate and water on the counter.

As Trinity stood opposite her husband, she could smell her mom's magnolia perfume on Camden. She always smelled of warm, sweet magnolia and transferred the scent to anyone who hugged her.

"How many times has Mom hugged you today?" Trinity laughed.

"At least twice."

"Did you ask her about coming for dinner?"

Camden rested his hand on the counter. "Yes, and she agreed."

"Good, because I don't have another option if I want to stay in town. I can't impose on Aurora. Honestly, I thought she would be over it by now. It's been two months."

"She genuinely seemed happy." Camden rubbed his chin.

Trinity sighed, tilting her head. "Thanks for lunch. Are you staying to join me?" She eyed the turkey club sandwich.

"Luis had a mad dash of customers coming in. The Lawrence family is throwing a baby shower for—"

Trinity paused as she picked up her sandwich.

"I'm sorry, forget I said that." Camden leaned over to pet Anderson on the head, both his paws on the counter.

"It's fine. Really. Thanks for lunch." She desperately wanted to confide in him about the phone call with his mother this morning but knew it would only upset him. And the only way to keep a secret in this town was to keep it locked inside your mind. Trinity didn't need to spread her anguish to Camden. Especially now with the possibility of ending the distance with her mom.

"I'm glad you can have Anderson here with you."

"Me too, but surprisingly, it's rather busy with residents coming and going."

Camden continued to pet Anderson in the same spot on his head. He had the habit of making repetitive motions when he was deep in thought or unsure what to do next. When they started dating, he used to take his thumb and rub it in circles on the top of Trinity's hand as though gaining the courage to lean in for a kiss. That tell had lasted for months, with him later declaring that he still fought off butterflies when he was around her.

"Are you sure you don't want half of the sandwich?"

"Yes." Camden withdrew his hand from Anderson's head and checked his watch. "I'd better go. Have a great rest of the day."

Anderson let out a whine and placed his paws back on the ground before shifting his focus to Trinity and the smell of turkey from the sandwich. She finished lunch, tossed a slice of turkey to Anderson, and returned to sorting the mail.

The bell over the door chimed, and Trinity peeked to see who it was through one of the mailboxes. A straw sunhat, which looked as though it belonged to Scarlett O'Hara, appeared. Under it, Mama, with cherry red lips.

"My, my. This heat," Mama stated. "Hello . . . Trinity?"

Trinity moved to the counter and found not only Mama but Judge Dunn, too. "Elizabeth, Mama, hi."

"Mama insisted we pick up her mail during my lunch break. She has something to ask you, as well." Elizabeth unwrapped Mama's arm from her own and put the key in the mailbox.

"Yes, Mama?"

Mama shuffled towards the counter, and Anderson popped his paws up on the counter, causing Mama to gasp.

"Your dog nearly sent me to my grave." Mama grabbed her chest. "He is darlin', though."

"Sorry, Mama. Anderson, get down." Trinity pushed Anderson down with the back of her arm. "Camden dropped off your cookies this morning, correct?"

"Yes, thank you kindly, he did. I heard you're rather handy, maybe even more so than R. J."

Where's she going with this? Trinity furrowed her brow.

"I'd love to have a screen door for the front. I fear I'm missin' home somethin' awful, and it would help bring a sense of that back."

"You want me to build you a screen door?" Trinity asked. "I'm afraid you won't be able to have much use of it except during the monsoon weather until the fall." Trinity leaned on the counter, hands clasped together as if in prayer.

"I don't care none about that. I want a screen door," Mama demanded, her right hand in a fist. "I would have asked your hubby, but his hands seem softer than mine."

Trinity bit her lip to keep from laughing. The vision of what a screen door might look like if Camden attempted such a building venture was comical. "Sure thing, Mama."

"I sketched it out for you. And here are the funds to cover materials." She removed a small white envelope from her purse and slid it across the counter to Trinity.

The sketch on the envelope was a basic screen door frame, with a strip of wood running diagonally to stabilize the middle on both top and bottom. Trinity could build the design in about thirty minutes. The hardest part would be attaching it to the frame of the front door. "I'll need to come over to take some measurements."

"How about tonight, after work? Bring your hubby. We can do supper."

"Mama, Gavin is comin' in tonight." Elizabeth stepped behind Mama, grasping a stack of mail.

Mama waved her hand as though a fly buzzed around her ear. "I didn't forget."

"I'd hate to interrupt family time." Trinity played with the wide hammered-silver band on her right middle finger.

"Gavin won't mind." Mama waved her hand again.

"Should I bring anything to eat? Or maybe some wine?"

"Just bring yourself, your hubby, and a tape measure. I only hope there are some of your cookies left by supper." Mama winked.

"Come on, Mama. We'll see Trinity later, and I need to get back to work." Elizabeth took Mama's hand and guided her toward the door.

"I need my lunch. Black-eyed peas with pork." Mama's feet shuffled forward.

"Mama, I don't have time to whip that up."

"Hush now. Yes, you do. Drive fast." Mama turned around, her face almost entirely hidden by the hat. "See ya soon, honey." She waved as the judge opened the door.

The thought of not having to cook for one night allowed Trinity to breathe a bit. But her mind continued to wander. *Who's Gavin?*

Something was going on in this town; Trinity sensed she was outside a secret. While it didn't happen much, she knew in the back of her mind that something in town was building with anticipation. Plus, she and Aurora had spoken so little lately, a sure red flag that she was hiding something.

With a cell phone in hand, Trinity called Aurora, but it went to voicemail. Maybe she was busy with the girls. Trinity pulled the lip balm from her pocket and applied a thin layer. She peered over at Anderson.

"Need to go potty?"

Anderson's ears went back, and he spun in an excited yes. They made their way outside through the post office's front door. The building, surrounded by Indian rosewood trees, provided much-needed shade from the noon sun. A slight breeze filled the air, causing the halyard and snap clips to clang against the flagpole. Trinity took a few steps closer to State Route 287, checking out Breakfast, Lunch, Dinner & Everything in Between.

Blinking as though she saw something off, she jetted her head forward. The parking lot overflowed with cars. After glancing at Anderson, who sniffed around at the flowers, she took a few more steps toward the road. Cars spilled out from the Hammer and Nail parking lot, too. How many people were at the Lawrence's baby shower? Did this many people even live in town?

Removing her cell phone from her jean pocket, she called Camden. On the fifth ring, he answered. "Hi. Everything all right?"

"Yeah, I'm outside with Anderson, and there are a ton of cars at the restaurant."

"Oh, I'm not there. Luis sent me over to the library to drop off lunch for William and Alexander."

"Were there all those cars when you left?"

"No, just the normal crowd, plus maybe a few extras for the baby shower."

They ended the call, and Trinity slid the phone back into her pocket, giving the crowd of cars one last look.

"Come on, Anderson. We don't eat flowers." Anderson gazed up with sad eyes. "Don't give me that look."

Anderson reluctantly followed Trinity back inside, stopping to lap up water before preparing for another nap on the floor. Then, with the post office silent, she noticed when a stream of vehicles on State Route 287 roared by. While there were houses spread all over Woolsey, traffic was unheard of in town unless you counted three cars at a stop sign as a traffic jam.

"What's going on around here?" Trinity asked a napping Anderson, who opened his eyes for a brief second. She continued to stuff mail into the boxes until her cell phone alerted her to a text message.

Camden: Back at Luis's, there's no one here. It's a ghost town.

Trinity reread the text before replying.

Trinity: Did you see any cars leaving?

Camden: I did. A whole line of them at the stop sign.

Trinity: Do you feel like we're missing something?

Camden: I think so.

Chapter 21

Camden

Camden didn't want to admit it, but when he parked in front of Elizabeth's house, he couldn't wait to eat whatever Southern artery-clogging meal the judge had prepared.

"Great call on the mums," Trinity said, climbing from the car. "It seemed wrong to show up without bringing anything."

Camden glanced over the top of the car to where the sun had started to set behind Trinity's head. Making his way around the hood of the car, his hand grazed the small of her back as he allowed her to go first on the path to the front door. Trinity gave the door a once-over as the wheels of construction turned in her mind. Sunlight captured the natural highlights of her hair, and her sunglasses rested on top of her head, holding the strands back from her face like a headband. Camden observed her as she worked the tape measure and tapped a note into her phone.

"What?" Trinity moved her hand to her face. "Do I have something on me?"

Camden shook his head as the front door swung open, Elizabeth on the other side.

"I thought I heard someone. Welcome, please come in." Elizabeth opened the door all the way and stepped behind it.

"Thank you. I'm just getting measurements for the screen door." Trinity hooked the tape measure onto her belt.

"Yes, thank you so much for doin' that for Mama. She's missing home somethin' fierce, and I fear perhaps movin' her at her age was a poor decision."

When Elizabeth closed the door, she motioned for them to follow her to the kitchen, where they found not only Mama but a man their age wearing a cowboy hat.

"Pardon me." Mama moved to hug Trinity and Camden. "Gavin, this is Trinity and Camden."

Gavin leaned against the kitchen island. A gray shirt was tucked into the front of his jeans, and he sported a belt buckle made of silver. A tattoo peeked out from the edge of his sleeve.

"Why, hi. I'm Gavin." He tipped his hat with one hand and shoved the other hand in the direction of Camden.

Camden took a step forward, switching the flowers to his left hand, and shook Gavin's hand. His grip was as firm as Camden expected, so he returned the shake with as much strength as he could muster.

Trinity reached her hand out, but Gavin pulled her in for a hug instead. "No handshakes for the ladies."

Camden cleared the lump of jealousy from his throat. "These are for you, Mama." He attempted to push the flowers between Gavin and his wife as the hug lasted a lot longer than needed.

"Quite an observant man." Mama beamed. "You took notice of the mums on the place mats."

"Please, everyone, have a seat." Elizabeth motioned to the chairs around the table. "Camden and Trinity are preparin' to divorce." Mama eased into her chair with Gavin's assistance.

"Mama!" Elizabeth scorned.

"I wanted the cat out of the bag before it tore it up, is all."

"It's alright, Elizabeth. It's not a secret." Camden and Gavin reached for the same chair to pull out for Trinity.

Trinity eyed them both and sat down as Camden helped her scoot in her chair.

"I'm sorry to hear such news. What a pity." Gavin sat. "But y'all are hangin' out together still?"

"Yes, you might want to ask Elizabeth about that." Camden's voice was snarky.

"I court ordered them to complete the restoration on their home before I grant the divorce. They have until September 1." Elizabeth set a shallow bowl of shrimp creole on the table, followed by a basket of sliced French bread.

"Lizzy has always been a believer in keepin' things old school. Divorce is not somethin' she grants often." Gavin leaned back in his chair, taking in the feast before him.

"Did she prevent you from divorcing, too?" Trinity inquired.

"Heavens, no, Lizzy was my babysitter. The only thing she prevented me from was gettin' was into the ice cream."

"Amazing. You've stayed in touch all this time?" Trinity took the basket of rolls from Camden and passed it on to Gavin.

"Yes, we were neighbors before Lizzy moved. So when I heard Mama was missin' home, I decided to visit and bring a little bit of home to her. Also, I wanted to make sure she wasn't gettin' herself into any trouble."

Mama reached out to swipe Gavin's hand. "Now, you hush. Y'all know I don't get myself into trouble."

Light laughter filled the kitchen as they all knew better.

"How long are you in town for?" Camden prodded. Every time he glanced over at Gavin he swore the cowboy was staring at his wife.

"Not sure, maybe a few days, maybe a week. I just finished up on a house, and I'm in between jobs until the next one starts up."

"Gavin does restoration work, preservin' the history of homes." Mama watched as Elizabeth loaded her plate with steaming shrimp creole.

Camden coughed, choking a piece of bread in his mouth. "You asked Trinity to build you a screen door?"

"My, my. I guess it simply slipped my mind." Mama returned her attention to her plate. "Senior moment."

However, Camden knew that while Mama was no spring chicken, she was still sharp as a tack.

Gavin looked at the elderly woman. "I can make you a screen door, Mama. I'm sure Trinity has plenty to do around her house." Then he turned his gaze to Trinity. "You know, Mama suggested I might be of some assistance with your home." Gavin leaned his head so his hat blocked all of Mama's face from Camden's view. Wasn't it rude to wear hats at the table?

"That would be amazing. We could always use an extra set of hands." Trinity smiled shyly. "Especially experienced hands."

"Because I know absolutely nothing." Camden clenched his jaw.

Trinity's head nearly snapped around at Camden. "That's not true." Trinity picked at her shrimp with her fork, clearly bothered.

He appreciated Trinity standing up for him, stroking his ego when it was a flat-out lie. The tinge of worried jealousy towards Gavin should have numbed a bit. But the Southern cowboy who clearly could fix anything made him beyond worried. Not that he didn't trust Trinity—he did. He just didn't trust the Southern romance novel cover model.

"It's a learning process." Camden set his glass down. "Trinity and I are more than capable of handling it. But thank you for the offer."

"If you should change your mind, make sure to give a holler," Gavin stated.

Give a holler? Sure, Camden thought, if he reckons. Maybe Trinity needed more help than he could offer. He didn't want her to hurt herself doing something too strenuous. "Thanks, Gavin. We appreciate it."

"I have some horseback riding planned down in Bisbee for a few days, but otherwise, my schedule is pretty open if y'all need me. As long as it's okay with Mama." Gavin looked at Mama.

"As long as you're here for supper each night, that's all I ask." Mama's smile warmed like a glowing candle. "Trinity, don't y'all have horses?"

Trinity nodded her head, finishing the bite in her mouth. "Yes, I'd be happy to take you out if you want to save some money. Starla is a great horse, and so is Stella."

"Gavin might enjoy seeing the beauty of the high desert," Camden added.

"I've not yet had a chance to explore your hometown."

Great, just great. Not only did Camden have to try and out-restoration him, but now he had to out-cowboy him too. "Trinity and I both work during the day, so I'm afraid it wouldn't work out well."

"I can spend the day with Mama until Trinity gets off work . . . assumin' there's still plenty of daylight in the evenin'?"

"Yes, indeed." Trinity wiped her mouth with a cloth napkin. "I should warn you, though, it's mighty hot out this time of year, especially in the evening."

"Heat doesn't bother me a bit." Gavin grinned.

Of course it doesn't. Camden tossed his fork, and it clanked on his plate. All eyes moved to Camden as he thought quickly to save himself from embarrassment. "Sorry, fork slipped." But he didn't think anyone at the table bought it. He shouldn't allow himself to be upset or even jealous. Come September, the men will flood to Trinity like monsoon rain to a wash.

"What are y'all doing for your home renovation?" Gavin asked, slathering butter over his bread.

"We're replacing the linoleum flooring in the bathrooms and kitchen with tile. We just removed the main bedroom wallpaper. The biggest challenge will be the dated kitchen. We removed the cabinets and countertops, and will be installing prefab cabinets, since they are much cheaper, and we'll paint them ourselves. The carpet is in good shape, so hopefully, we can keep that. We need to replace the toilets and baseboards. I hope we can update the bathroom vanities, but we're not sure. We have a limited budget." Trinity sipped some iced tea. "The countertops worry me the most. Everyone wants high-end, which means—"

"Granite," Gavin interjected.

"Exactly." Trinity waved her empty fork. "I'd love not to have to do laminate and do concrete countertops, but I don't have the skill set. Or the funds to risk messing it up."

"I just did a concrete counter in Louisiana. I could do it for you."

Camden rubbed his forehead. Of course the cowboy knew how to do what Trinity wanted.

Trinity reached out towards Gavin, touching his wrist. "Could you? That would be amazing! Right, Camden?"

Camden nodded his head, but the words stuck in his throat until he finally scratched out, "Yes, that would be. Thanks."

"No problem." Gavin patted Camden's shoulder.

"Ain't that somethin'? Y'all will have the kitchen of your dreams." Mama winked.

Camden's heart sank. *Not long enough to enjoy it.* He needed to change the subject. "Gavin, do you know Mama's name? She insists we call her Mama."

"I do, but if Mama wants you to call her Mama, then you best do it." Gavin winked at the old woman.

Camden returned his focus to his plate but couldn't shake a suspicious feeling. All the cars at the stop sign today, Mama asking for Trinity's help with constructing a screen door when Gavin the Cowboy Handyman was a willing helper, the wine from Utah for watching Jasmine but never hearing about a fire up north. Plus, Mama's investigative adoption questions were just as suspect as her throwing a cowboy at his wife. Something didn't add up. And he started to think Mama might be running the whole show.

Chapter 22

Trinity

Trinity checked her phone for the third time since she and Camden arrived home from supper. They shared the couch, with Anderson in the middle, as music played on the television and a home improvement book rested in her lap.

"What's on your mind?" Camden gulped ice water.

Trinity turned to him and folded her legs onto the couch under her. "Remember all those cars I saw earlier today?"

"Yes." He set his glass on a coaster.

"I called Aurora, and she never called me back. I haven't spoken to her in days. Which is so unlike us."

"Did you find it odd that Mama asked you to build the screen door when she has a professional carpenter staying with her?" Camden turned toward Trinity, his left leg resting on the couch.

"I didn't buy the senior moment, either. I mean, why ask me when only two hours later Gavin was arriving?" Camden scrunched his face in disbelief. "Yeah, you're right." Trinity snatched her wine glass from the coffee table. "Did dinner seem like a setup?"

"Yes!" Camden slapped the side of his knee. "Mama was pushing Gavin like a prize onto you. She must have requested the screen door so she could show your handy skills off to him."

Trinity leaned toward Camden, resting her arm on Anderson's side. "But why?"

"First, you didn't have to offer horseback riding to him."

"Way to veer off subject." She smacked his leg. "I thought it would be a nice gesture. He can help us. He knows a lot more than me. Imagine how much quicker we could knock out the kitchen. Plus, the countertops I've always wanted." Trinity placed her hand on her chest. "Concrete countertops."

Camden glanced at what was left of their kitchen.

"Think how fast I could be back to making dinners, desserts, and my cookies again. Plus, I'd get to use it for a little bit before we move."

He sighed in defeat. "You make a decent point."

"Decent?" Trinity smirked. "Okay, Mr. Not Green Hammer."

She turned over the book in her lap, swirling the wine around with her elbow resting on the couch's armrest.

"Fine, it was a good idea to invite the cowboy horseback riding. But don't tell me he's not sweet on you."

Trinity turned to Camden. "Sweet on me. Why, whatever do you mean?" The words rolled out Southern-style as she batted her eyelashes and giggled. "You're always welcome to join us."

"On what third horse?"

She tapped her silver ring against the wineglass. Thoughts flooded back from her morning phone call with his mom. Knowing full well that Mrs. Moore wished she would ride off into the sunset with anyone other than her son, maybe Gavin was divine intervention. And she couldn't lie—the man was attractive.

"Not in the mood for jokes tonight?" Camden reached for her arm. His fingers grazed her right elbow. "Why do I think the town isn't the only one concealing secrets?"

She could never hide anything from him, no matter how much she reminded herself not to let her face show her emotions. It was essential to keep a marriage honest, but not when she knew the secret would only hurt Camden. Yet, it was starting to itch at her like a wool sweater.

"It's only the town," she lied.

Camden set the book on the coffee table and took Trinity's hand. Anderson didn't mind his parents' arms resting on his side.

Trinity took a deep breath.

"We've never lied to each other in all our time together. At least, I never have." Camden's eyes burned into hers.

"I never have, either," Trinity whispered.

"Until today." Camden traced his thumb over her knuckles. "The ride over to the judge's house was silent. Usually, we always have something to talk about."

"Fine. Gavin is cute. There, I said it."

Camden smirked. "That's not a secret."

Trinity took a long sip of her merlot, setting the glass on the end table before turning to face Camden. She placed her other hand over his. Closing her eyes, she released a breath. "I called your mother."

Camden's eyes went blank. She watched as his fingers slid from her grasp. He rose from the sofa in slow motion. Trinity's heartbeat sped up, fearing his response.

"You called . . . her?" he snapped.

Rarely did Camden become upset. Nothing really bothered him outside of desert creepy-crawlies and his family. Trinity moved to stand, stepping closer to him.

"I'm sorry. I thought maybe your mother had changed her mind about us. Maybe she'd grown tired of missing you and might reconsider helping us out financially with the adoption."

"If you'd thought, then you would've known nothing has changed her perception of you and about my choices to be with you. You went behind my back to call my mother, a woman who I don't even speak to." Camden's voice rose, his tone sharp like a stern nanny—undoubtedly he'd heard the inflection in his past. A past full of maids and gold-plated everything.

"I'm sorry for trying to save our marriage. Save us!" Her cheeks warmed from all the blood pumping to them with the added help of the alcohol.

"Save us?" Camden snapped. Anderson hopped off the couch and stood between them. "Don't you think I've tried? Don't you think I *hate* this? I hate the thought of not saying good night and good morning to you. But you proved your point today by calling my mother, a woman who hates you—who hates us."

"Because I love you. Because I don't want September to come. Because I want to be a family!"

Camden formed and unformed fists at his side while Trinity's eyes watered, the tears producing on her bottom lids like a wave about to crash.

"The one thing I asked you *never* to do," Camden hissed, "you did."

"I don't understand why this makes you so upset, especially if she would've agreed to help. And I found out you already asked her."

"She hung up on me."

"You're mad at me for doing something you already did. So you also hid it from me until just now."

"She's my mother. I don't need your permission. But I've made it clear to you that I want nothing to do with her. By calling her, no matter the reason, you broke my trust. My mother doesn't respect you, and that is something I'll never forgive her for. Even if she had agreed to give us money, I wouldn't accept it now."

Tears spilled from Trinity's eyes, wetting her shirt as it soaked them up. "I don't understand . . . you asked her before, but now you won't take money from her? Are you not going back home to Chicago come September anyway?"

"I don't know yet what I'm doing, but I assure you I'm not going back to my parents. If I return to Chicago, it'll be because I have connections there and no family here anymore." Sighing in frustration, he stared at his wife. After a beat, he stepped forward and took her head in his hands, his thumbs grazing her cheeks, wiping the tears. "I realized if we took their money, they would always have a way of holding our child over our heads. Create some loophole with their mass of lawyers . . . they'd do whatever to break us up."

"But we're breaking up because we can't have a baby together," Trinity sobbed.

"I'm sorry." He kissed her forehead and disappeared down the hall.

Trinity sank into the couch, and Anderson followed, cuddling up against her. She cupped her wineglass in one hand and rubbed her fingers through the dog's fur with her other. Around her were memories of love and life. Couples didn't divorce when they were surrounded by happiness and warmth. Couples didn't renovate their home together only to have another couple create a lifetime of memories in it.

Anderson rolled onto his back, and Trinity's hand moved to rub his belly. Not only would she miss their home, but she feared starting over, feared moving in with her mom, and she mostly feared the unknown. She reminded herself that Woolsey would still be her home, even if she was no longer *in* her home.

As Trinity slumped lower into the comfort of the couch, a glint of hope remained—somewhere, deep down—she could feel it and didn't know what it could be. Yet, she felt it all around her; she felt it in Woolsey.

Chapter 23

Camden

Camden approached the bundles of tile stacked in the corner of the kitchen. "I got this. How hard can it be?" Anderson peered over the back of the couch, his eyebrows raised and lowered as if trying to find the answer.

"We can show your mom we don't need Gavin's help." He let out a deep sigh.

Taking the *This Old House* book, he skimmed through the pages on tile. It was basic as could be. Measure your area, purchase tile and supplies, add spacers, let dry. He examined the pages again. *Had the book missed a step? It didn't say anything about applying the mortar. Probably because it's easy, and no explanation was needed.*

Camden picked up the trowel, examining the flat edge and the toothed edge. *Two sides. The book also didn't specify which to use. It must be the flat side, and the toothed side must be for tile that goes up a wall to help it hold better.* He double-checked the book again and read about mixing. Then he turned the page, and it went on to discuss how to place spacers. *It must not matter which side at all then.*

Already having prepared the concrete by clearing every last piece of dog hair possible, he opened the tub of premixed mortar. "Wait, did I get the right stuff? I thought I needed grout." He squatted down and read the fine print on the bucket. "They must be interchangeable words."

He took the drill, attached the mixer, and squeezed the trigger while squinting with one eye and leaning his head back as though afraid of the torque from the power drill. Getting the hang of it, he smirked and mixed everything to the consistency as noted on the bag.

Camden set up the manual tile cutter, placing the measuring tape and marker next to it, and then he examined the kitchen around him. *Really how hard can it be? It's not any different than . . . well, something easy.* He took the trowel, scooped up a glob of mortar, and tossed it onto the concrete below, starting at the edge of the carpet. He would work his way backward, that way the new cabinets could hide any cutting mistakes.

Making smooth swirl marks with the trowel's flat side, he covered a section big enough to lay a piece of tile down. With both hands, he smooshed it firmly and wiggled it slightly.

He leaned back on his knees. "See Anderson, easy. I can have this finished by the time Trinity gets back from her horseback ride with Gavin." As the words rolled off his tongue, his jaw tightened.

He'd moved past his anger about Trinity calling his mother, yet, his teeth clenched at the thought of her and Gavin in the desert. He loathed the idea of her smiling and giggling at Gavin's stories because he probably had good ones to tell. Times of wrangling alligators and roping mosquitoes, or whatever Southern men did in their free time. Camden didn't have stories to tell. At least nothing about belt-buckle adventures or anything with Southern cowboy charm.

Camden moved onto the next piece of tile and smeared the mortar down in a natural swirl pattern, making sure it was smooth as butter. Sitting back on his knees each time, he reviewed his handiwork. It almost seemed too easy.

He returned to the mortar and laid six more tiles, placing the white spacers in between. As he worked toward the corner of the kitchen, he realized the tile cutter and supplies were out of reach. Camden tiptoed on the bare concrete edge, gathered them, and went back to his spot.

"Maybe I shouldn't have tiled myself backward like this, but I'm sure I can carefully step out when I'm done, right Anderson?"

The dog snored away on the sofa while Camden returned to the tile work. In less than an hour, he'd nearly laid the entire kitchen floor. The only thing left was the corner. As he squatted on the remaining concrete floor, Camden rubbed his chin.

"It's going to be tricky, but I can do this."

The good news was Camden had watched a video on tile cutting with the device and knew precisely how to go about it. He measured the tile, marked it, and placed it on the cutter. The horrendous scraping noise produced by scoring the tile caused his ears to try and fold in on themselves. Anderson sprang up on the sofa and barked.

"Sorry, buddy. That's a horrible noise. Good thing Trinity isn't here. Sounds like nails on a chalkboard."

With each cut, Anderson barked and Camden's teeth grit. Yet, he continued until only four tiles were left to be laid, right where he stood. Maybe tile laying was like Twister for adults, only all the circles were the same color and it was necessary to step off the game board.

To keep his weight more even, Camden stretched his body across the completed tile and then maneuvered around to face the remaining section. Tilting the bucket on its side, he scooped out the remaining mortar and smoothed it as best as he could into the spot. Cutting the final two tiles while lying on his stomach proved his greatest challenge. Plus, his ear was much closer to the horrific noise of the tile cutter.

Camden laid the final tiles, gathered the supplies, and softly but quickly got to the carpet. With his hands on his hips, he observed his job well done.

"No wonder Gavin works in construction; it's easy work!" Taking his glass of wine to the sofa, he plopped down next to Anderson. He propped his feet up on the coffee table and turned on the baseball game. Come morning, they could walk on the tile and start to plan out the next job. Furrowing his brow, he checked his watch, wondering how much longer Trinity and Gavin would be gone.

Anderson's head popped up, swiveling to the front door, his ears folded back. The sun had disappeared behind the mountains some time ago, and only a sliver of light remained. Two shadows on horses made their way up the road. Anderson jumped from the sofa and went to the door, letting out a whine.

Camden didn't move. He needed to play it cool, as though he didn't care. Of course, he *did*, but he didn't have a right to, not anymore. Anderson's whining continued as the minutes passed. *What's taking them so long?*

He finally rose from the sofa and set the wineglass on the end table. "Gotta use the restroom, buddy?"

Camden slipped on his loafers by the door and opened it. Anderson took off in the direction of the horse stable while Camden busied himself inspecting a plant on the porch.

Trinity and Gavin's voices traveled through the hot air around the side of the house. *What could they possibly still be talking about?* Practically on tiptoe, Camden made his way to the side of the porch closest to the horses. While he could hear voices, he couldn't make out what was being said. Then silence. *Are they kissing?* Camden bolted down the steps and around the house. *Not on my watch!*

"Camden," Trinity's voice broke through the night.

Since he was too busy looking out for snakes and other creatures, he hadn't noticed them coming around the house.

"Hey, hi, hello," Camden said. "I didn't even know you two were back yet." He placed his pointer finger in his right ear and wiggled it around, wondering if he'd done permanent damage by not wearing ear protection during the tile cutting. "Just letting Anderson out to do his bathroom stuff." *Bathroom stuff? Way to play it smooth.*

"Gavin accepted my offer to join us for some wine. We were heading inside." Trinity smiled.

"Be careful not to walk in the kitchen. I laid the floor," Camden boasted, his chest high, shoulders back.

"You did what?" Trinity stopped mid-step on the porch.

"The entire kitchen floor is tiled. Can't walk on it for at least twenty-four hours."

Trinity opened the front door. "Well, I need to see this, then."

Anderson joined them as they piled in the front door as if coming in from a snowstorm.

"Hi, you must be Anderson." Gavin bent down to pet the dog. "He's a good-lookin' rescue."

"Thank you," Camden offered.

"I have to say, Camden, it looks amazing." Trinity approached where the tile met the carpet. "Good thing we have a few bottles of wine in the hall closet along with some plastic cups. The wine might be a little warm. Unless there's any left from the bottle you opened, Camden?"

Camden shook his head. "Last of the bottle."

Trinity made her way to the closet while Camden's focus remained on his wife.

"Tile can be easy to lay as long as you put the mortar down correctly." Gavin moved closer to the tile to examine it.

For someone who'd been out in the heat, Gavin didn't even have a drop of sweat on him. How did he manage that?

"Yes, I used a trowel and plenty of mortar. I even got out the level." Camden cracked his knuckles and rocked on the balls of his feet.

"That's all good, as long as you troweled it in straight lines and, of course, used the correct side of the trowel." Gavin stuck his thumb behind his belt buckle and chuckled. "But everyone knows how to use a trowel . . . except maybe Anderson over there. Most first-timers often make the mistake of swirling the mortar. It leaves air pockets under the tile, so it'll break when anything heavy lands on it. Sometimes even walking on it is enough to crack it."

Camden tried to lessen the shock spreading across his lips with his hand, rubbing it over his forming five-o'clock shadow. "Straight mortar lines." It came out sounding like a question. *Did I use the wrong side of the trowel?*

"Yeah, it's easier to swirl the mortar on, and it doesn't seem to be the wrong thing to do. But after talking to Trinity, it sounded like you read up on tiling, or at least watched some how-to videos."

Camden lowered himself onto the sofa, his mind raced. He swallowed the imaginary rock forming in his throat. Tiling seemed so easy, he hadn't felt the need to spend hours watching videos. He'd read through the book. Okay, he'd flipped through the book. *What have I done?* Snatching the wine glass off the end table, he gulped the rest of his drink.

"I hope a 2017 merlot is okay with you, Gavin?" Trinity entered the living room with two plastic cups and an unopened bottle.

"Oh dang, the bottle opener is in the kitchen." Camden pointed to it sitting on the window ledge over the kitchen sink.

"No problem, it's a twist off. No cork." She waved the bottle.

Camden fought the urge to sigh aloud. Instead, he ran his hand through his hair a few times. He held his glass out, and Trinity poured wine into it. Camden waved her on to keep pouring until the glass was nearly overflowing.

Gavin took a filled plastic cup from Trinity and made himself at home in the single royal-blue armchair which sat next to the sofa. His wife joined him on the couch but at the other end, nearest Gavin. Anderson decided to make a new best friend in the cowboy and took up residence at his boots.

Great, even the dog's ready for the divorce.

Chapter 24

Camden

"Trinity showed me some amazing views on the ride." Gavin lifted his wineglass. "A delightful surprise to see such much beauty in the valley of the desert."

"I'm surprised you like wine," Camden blurted.

It didn't look natural, a cowboy sipping wine. Maybe a beer would suit him better.

"Gavin offered to help with the cabinet installation," Trinity interrupted, clearly trying to prevent him from replying.

"I think you and I'll manage fine, but thank you, Gavin, for the offer. I'm sure you probably want to get going." Camden stood.

"No, we just opened the wine but two minutes ago. Don't be a rude host." Trinity leaned back on the sofa. "Gavin was telling me this amazing story of the time he was down in Key West marlin fishing. He's been on so many adventures."

Camden nodded though his focus returned to the tile and how he didn't do one single straight line with the mortar and most likely used the wrong side of the trowel. So what if Gavin is some prominent hotshot construction worker? Maybe he didn't know a thing about tile. Maybe down in the South all the humidity made it so he couldn't swirl the mortar.

Gavin waved off his adventure and changed the subject. "Y'all doin' new baseboard trim, too?"

"Yes, once the painting and all the tile is complete. I've done it before with my mom, back when I was a teenager." Trinity switched her plastic cup from one hand to the other.

"Is there anything you can't do?" Gavin beamed. "You're such an amazing woman."

"Oh, please. I simply grew up with a hardworking single mother who taught me a great deal about life. Not to mention I spent many days hanging out at Hammer and Nail."

Camden glanced at Trinity, watching as her cheeks turned rosy from Gavin's flattery. "Yes, Trinity is amazing. I'm lucky to be married to her."

"I feel like we need something more than the wine." Trinity stood. "There should be a box of crackers or something in the pantry that I can reach without stepping on the tile."

"It's alright, Trinity. I should probably be goin'." Gavin stood.

"Nonsense, sit down. We haven't had much company lately." Trinity turned her head over her shoulder. "Besides, I'm sure you have more stories to tell about all your adventures."

Gavin eased back down into the chair, resting his boot on his knee like he was John Wayne, comfortable in his skin.

Camden rubbed his thumb over his opposite hand in small circles. Maybe he could grow a beard like Gavin's. It would make him look more . . . country. But it felt and looked messy. Plus, he'd tried a five-o'clock shadow, and by four it was an itchy annoyance. The only time Camden felt comfortable was when he was in a suit with a tie and wingtips and a freshly shaved face.

"Found some cheesy crackers." Trinity poured some into two plastic cups and handed one to Gavin before returning to the sofa.

Anderson perked up and spun around, placing his chin on Gavin's knee.

"Can he have one?" Gavin clutched a cracker between his fingers.

"Yes," Trinity said.

"No," Camden said at the same time. "They don't agree with him."

Gavin held the cracker midair as Anderson's drool soaked through his jeans.

"Of course he can," Trinity insisted.

Gavin held out the cracker, and Anderson sniffed it before snatching it from the cowboy's fingers.

Camden glared at Trinity.

"One cracker is fine, Camden. Come here, Anderson, no more begging."

Reluctantly Anderson left the prized spot and curled up at Trinity's feet.

"He listens well." Gavin dropped a few more crackers into his mouth.

"We're lucky. He was easy to train. I think most shelter dogs are simply happy to be in a forever home, so they want to show you how grateful they are." Trinity leaned down and gave Anderson a few pets before sitting back up.

"You must not have time for any pets?" Camden inquired. "Being such an adventurer and all."

Camden chuckled to himself, knowing how much Trinity loved animals. That will show her Gavin's not the right kind of man for her come September. Even if he couldn't remain her husband, he could at least prevent a cowboy from replacing him.

"I've fostered many dogs. Workin' in construction and bein' my own boss, I can often bring the dogs with me to the site. They're safe, of course, but being around different people and noises helps some of them to become better equipped for a forever family." Gavin scratched at his beard. "I usually take a three-month break so I can travel, then when I return, I open back up for fosters."

"Oh, dear God," Camden whispered.

"Pardon?" Gavin leaned forward.

"I said, oh, good job," Camden lied.

"What a wonderful thing you do for all those dogs." Trinity leaned forward like a princess observing her prince.

Reaching in front of Trinity, purely to block the staring, Camden snatched the wine bottle and emptied the last of its contents into his glass. He helped himself to some of the cheesy crackers from Trinity's cup since she hadn't bothered to offer him any.

"Sorry, Camden. I didn't think to get you a cup."

"No need." He grinned. "We can share."

"What else are you thinking of doing for the renovations?" Gavin inquired, squirming in the chair a bit.

Trinity stood from the sofa. "Oh, let me show you."

"Thanks, hey, ya never know, I might move here. Maybe I'll buy this place."

Camden ran his hand through his hair, pulling at it between his fingers.

Gavin followed Trinity as she took him on a tour of the rest of the home. Telling him the plans for the two bathrooms, Camden listened to his wife speak as he drank a good deal of his wine in a few gulps. The warmth of the alcohol spread through his body as dizziness came over him. How many glasses had he drank? Holding out his hand, he counted three. It wasn't normally too many for him, but he hadn't eaten dinner yet. Plus, laying tile was a workout of its own he'd not expected, especially in the mid-June heat. *Crap, I'm buzzed.*

He always did stupid stuff when he was buzzed, like attempting to hang curtains. The first night in their home, he wanted to hang curtains to keep people from looking in. Trinity had insisted no one would be looking in and they should relax and celebrate on the first night. After about four glasses of wine, Camden could no longer relax with the thought of someone watching them. He removed the curtain rod from the box and read the blurry instructions a few times over. With a raised glass of wine, he declared himself the man of the house, and he needed to hang the curtains himself. Five holes later, he threaded the fabric on and slid the rod into place only to have it come crashing to the floor seconds later. Trinity laughed so hard he thought wine might come out of her nose. In the morning, he nursed his hangover on the sofa while Trinity patched up the holes, installed the anchors, and rehung the rod properly.

"I think the renovations are goin' to be great," Gavin announced they returned to the living room.

"Thanks, I just wish we could've done all this when we bought the house, or at least—" Trinity poured more cheesy crackers into her and Gavin's cups, then resumed her spot on the sofa. "Well, I just hate doing all this work and spending all this money to not be able to stay and enjoy it."

"You can't afford to live here on your own?" Gavin tilted his head like a dog questioning a command.

"Not on my teacher's salary, and I don't want a roommate. Not that I would be able to find one out here." Trinity took a long sip of wine.

Camden knew Trinity was holding back tears. She loved this house, and he knew she didn't want to give it up. He leaned forward, buzzed, and reached for her arm.

"What a shame." Gavin shook his head. "Where will you go?"

"I'm moving back in with my mom. Which shouldn't be a big deal, except our relationship has not been the best lately."

"But you don't have to leave your hometown or give up your job." Gavin leaned forward, elbows on his knees as if getting closer to Trinity would solve her problem.

Camden leaned back, watching them as though he were observing them from behind a secret two-way mirror. Could he be losing his wife even before September? *No, I'm overthinking all this.*

"Earlier, you mentioned you might be moving here. You must have been joking." Camden's words slurred. *Crap!* The wine was controlling his mouth.

Camden caught Cowboy Gavin glancing at Trinity before he answered. "Jesser really ain't the same without Mama next door."

"Life always figures itself out, doesn't it?" Trinity said between sips of wine. She glanced at Camden out of the corner of her eye. "My mom and I'll work out our problems in time. Hopefully, when she is over for dinner."

"Mind if I ask . . .?"

"I went in search of my father and called him up. It didn't go over well with her."

"I'm sure everythin' will be fine. After all, she's your mama." Gavin sighed, swigged the last of the wine from his glass, and stood. "Thank you for your hospitality, Trinity and Camden."

Trinity eased off the sofa. "Most welcome." She stepped forward as Gavin made his way to the front door.

Don't hug him. Don't hug him. Camden clenched his jaw.

Gavin leaned toward Trinity and wrapped his toned construction arms around her. *Why does Cowboy have to hug his wife?* The quick hug seemed to last minutes.

"Nice seein' you again, Camden." Gavin lifted a hand to wave goodbye.

Camden nodded his head and remained seated. "Yeah, you too."

As Trinity closed the door, Camden wrinkled his forehead. *Yeah? When did I start saying* yeah *instead of* yes*?* Maybe moving back to the city would do his speech some good. Land a job at a nice Ivy League college. Earn enough money to live in a loft. Could his mother have been right all along?

"It's nice having people over. Especially friendly, down-home people." Trinity returned to the sofa, tucking her feet under her bottom. "You drank too much." She glanced over into the kitchen. "But I'm impressed by the tile work. I think once the mortar dries and we put the grout down, it will look amazing."

"There might be a slight unseen problem with the tile, maybe two problems. I didn't do straight lines. I did swirls." Camden wiggled his hand like a moving snake.

"You did what?" Trinity's eyes grew wide. "Why would you do swirls? They'll crack with any weight on them—like the new cabinets, appliances, or our feet."

"I didn't think it mattered, straight, swirled. It's mortar." Camden raised his hands in the air. "And which side should I have used for the trowel? The smooth side, right?"

"The smooth side?" Trinity jumped up from the sofa. "Why would you use the smooth side!"

"The book didn't say which side. It left it out!" Camden pointed at the *This Old House* book laid open on the kitchen table.

Trinity stomped over to the book and turned the pages, then turned them back, then forward again. Camden hovered over her, his hands on his hips, his foot tapping on the carpet.

"See, it doesn't say how to use the trowel and which side." Camden folded his arms.

Then Trinity examined the page, flipped it forward, and then back. She feathered the bottom of the page with both hands and pulled it apart like a peanut butter and jelly sandwich.

"It does say. If you noticed the skipped page numbers, you would've figured out the pages were stuck together." Trinity rubbed her fingers together, trying to get the stickiness off them.

There it was. The pages, unstuck, revealed how to trowel the mortar (in straight lines) and which side of the tool (the toothed) to use.

"We need to try and save these tiles before the mortar sets." Trinity kneeled at the edge of the carpet. "I'll pull them up, and you run them outside to the hose and rinse them off. Where is the scraper?"

Camden located one on the end table and handed it to her. "I don't want to be outside in the dark. The geckos are . . . everywhere . . . and . . . bats."

Trinity popped up one tile, able to save it. "Camden, put on your big boy pants and get your butt outside to rinse these off. Unless you think you can pop these all up without breaking any."

Camden's feet paused. He didn't want to do either. Anderson stood waiting to see what was going to happen next between his parents.

"Camden!"

"I'm too buzzed to argue." He slid on his shoes and took the first tile out to the hose.

"Take Anderson with you."

"Nope, you insisted Cowboy give him a cracker. Now you deal with the stink from his back end."

Trinity scrunched up her nose at the thought and began to free another tile.

Chapter 25

Trinity

Outside the post office, the clouds built by the moment, flat on the bottom with ice cream scoops for the tops. Temperatures in Woolsey the last few days had reached 115 degrees. The atmosphere was geared up to drop some monsoon rain. At least, that's what everyone in town hoped for. Unlike most states where rain was common, in Arizona, residents stood at their windows like children hoping for a snow day. Although rain often caused Arizonians to forget how to drive, it brought them joy. Not to mention, residents conversed about it as though the president were coming through town.

The bell chimed and several residents entered.

"Wanted to get my mail, just in case a monsoon comes through." Mrs. Ebbinga jingled her keys.

"Oh yes, I hope we get some rain. And not just a lot of dust for nothing," added Mr. Kellogg.

"Mrs. Moore." Mrs. Ebbinga approached the counter. "Don't you be staying open for the sake of the mail. You see that haboob coming, you hurry home."

"You know how 287 floods," Mr. Kellogg warned.

Trinity folded her hands on the counter and allowed Anderson to put his paws upon it as well. "Thank you, Mrs. Ebbinga and Mr. Kellogg. I'll be okay."

"Tell Mr. Moore I said hi." Mr. Kellogg held the door open for Mrs. Ebbinga.

"Will do." Trinity waved as they exited.

Before Trinity could return to sorting mail into boxes, the bell chimed again.

"Trinity?" Mama called out.

"Yes, Mama?"

Mama stood next to Elizabeth, who held a chunky black puppy.

"Oh my goodness," Trinity squealed with delight. "It's a puppy!" She bolted to the door and swung it open as Anderson followed.

Without asking, Trinity scooped it up from Elizabeth and proceeded to kiss its head. "I'm sorry, Elizabeth, I didn't mean to take it from you."

Mama laughed and elbowed her daughter. "It's quite fine, honey. Puppies can be excitin'."

Trinity lowered herself and the puppy to Anderson's level; the dog's tail swayed back and forth like a boat at sea. Anderson had spent time with other dogs during all the town's get-togethers and Saturday lunches, so Trinity knew it would be safe to allow him to meet another dog. Anderson's nose twitched a mile a minute, sniffing in all the puppy's smells.

Upon closer examination, the black puppy had a cream spot on his chest and his back leg. He appeared to be a mix of Labrador and maybe a border collie.

"I didn't know you ladies were getting a puppy."

"We didn't," Mama stated. "We found him. He's a stray."

Trinity slowly rose back to standing, the puppy in her arms. "A stray?"

While it could be possible for someone in town to lose a dog, residents would have known, and she would've heard about it. There had been occasions when out-of-towners deliberately drove out to dump their unwanted cats and dogs, hoping someone would take them in unless something in nature got to them before a ranch hand found them.

"We found it . . . w-w-wanderin' the road," Mama stuttered.

"Oh, you poor thing." Trinity continued to snuggle with the puppy. "Thank goodness they found you." She checked its paws for signs of injury. If the temperatures were over ninety degrees, the pavement would be like lava to a dog's pads. "Where did you say you found the puppy? He has no burn marks on his paws, so he must have been walking in the dirt."

Mama nodded. "Yes, yes, indeed. Found him in the dirt. That's where he was. In . . . the . . . dirt."

Why was Mama struggling to find her words? Trinity furrowed her brow. "Good thing you found him before the monsoon starts up." Trinity eyed the clouds building outside. "He doesn't even feel hot, and he isn't panting."

"Yes, because," Mama turned to Elizabeth. "He had a water bottle."

"He had a water bottle?" Trinity peered at the puppy.

Mama nodded her head. "He's in good hands now."

"Me? You want me to take care of it?" Trinity continued to hug the puppy against her chest.

"Yes, honey, looks like Anderson would love the company." Mama smiled at Anderson, sitting politely at Trinity's feet.

"I would love to take him home, but with the house renovations and the . . . divorce. I'd hate to get attached only to lose him." Trinity kneeled back down so Anderson could get another sniff in.

"It's only the middle of June." Mama waved her hand as though the calendar didn't matter. "He needs a home."

"I don't know, Mama. I think we should take him into Cactus City and get him scanned for a chip, find out if someone is missing him."

Mama shook her head. "Keep him safe with you. Don't even worry about that. A pup that young won't have a chip. Right, Liz?"

Elizabeth glanced at Mama, then back at Trinity. "Right."

Mama pulled at her daughter's shirt. "Better get goin' before the storm. What do y'all call it? A boob?"

Trinity brought the puppy to her lips to hide a chuckle. "It's a *ha*boob."

"A highly inappropriate name." Mama pivoted toward the door as fast as a ninety-year-old could. "See you soon, honey."

Trinity let the puppy down onto the post office floor as the door closed behind Mama and Elizabeth. *A water bottle?* She placed her hand on her hip, watching Anderson and the puppy romping around.

To be honest, she didn't hate the idea of a puppy. She'd brought it up in conversations a few times with Camden, but they'd pushed it to the back burner with all the depressing baby news. A part of her wished she could keep the puppy, but it must belong to a family who missed it dearly.

"For now, we'll call you, Puppy." Trinity got down on the post office floor and admired Puppy and Anderson playing.

Thoughts swirled in Trinity's mind about Mama and Elizabeth bringing the puppy into the post office but they neglected to pick up their mail.

She went to the other side of the mailboxes and opened the back slot for the Dunn's. Full. Could they simply have forgotten to pick up the mail with the discovery of Puppy?

Chapter 26

Trinity

The storm didn't wait long to build as the white clouds puffed higher into the sky. The fading blue sky turned tan as the winds picked up and grabbed the dirt. Birds fluttered as the gusts blew them around like lost plastic bags. Palms whipped, and branches danced as the haboob pushed through Woolsey.

Trinity leaned against the post office door as it vibrated with each gust. "We should probably wait it out here, but if there is rain behind this, we'll be stranded."

The post office closed at five. She checked her cell phone—4:35. "Close enough."

She shut off the lights, locked the office door, and scooped up Puppy. "Come on, Anderson, let's go." Trinity exited the back door and held her balance against the whirlwind.

Puppy's black ears flopped in the wind. "Anderson, car!" she yelled over the gusts of wind. Dirt smacked her face, sharp like mini pushpins.

After she locked the back door, Trinity bolted to her truck and opened the driver's side door for Anderson, holding it against the wind. Sliding in right behind him with Puppy, Trinity slammed the door closed.

She brushed the hair out of her eyes. With the taste of dirt in her mouth and the smell of it in her nose, she started the truck. "Let's get us home, boys."

Shifting onto the main road, the visibility was decent and not the worst she'd ever encountered. Puppy rested in her lap as she shifted through the gears and turned onto State Route 287. Dust blew over the road, the last of spring's dried blossoms danced in the air with it. She knew better than to drive in this weather and scolded herself for not leaving ten minutes earlier.

The wind pushed at the side of the truck as Trinity white-knuckled her way to the stop sign. As far as she could see, which was not far, it was a ghost town as the stop sign flapped in the wind.

Double-checking one more time, she drove on, making her way closer to the house. A gust of wind howled as it shook every part of nature into a tailspin. In her pocket, her cell phone beeped, but whoever it was would have to wait until she was safely home and on the couch. What if it was Camden? Maybe he was in trouble?

She gripped the steering wheel tighter in one hand as she removed the cell and glanced at the screen. A missed text from Camden caused her to wish she'd taken his advice and added a stereo with Bluetooth. Tapping at the screen she pulled up his number.

"Hi, Trinity. Are you still at the post office?" Concern filtered through Camden's words.

"No, I'm on the 287. Where are you?"

"I'm still at the restaurant with Luis and your mom. Why are you driving? You know better."

"I didn't want to take the chance of the roads flooding out." Trinity leaned closer to the wheel. "Everyone is going to be stuck at the restaurant if you don't leave now."

"It's too late. Hang up and text me when you are home."

"I will, Camden. Be safe. The same goes for Mom."

The phone call dropped. She tossed the cell onto the dash. Knowing Camden was safe at the restaurant allowed her to sigh with relief for him. She kept the truck on the road as best she could while the air thickened with dust.

The truck rocked as a dead palm leaf smacked into the passenger side. The wind picked it up, pushing it over the fender and across the hood. The palm leaf's sharp shark-like teeth scratched the paint along the way.

"Almost home, boys!" The street narrowed as she turned onto Mountain View Road. She noticed the white-and-black street sign trying to spin like a whirligig on the top of the post.

The dust continued to blow sideways as Trinity pulled into the driveway and finally the comfort of the garage. She sighed and rested her head on the seat back before texting Camden that she had made it home.

Once inside, Trinity placed the puppy in Anderson's crate and headed to rinse off the dirt caked in her hair and every inch of her body.

Dressed in clean clothes, she released Puppy from the crate where he now sat whining.

"You're okay, Puppy." She scooped him up into her arms. "A crate is a safe place for you when I need to make sure you stay out of trouble."

At the window, Trinity saw the dust had died down but didn't bother to bring any rain with it. "Looks like we risked driving home for nothing."

She snatched the remote off the coffee table and turned on the Diamondback game, which was already in the second inning. Examining the mess of dried mortar swirls on the kitchen floor, she set Puppy down. "Can't hurt anything that's already a mess." She crossed her arms and wondered how they would get all the mortar up.

Puppy tilted his head at the mortar mess, barked at it, and then became distracted by the door stopper for the garage door. Reaching out to paw it, Puppy caused the spring to bounce back and forth. He lowered his head and dove for it. Anderson wandered over, unsure as to all the commotion. Soon he lay down to observe Puppy enthusiastically playing with his newfound toy.

"You boys have fun. I'm going to see what I can make for dinner."

Above the sink, through the kitchen window, was a view of the backyard. The sight spanned past the mountains, which surrounded the north and south landscapes of Woolsey. The dust left a thick coat of dirt on everything in sight. A bit of worry settled into her chest since Camden had yet to make it home. While he was not in any danger from the storm, she didn't feel complete without him, especially with how they left everything last night. At that moment, an intense feeling of love hit her directly in the heart. She needed Camden. She needed them to be together. Baby or no baby. She didn't want to be without him; she couldn't live with him.

The garage door swung open, Camden on the other side. "Hi."

Trinity dove for Puppy. "Watch out!" She scooped him up before the door hit him. She hadn't come up with a way to tell Camden about Puppy.

"What is that?" Camden pointed.

Trinity's eyes followed his finger. "This is . . . Puppy."

"I can see it's a puppy. Why is it here?"

She smiled. "Mama found him wandering outside the post office."

Anderson greeted Camden as Puppy wiggled to break free from Trinity's embrace.

"Hi, buddy." He kneeled to pet Anderson.

Trinity set Puppy on the floor, and immediately Puppy attempted to hide behind Anderson's whooshing tail, unsure of this new person.

Camden held out his hand for Puppy to sniff. After approving the smell, Puppy leaped forward in a puppy hop and set his paws on Camden's knees. He ruffled the fur on each dog's head, then stood up.

"Have you called the vet in Cactus City yet? I don't remember hearing about anyone losing a pup in town."

"Not yet."

"Oh. No, no, no." Camden waved his finger. "We're not keeping the puppy."

"When Gavin spoke about being a foster to dogs, it warmed my heart. What if this poor puppy is homeless? He can't go sit in some shelter." Trinity picked up Puppy and snuggled her face next to his.

"For starters, we're in the middle of renovations."

"Come on, let us have this one last adventure before it's over." Trinity frowned as she pressed her cheek up against Puppy. "At least for Anderson's sake, he needs a brother."

Camden ran his tongue over his teeth. "Fine, but only until we find out who he belongs to."

"And if he doesn't have a family?" Trinity kissed the top of Puppy's head.

"Then"—Camden shook his head—"we'll deal with it."

Trinity hugged Puppy before returning him to the floor.

Camden removed his shoes and set them near the garage door. "Why couldn't Mama and Elizabeth keep the pup?"

"He's probably a tripping hazard. Mama is already pretty unsteady on her feet without trying to maneuver around a dog."

Camden snickered as Anderson and Puppy played chase around the couch. Trinity returned to the kitchen, gathering a cutting board, potatoes, asparagus, and radishes. Taking them to the dining table, Trinity prepared dinner.

"I wanted to apologize for getting upset with you about calling my mother." Camden pulled out a chair at the table.

Trinity paused, the knife over the potato. "It's okay. I understand why you were upset. I didn't mean to break your trust. I wanted to . . . I wanted to make sure I didn't give up on us without giving *every* attempt. The regret of not knowing would have been far worse. I couldn't ignore a chance to save us."

The dogs made a final romp around the couch before Anderson lapped up some water, showing Puppy where it was located. Soon both dogs' faces were shoved deep into the bowl. Trinity's gaze landed on the dogs, as did Camden's. Joy welled up inside her heart, warming her like a crackling fire on a chilly night. *Please don't let me forget this moment.*

Trinity added the chopped veggies to the small roasting pan, slid it into the oven, and then poured them each a glass of wine. Camden lowered the volume of the baseball game, and together they sat watching the boys snuggled up on the cool of the mortar-mess floor.

"When's my mom coming over?"

"I suggested a Sunday brunch, actually, over dinner. Luis gave her a later shift."

Trinity rested her head on the couch; her shoulders relaxed as she sighed. "Thanks, I think that'll work well. I can pick up some muffins and fruit and whip up some scrambled eggs without too much of a cooking nightmare."

Trinity's arms ached to wrap themselves around Camden, to nestle her face into the crook of his neck where she could smell the scent of his cedar and peppermint aftershave, and she longed to have his embrace around her, too. Instead, Trinity closed her eyes and let the pinot noir rest on her tongue.

Chapter 27

Camden

Camden stacked the library books on the coffee table and set three places at the kitchen table. Next, he gathered three mugs while Trinity scrambled eggs in a bowl with a pinch of pepper and salt.

"Can you grab me the milk and shredded cheese, please?"

Camden held the items out for Trinity as she added a splash of milk and then a handful of shredded cheese into the bowl. Anderson ran to the living room window as a shadow moved outside.

"Looks like your mom decided to ride over." Camden pointed as he returned the milk and cheese to the refrigerator.

Lillian had two horses, Elliot and Eastwood. Today, he noticed she had brought Eastwood, her chestnut quarter horse. Elliot was a beautiful tobiano American Paint.

Camden heard the gate for the stables close, followed by boots coming up the back patio steps and then a knock at the slider. For as long as they'd owned the home, Camden never knew of Lillian coming to the front door, always the back patio slider.

"Hi." Trinity pulled the slider open and allowed Lillian to enter.

Anderson and Puppy rushed to greet the new person. As the days grew closer to July, Puppy had bonded with Anderson and became his shadow for everything.

"Hi, pups!" Lillian cheered and lowered to give hugs while the dogs licked her with happiness. "How are you boys doing? I bet you're being so good."

When Lillian stood up, her eyes met Trinity's, and the tension in the home froze. Her hair was hidden under a pale-violet bandana, and her left wrist was covered in multiple homemade mismatched bracelets. This was the first time in months that Lillian and Trinity had seen each other, a challenging feat in Woolsey, to avoid someone, anyone. Camden knew that Lillian still loved her daughter as much as always, but the anger lingered under the surface. He hoped this morning the women could move past it.

"Trin." Lillian shoved her hands into her jean pockets.

"Thanks for agreeing to come over. Have a seat, I'll throw the eggs on, and we can eat in a few minutes." Trinity moved to the stove and poured the beaten egg mixture into the heated skillet.

Lillian gave a quick hug to Camden before sitting at the table. Camden poured her some coffee while his mother-in-law snatched a muffin and scooped the fruit into a small bowl.

"Looks like your kitchen reno is going . . ." Lillian's eyes focused on the mortar mess.

"It's a new style, Lillian. Everyone's going for this new style called rough mortar. Very fashionable."

Lillian covered her mouth as she giggled. "I'd like to see this new trend in magazines."

Camden joined her at the table. "It's so stylish that it's a secret."

She winked at Camden as Trinity approached the table with a serving dish of steaming cheesy scrambled eggs.

"Smells great, Trin. Thanks for having me over." Lillian reached for the wooden spoon.

"Mom, let's not dance around the obvious." Trinity sipped her coffee.

"That's a nice way to start an apology." Lillian stabbed a strawberry with her fork a little harder than needed.

"Mom, come on, don't be ridiculous."

Camden focused on his plate, not picking sides by making eye contact with either woman. Observing Trinity and Lillian's relationship over the years, he'd noticed they were more like sisters than mother and daughter. Of course, he couldn't be sure what a normal parent-child relationship looked like, thanks to his nanny-raised experience. He figured their relationship was sisterly because they only had each other and had gone through some significant challenges together.

"Yes, let's argue about this again, instead of admitting you did what I asked you not to." Lillian shoved a forkful of eggs into her mouth.

"Mom." Trinity set her fork on her plate. "He doesn't know where we are. I blocked the call. I didn't give him any information on us. I didn't go see him in person."

"Why? Why did you need to talk to him? Your father was—maybe still is—a horrible man. Talking to him won't change what he did."

Trinity sat back in her chair and crossed her arms. "I didn't expect him to change, and it's not why I called him. I needed to ask him why. Why did he do what he did? I needed closure."

"We had closure when I put our entire life in the car and drove away." Lillian crossed her arms. "He hurt me. He damaged me, physically and mentally. You would've been next."

Silence fell over the table like dust after a haboob.

"I had to know," Trinity reiterated after moments passed.

Lillian rubbed her forehead. "And did you get your answer?"

Camden had held Trinity's hand through the short conversation, but he knew it felt like an eternity to his wife. When the call had ended with her father, he'd wiped her tears and hugged her before she'd disappeared into the desert on Starla.

"He . . . he said you did the right thing. He said he never looked for us." Trinity's voice was soft. "He said he was sorry, that he wished he could go back and change his choices, but he couldn't. Mom, he was drunk. His words slurred together. He said he didn't know why he did what he did, but that it was who he was and always will be."

"So, was that the answer you wanted?" Lillian glared at her daughter.

"I wasn't looking for the answer *I* wanted. I was looking for the answer he had to give." Trinity reached out a hand and placed it over her mom's. "I'm sorry I did what you didn't want me to do."

"It's done and over with now. And I guess I can see, from your standpoint, that you needed to speak with him. You were so little when we left." Lillian's eyes focused on Trinity's hand. "I'm sorry I didn't understand that you needed to have closure."

"Mom, I have enough change coming in my life. I need you."

"You need my hospitality." Lillian tilted her head.

"I need you because you're my mom."

"Aww," Camden intoned, unaware he said it aloud.

Lillian and Trinity glanced at him as he covered his mouth, his teeth clenched together.

"I didn't mean for that to come out." Camden forced a smile.

Mom and daughter stood up and embraced, and he was happy to have the rift between them mended. Not only did he want his wife to have her mom back, but he also wanted his mother-in-law back, too.

"Now, tell me what I have been missing out on?" Lillian sipped some coffee before diving back into her eggs.

"I wanted to ask you about using your kitchen," Trinity asked, trembling in her voice. "I'd like to try and sell my coconut chip cookies, bring in some extra income, regardless of the divorce. It would not be a lot, and I could bring over all my supplies until I moved in, of course."

Lillian put her fingers to her lips. "Trin, that's an amazing idea. You're right, it might not be a lot, but it might turn into something bigger. I'm proud of you for taking this step."

"Even if it's too late to save Camden and me." Trinity lowered her head.

"It's never too late for anything."

"Mom, have you noticed everyone around here is acting strange?" Trinity removed the liner from around the bottom of her muffin.

Lillian shook her head and lifted her mug to her lips.

"The Hackenburgs brought us wine from Utah when they returned from fighting a fire up north." Trinity leaned forward over the table. "There was a line of cars leaving the restaurant, too."

"Let's not forget Mama dropping off Puppy with you." Camden pointed at a mass of fur roughhousing on the living room carpet.

Lillian glanced at her watch. "I hate to cut this short, but I really should get to work."

"Luis gave you the morning off," Camden reminded her.

Lillian paused halfway while rising from the chair. "Yes, but I left a ton of laundry on the line at home, and with it being monsoon season, you never know how early those rain showers can build."

Trinity's forehead wrinkled as she mouthed at Camden, "What?"

Before Camden or Trinity could stand all the way up from their chairs, Lillian was at the slider.

"Thanks again for brunch. It was lovely. Love you both." Lillian waved a hand in the air and exited out the patio sliding door.

"Monsoons don't have the energy to build until the afternoon, even I know that." Camden placed his hand on Trinity's shoulder.

She leaned her head against Camden and placed her hand on his chest. "What's up with everyone?"

Chapter 28

Trinity

"Mama, Trinity is here to see you, as requested." Elizabeth knocked on Mama's bedroom door and opened it. "I need to get back to work. Mr. Kellogg is not lettin' it go that Mr. Cooper's horse ran into his truck. Can a horse get drunk? I mean, what other explanation is there?" Elizabeth shook her head. "You can't see the dent unless you look at Mr. Kellogg's truck from the front."

Trinity went to Mama and sat at the bed's edge. She took hold of Mama's hand and gently squeezed it. Anderson and Puppy followed behind, lying at the foot of the bed.

"How are you feeling, Mama? Any better?"

Mama held a tissue tight in her other hand and rubbed it under her nose as she sat propped up with pillows.

"Not much, sweetie. I'm not sure how long this cold will hold on for." Mama closed her eyes.

"You'll be just fine. You're a strong woman, and it's a simple cold. Your feistiness should be enough to knock it right out of you." Trinity winked.

Elizabeth had shown up to get Mama's mail and insisted Trinity visit her immediately. Trinity had grabbed the dogs, locked up, and jumped into the truck.

"How are the dogs?" Mama turned her head.

"They're doing great." Trinity scooped up Puppy, who was at least five pounds heavier.

She held Puppy closer to Mama so she could pet him. "What happened with Gavin? I heard he up and left already. I thought he was staying longer?"

"Emergency restoration," Mama whispered. "Tell me how you and your husband are doing."

"Mama, you should rest. We can chat later." Trinity set Puppy on the floor next to Anderson. "Can I get you some water or juice?"

Mama shook her head and coughed. "Did you make up with your mama?"

"Yes, the other morning. All is well now." Trinity watched as Mama closed her eyes again. "I'm going to let you rest."

"Bring Camden by, please. And name the puppy. He is family."

"Yes, Mama." Trinity tucked the elderly woman's hand under the covers and rose from the bed. "Take care, Mama."

"I think I am close to death," Mama whispered as Trinity made it to the doorway.

"Now hush, Mama. You're not even close." Trinity turned back around and returned to Mama's bedside. "Look at me, saying *hush*. You're rubbing off on me, Mama."

"You need to grant a dyin' woman's wishes." Mama's eyes were still closed.

"And what would that be?" Trinity kneeled beside the bed.

"That you and Camden get your baby. That you two stay together."

Trinity's chin quivered and she rubbed her hand over Mama's shoulder. "I wish we could." Trinity paused, holding back her tears as best she could. "Unless you're a genie. Just rest, Mama."

She took a breath and stood, pushing herself up with her hands on her knees. Trinity straightened out her shirt and held her head up in hopes of keeping the tears from falling from her eyes.

But as she reached the doorway, Trinity heard Mama whisper, "I am a genie."

After Trinity left work, she could only think of one place she wanted to go. She dropped off the dogs with her mom and headed west. It'd been some time since she and Camden last visited their special place, and it was as though her truck drove itself in the direction, like a magnetic pull.

She turned off the highway and eased the truck around dried-up brush, following a dusty path. She spotted fresh tracks. *Dang, someone is probably there.*

Just as Trinity was going to turn around and head back, she spotted a familiar Honda parked in the distance. Getting a car back there was not easy, but it was doable if the driver knew the area well.

"Camden?" she asked the empty cab of her truck as she parked next to his car and climbed out. "What are you doing here?"

She approached the historic slab of concrete and stepped up onto it. The only thing left of the house was its red brick fireplace and chimney which seemed to touch the heavens. Trinity had stumbled upon it back when she started dating Camden, and she'd taken him out to explore the desert. It was more accessible by horseback, but it was a long ride without any nearby water.

"I can't believe this thing is still standing. I'm surprised some teenagers have yet to come and destroy it." Trinity sat next to Camden on the brick hearth, pressing her hands on her knees.

"Some things are meant to last forever." Camden glanced at her and rubbed his palm on the brick. "A memory of us here popped in my head, and I had to come."

"You remember?" Trinity blushed.

Camden's nose reddened. "How could I ever forget?"

Trinity thought of their first night together, and her heart raced, reliving it. The sun had set behind the mountains, and the hum of the highway was barely audible. Camden had laid out a blanket on the concrete, and they'd reclined on their backs, watching the stars come out. She'd built a fire, the dried timbers crackling in the silence surrounding them. The burnt pizza box, in an attempt to keep the pizza warm, had been tossed into the fire some time ago. Half a bottle of wine sat nearby. And when he rolled over to kiss her, Trinity knew that the wine, pizza, and view would take a back seat to what was about to happen.

"This is where I was when I knew." Camden wrapped his hands into a ball.

Trinity leaned over and bumped his shoulder. "That you'd be getting lucky."

"No, that I wanted to give you the rest of my life. I wanted to, I had to, marry you." He focused his eyes on the ground.

Trinity's heart felt as though it disconnected from her organs. She pressed her eyelids closed, and when she opened them, tears ran down her cheeks.

She pushed past the lump in the back of her throat. "Why did we stop coming here?"

"Because life got in the way. Because we let life get in the way," he corrected himself.

"Remember we were going to take some of the bricks and build a fire pit for the backyard? I guess it doesn't matter now."

"I guess you're right."

And she didn't want either of them to be right.

Chapter 29

Camden

Camden entered Hammer and Nail to find R. J. sipping coffee behind the counter with a paperback open.

"Camden, good to see you." R. J. raised his coffee mug in greeting. "How's the new puppy working out? Anderson getting along with it?"

"Yes, they've become best buddies over the last week." Dressed in slacks and a button-down, Camden had taken a break from the restaurant at the end of the morning rush to stop by to see R. J. "I find it rather enjoyable to watch them romp around. Of course, it has put Trinity and me a bit behind on the renovations."

"What can I do for you today?"

Camden didn't know what to say. How had the town not found out about his poor tile job and the mortar mess fiasco? Had the Hackenburgs not seen him hosing off a hundred tiles in the front yard?

"I need something to remove dried mortar from a concrete floor."

R. J. closed his book and took another sip of coffee. "I reckon there was an issue at the house?"

Camden nodded. *How does the town not know this?*

"You're probably referring to what is called thinset. You have a few ways to go about it. There's the hammer and chisel method, which would probably take you a few months. Or you could use a rotary hammer with a chisel attachment. However, I would recommend a dustless grinder."

"Perfect, I'll take it." Camden removed his wallet from the back pocket of his slacks.

"Don't have one."

Camden squeezed the wallet and his shoulders slouched. Of course not. He would need to take time and drive into Cactus City.

"You'll want to protect the area." R. J. walked around from behind the counter. "Make sure you tape off the rest of the house as the dust will get everywhere."

"Do you have those items?" Camden slid his hands into his slack's pockets. "I can at least get started on that part."

"Sure do." R. J. moved about the store, collecting plastic draping and tape. "Are you taking the pup to Cactus City?"

Camden followed behind R. J. as he stacked the supplies into Camden's hands. "Since no one in town is missing him, Trinity and I have put off taking him. At this point, neither of us wants to give him up."

"You give him a name yet?"

"Not yet. We don't want to name him if we aren't going to be able to keep him."

R. J. patted Camden on the back and motioned to head to the register. "Might be best if you keep the pup. If you take it to the shelter, who knows how long it will be there." R. J. placed another roll of tape onto Camden's stack.

"Trinity and I agreed to have Puppy scanned for a microchip at the vet in Cactus City and then decide from there."

"Great for relationship building."

"I guess. If there was a relationship that was remaining a relationship." Camden's voice was riddled with disappointment.

What does R. J. know about relationships in the first place? He was a single man who spent his days reading and sipping coffee, flirting with the judge, but too afraid to make a move.

"Have you ever been married, R. J.?" Camden set his stack of supplies on the counter as the man began ringing up the items.

"Yes, right out of high school to my high school sweetheart. Rosaline. Smart, funny, and handy. She was always willing to learn a trade and never stopped amazing me, married for a wonderful twenty-three years."

Maybe R. J. did know what he was talking about after all.

"If you don't mind me asking"—Camden handed R. J. his credit card—"what ended the marriage?"

R. J. leaned back on the stool. He took a sip of coffee. "A horseback riding accident. A rattlesnake spooked the horse; it took off and threw Rosaline off." Camden's heart sank. How could being thrown off a horse cause a person to die? He figured horseback riding was reasonably safe. "Had she fallen on the dirt, maybe she could've survived with only some broken bones, but there was a rock . . . more like a boulder." R. J. sipped his coffee, blankly staring into it.

"Sorry to hear." Regret spread through Camden's heart; he hadn't meant to stir up any old emotions for R. J.

"It's always the good ones, right, Camden? To this day, I wish it had been me. She could easily have run this store or sold it, moved on with her life. Instead, an old man without much of a life sits in front of you." R. J. swiped the credit card through his tablet attachment and then handed it back.

Camden's mind went to Trinity and all the times she rode Starla. He never once thought about losing her in a horseback riding accident. He'd imagined a rattlesnake bite, car accident, or health problems. But horseback riding? Never.

"Do you think you'll find love again? Marry again?" Camden slid the card back into his wallet.

R. J. placed the items into a bag for Camden. "Not sure. I should move on, but . . ."

"The judge seems to enjoy your company," Camden hinted.

Was R. J. blushing? "She's a great woman, but I doubt she would want to date someone like me."

"You won't know unless you ask." Camden took the bag in his hand.

"Thank you, and good luck with the pup."

Camden left the store with two things on his mind: keeping Trinity safe with his newfound horseback riding information and wondering how many bricks from the fireplace he could fit into the trunk of his Honda.

"You bought me a helmet?" Trinity held up the shiny black contraption.

Camden had picked it up in Cactus City during his extended lunch break from the restaurant. He'd swung by the post office and picked up Puppy to take with him to the vet, much to Anderson and Trinity's dismay. Trinity wanted no part in finding out if they were going to lose the dog.

Puppy, as ecstatic as Anderson to see each other again, romped with his too-big paws, running as though he wore clown shoes.

"Yes, for when you ride Starla," Camden instructed. "Horses can be easily spooked, and I don't want you falling off and hitting your head on a rock."

"Starla and Stella don't spook easily. I trained them."

"Trained them?" Camden removed his shoes.

"Yes, when they were colts, I put a bunch of garbage in their pen. Plastic bags, rubber snakes, helped them get used to different things."

"Still, just to be safe, wear it, please."

"Okay." Trinity patted Camden's shoulder. "I will. What has you so worried?" She glanced at the table. "Ah, R. J. told you about his late wife."

Camden nodded.

"Let's change the subject; I hate even thinking about Rosaline."

"You knew her, then?" Camden loosened his tie and yanked it off from under his collar.

"Yes, she had the biggest heart. Full of love, adventure, and stories of her family." Trinity clapped her hands as if to break up the thought. "What happened at the vet's office?"

"That's why I called you on my way home."

"Sorry I missed your call, I was finishing up the mail sorting when Margie stopped in. I figured you were calling with bad news. She helped me outline a plan for my cookies, but we can talk about that later. So . . . what happened at the vet?" Trinity scrunched her face up like she was about to be hit with the news, literally.

"Puppy has a microchip. He's registered." Camden could almost feel Trinity's hope leaving her body and melting onto the floor. He took her hand. "However, Puppy is registered to a Mr. and Mrs. Moore."

"What?" Trinity's mouth hung open as she placed her hands around Camden's shoulders.

"And Puppy was not reported as missing. The vet called the prior registered owner, Jolie Belle Dunn. It turns out the dog was adopted at a shelter in Phoenix, and the microchip was updated to reflect its new owners—us."

"Jolie Belle Dunn?" Trinity crossed her arms. "Could that be Mama's name?"

"Well, I should say so. And do you want to know the date of us being the new owners?" Camden took a breath. "Remember the day of the storm when Mama and Elizabeth showed up with Puppy at the post office?"

Trinity uncrossed her arms, only to cross them the other way. "Same day."

"Same day. And today, when I was in Hammer and Nail, R. J. mentioned a puppy could mend a relationship, but he acted as though he didn't know about my mortar mess up. Like he was too busy to remember town gossip because he was focused on something more important."

"So, Mama, I mean, Jolie, orchestrated this whole lost puppy thing in an attempt to save our marriage?" Overwhelmed with thoughts, Camden dropped into a chair at the kitchen table.

"Speaking of Mama, I saw her today. She's not feeling well and wants to see you. She was talking nonsense, too, calling herself a genie. This whole town isn't making sense lately." Trinity sank into the chair next to Camden at the table. "And Aurora's silent treatment —"

"You still haven't spoken with Aurora?"

"For two weeks! Every time I call, she says she's busy with the girls or has a doctor's appointment. It's always something. I don't know why she's avoiding me."

"This whole town has gone crazy!" He threw his hands in the air.

Puppy and Anderson froze mid-romp at the commotion but quickly returned to playtime.

"Does this mean we can finally give Puppy a proper name?" Trinity beamed.

"I know you already have one picked out, start using it." Camden unbuttoned the top two buttons on his shirt.

Trinity clapped her hands. "Dean!"

"Great name." Camden tried to smile, but an unsettling fear washed over him for the first time since he moved to Woolsey. A town that once held no secrets now appeared to brim with them. He ran his hand through his hair and reached his other hand out to Trinity.

"I know you're thinking all this is adding up to no good, but my heart feels like it's adding up to something big. And now we know Mama's real name." Trinity leaned in and kissed Camden on his cheek.

Camden's heart skipped, craving the need for comfort. He wanted to pull Trinity in and kiss her on the lips. He tried to do so many things because he still loved her as much as always. He wanted to have this unsettling fear erased from inside him.

"Sorry." Trinity leaned back.

Camden lifted his hand to Trinity's cheek, wrapping his fingers into the hair behind her ear. His heart raced with his skin on hers. He needed her, and he didn't want to let her go. He couldn't. *So we don't have kids. We can have puppies.*

"We shouldn't," Trinity whispered as her eyes locked on his.

"I know." Camden pulled her into his lap, wrapping her up in his arms.

With Trinity's breath on his shirt and the smell of jasmine in her hair, he moved his lips toward her when a jolt hitting the bottom of the chair interrupted them. Camden released Trinity from his grasp to find Anderson and Dean wrestling against the chair legs.

"Okay, boys, let's get you some dinner." Trinity eased herself off Camden's lap.

So much for Dean helping their relationship.

Chapter 30

Trinity

When it came to celebrating the Fourth of July, Woolsey didn't hold back. From the earliest childhood memory Trinity had, she recalled the Shop and Save had served up a feast for the town each year, even some years when a monsoon tried to dampen the celebration.

Charlie operated the grills and smokers, just as he did every Saturday on the store's patio. The scent of mesquite and hickory floated throughout the town, reminding anyone who might have forgotten to be ready to celebrate. Of course, Saturday get-togethers were always a barbecue feast, but nothing rivaled the one on the Fourth. It was the most beloved event in Woolsey over all other holidays. Because unlike the rest of the United States, who had cabin fever in the winter, Woolsey had a touch of it in the summer.

Excited for the gathering, she pulled the truck into the parking lot around four thirty in the afternoon.

Camden and Anderson climbed out while Trinity helped Dean down. His attempts to jump from the truck proved to be more of a stumble than a leap. Hopefully, Dean could work on that once he grew a bit bigger.

"Moores!" several residents cheered as the pair approached the row of picnic tables.

Forceful, like long-lost aunts, residents gathered to hug and squeeze hands with Camden and Trinity.

"We heard about the puppy," Jennifer stated, waving her husband, Greg, over. "Dean, right?" Jennifer bent down to pet the dog as he wiggled around between her legs.

"Is Fred here?" Trinity asked, peeking around for Jennifer and Greg's bulldog.

Greg pointed to one of the grills. "He has taken up residence in hopes of catching a burger."

"I doubt any playtime will happen with him today." Jennifer moved on to pet Anderson. "I think Dolores brought her boys, though."

Trinity knew Dolores's "boys" meant her four mutts. They ranged from about eight to ten years old. Dolores had adopted them during a Cactus City animal shelter Christmas event five years ago. She went in looking for one and left with four.

"Great." Trinity placed her hand on the edge of her baseball cap, providing extra shade as she searched for the boys. "I know Anderson would love to play with them, and it would be good for Dean, too." She spotted several blue kiddie pools full of water under the shade of some trees for the pups to enjoy.

The only thing missing in Woolsey was a dog park. Residents didn't complain, though. If an owner wanted to have playtime, they set a date, time, and place. It would be a challenge to keep up a grassy dog park in the desert. The nice part about Woolsey was nearly every area was dog friendly. Be it the grocery store, the post office, or Hammer and Nail. Having all dirt parking lots helped a lot because it wasn't as dangerous on paws as scorching pavement. Although no one had taken a dog into the courthouse or library, Trinity was sure it wouldn't bother anyone at all. While dogs were not allowed inside Breakfast, Lunch, Dinner & Everything in Between, they were allowed outside on the patio.

"Who is in charge of the fireworks tonight?" Camden asked.

"Barrett, as long as he puts on pants." Jennifer laughed.

Dolores's husband, Barrett, had a thing about walking around his property in the morning in his T-shirt and boxers while pairing his knee-high black socks with flip-flops. With a coffee mug in hand, he would check on his roses. In the winter, he was nice enough to put on a wool hat. Barrett had the most beautiful roses, even if he wasn't big on appropriate attire outside the house.

"I'm starving." Camden faced Trinity before he spun in the dirt. "I'm going to check on getting a plate of food. Want anything?"

"I'll grab something in a few." Trinity shoved a hand in her pocket. She watched as Dean and Anderson found Dolores's boys.

Jennifer reached her hand out and placed it on Trinity's arm. "How are you doing? I mean *reeeally* doing." Jennifer taught fourth grade at Woolsey Elementary and tried her best not to meddle too much in other people's businesses.

"I'm doing well. The house is coming along as best as it can, even with the addition of Dean."

"You must have me over soon. I'm eager to see the updates." Jennifer eyed her husband and Fred like a mother checking on how her children were behaving.

"Are you already planning for Halloween?" Trinity watched as a dragonfly circled.

"Yes! This year, I have a Frankenstein theme planned." Jennifer smiled big enough to see all her teeth, even the molars.

With the houses spread out in Woolsey, it made trick-or-treating a challenge for the kids, especially since it was usually in the eighties temperature-wise. Chocolate candy often melted being out too long. That's why Jennifer's passion for Halloween meant a great deal to the town. Residents all pitched in and brought bags of candy. Jennifer and Greg's home never disappointed and even had adults without kids excited to see it from year to year.

"I'll have the garage decorated, as always, and a Frankenstein haunted path in the yard." Jennifer rubbed her hands together in glee. "I think I'm going with twenty stopping stations for candy. And of course, refreshments and treats for the parents, as well." Jennifer's mouth froze. "I mean adults, for adults." Jennifer reached her hand out and rubbed Trinity's shoulder. "You and Camden must come."

Just as Trinity was going to agree to come, it hit her. She would be coming alone, as a divorcée of sixty days.

"You don't have to be a parent to join the fun. You know that by now, right?" Jennifer kept going, trying to undo the damage of saying the p-word.

Clearly, Jennifer was too focused on the p-word, forgetting that Camden would be nowhere near Woolsey for Halloween. And if, for some odd reason, he happened to be, they wouldn't be spending the evening together.

With a flustered look on her face, Jennifer said, "I think Greg needs me. Excuse me."

Trinity watched Jennifer hurry off into the crowd. Looking around, she located Camden with a stacked plate and Anderson and Dean lapping up water with the boys over on the grocery store's patio. The realization that Halloween, Thanksgiving, and Christmas would be incredibly different and challenging this year hit her in the heart, nearly taking her breath.

"Hi, Trin." A familiar voice came up from behind her.

"Mom, hi." Trinity embraced her mom.

"Trin, what's wrong?" Lillian ran her hand over the ponytail popping out of her hat.

"Nothing." Trinity wiped her tears and gathered her composure. "Did you bring your potato salad?"

"Yes, I see Camden has already located it on the table and has taken more than his fair share."

Lillian's potato salad was legendary in Woolsey, especially since she didn't make it for the restaurant. She made it with potatoes from her garden.

"Where are my grand-pups?" Lillian rubbed her daughter's back as they peered out over the crowd of residents milling about.

Trinity's heart warmed at her mom's touch. She'd missed it.

"They're taking a rest over by Fred." Trinity pointed toward one of the grills. "Have you seen Aurora lately? She has been distant for weeks."

"Did you hear my phone?" Lillian pulled her cell phone out of her back pocket.

"No," Trinity tilted her head. "Mom, do you know something I don't know?"

Lillian slid the phone back into her jeans pocket and shook her head. "No, Trin." She paused. "That storm the other day was pretty bad over by Aurora and me."

"Mom, you don't live that far away from me. It was the same everywhere in town."

"I think we got it worse over by us. You know how it can be. Dust in the front, rain in the back." Lily grabbed Trinity's hand. "Come on, let's go eat. I'm hungry."

Trinity scrunched her brow as her mom pulled her across the parking lot over to the tables.

Camden chatted away with Greg as they noshed corn on the cob and ribs at the table nearest to the grill. Dolores's boys were fighting over who got to drink from the multiple water bowls. Fred, Anderson, and Dean rested by the mister fans;

they made a huge difference when the temperatures were in the hundreds.

Trinity piled her paper plate with potato salad, corn, ribs, and one of Dolores's homemade rolls. She set her plate on the table across from her mom's and went to grab ice water when Gavin appeared at her right.

"Water?" Gavin handed her a chilled bottle.

"Gavin! Thank you." She hugged him before taking the bottle of water.

Gavin slid onto the picnic table's bench next to Trinity along with his plate and a sweating bottle of beer.

"I didn't know you were back in town." Trinity opened her water bottle and took a swig. "I thought you went back to Jesser."

"I got in last night. Mama had a fall, and Lizzy needed some extra help. Plus, she still can't shake that cold."

"I heard about the fall, but I thought she was okay."

"She's on the mend. Upset that Camden hasn't stopped by as asked."

"I know. He will see her soon, promise. Oh, Gavin, this is Lillian, my mom." Trinity gestured to her mom across the table.

"Yes, Lillian and I have met." Gavin grinned.

"Oh." Trinity ripped off a piece of the roll and forced it into her mouth. "Are Mama and Elizabeth going to make it?"

"No, Lizzy was worried about Mama being out in the heat for too long, especially with her being weak after the fall," Gavin stated. "I mean Louisiana gets mighty hot, but not dry like this. I can feel my skin cracking under my shirt. I could use an IV drip to keep me hydrated."

Trinity covered her mouth and laughed. "It's true. But I'm not sure how you handle all the humidity in the South. A monsoon rolls through, and for three hours we all feel as though we're swimming in molasses. It's so dry, you can smell the rain coming here."

"Sure can't smell the rain comin' in the South. It's a permanent resident." Gavin nibbled on his ribs, then, without warning, Camden slid onto the edge of the bench next to Trinity.

"Was getting seconds." He glanced around Trinity at Gavin. "Hey, you're back."

Gavin raised a rib. "Indeed. Couldn't stay away forever."

"There isn't room for you here." Trinity's left arm squished against Camden's right arm.

"Sure, there is. Gavin, can you please scootch down a touch? I want to sit next to my wife."

Trinity's eyes widened, and she shoved a rib into her mouth to keep from gawking. Was Camden jealous of Gavin enough to be bold? The closest Camden ever got to bold was with his brightly colored ties.

"Pardon me, my apologies." Gavin scooted himself, his beer, and his plate a few inches to the right.

Dean and Anderson trotted over to flop at their feet. "Gavin, have you met Dean?" Trinity asked, trying to lighten the jealousy that hung thick in the air.

Gavin snatched up his beer and took a long time drinking before setting it down. He wiped his mouth with a paper napkin. "No, but Mama did mention him."

Trinity squeezed out from between Camden and Gavin. She scooped up Dean, still able to carry him, but barely.

Gavin set his hand on top of Dean's head and then rubbed under his chin. "Well, you're a fine-looking dog," he oozed. Dean wiggled in Trinity's arms, and she set him back down on the ground before wedging her way back between the men.

With eyes laser focused on Camden, in a way only a wife to a husband could do, she silently communicated her displeasure. With a huff, Camden returned to focusing on his plate.

"Don't be getting into a jealous fight," Trinity said through clenched teeth.

This would be their last holiday celebration together, and she didn't want Camden and Gavin getting into it. She wanted to enjoy every part of the evening.

"Great potato salad, Mom, yet again." Trinity winked.

"Thank you, Trin." Lillian continued to eat, not seeming the least bit aware of the tension looming over the table. "Charlie did a great job with the ribs, but he always does." Lillian licked another rib clean to the bone.

"I would agree," Camden added. "I had both a burger and the ribs."

"You had both?" Trinity laughed and placed the back of her hand on Camden's forehead. "Are you feeling okay?"

"Yes, I figured since it's the last time I'll be here for the Fourth of July, I'd better get it all while I can."

Trinity and Camden stared at each other, their faces distraught.

Abruptly, Lillian pointed across the way at nothing. "Gavin, would you mind helping me over there?"

"Sure thing, ma'am." Gavin sprang up, and together, they hurried away, taking their plates with them.

Trinity's eyes squinted, but it wasn't from the sunlight. "It's like they know each other a lot more than I thought. What's going on?"

"Do you feel as though we're being hoodwinked?" Camden asked.

Trinity nodded her head. "Something is going on. I've just about had it with being on the outside of it all."

"Then why don't we ask Mama and Elizabeth about the dog?"

"Because I don't want to upset Mama, especially with her feeling poorly, and you haven't visited as asked. Whatever this town is hiding, they can't hide it for long." Trinity finished her roll. "And because, like you said, this is our last holiday celebration here and your last one with me. We need to enjoy it."

Camden took her hand and wrapped his around it, watching as the clouds formed, reaching up into the sky, sending shade to sections around the grocery store. This might be one heck of a Fourth of July, even without the fireworks.

Chapter 31

Camden

Camden wanted to stay in this moment forever, watching the reflection of fireworks in Trinity's eyes. Her mouth was oohing and aahing at each explosion. However, the threat of being struck by lightning was far greater, at least to him.

"Trinity, come on, let's get the dogs and head home." Camden pulled at her arm.

"The boys are safe." Trinity pointed behind her without turning around.

Yes, Anderson and Dean were safe under the cover of the patio with the rest of the dogs. By strategically moving the picnic tables around, they'd blocked the dogs, undercover, just in case.

"Barrett had been looking forward to this since New Year's Day," Trinity yelled over the gust of wind, bang of fireworks, and the rumble of thunder. "We can't bail on him."

She had a point. Barrett spent July fifth to the last day of December planning the fireworks for the New Year's Eve get-together, though it was not as big an event as the Fourth. Then Barrett spent January to July planning the Fourth of July celebration.

The lightning danced across the sky like veins between the clouds. It wasn't raining, but he could smell the moisture in the air. Bright reds and blues sprinkled the sky along with sparkling gold. The clouds continued to push forward, making the last of the fireworks a hide-and-seek show. Then, with an explosion of all the colors in the rainbow, the sky lit up with the grand finale. Behind them, the group of dogs barked their disapproval at the noise.

Camden wrapped his arms around her waist, and the alcohol of the night allowed him to not care about what he should and shouldn't do. Trinity didn't fight it either, which caused him to smile. She wrapped her arms around his, pulling him closer against her back. *Please, do not let this moment end.*

"I think I felt a drop of rain," Trinity said, touching her nose. She removed her hat.

The firework show ended, and everyone stood around, wishing there would be more. Barrett approached the crowd of residents, and the applause started. He bowed as though it was the curtain call after a Broadway show.

"It's picking up," Camden said as thick drops of rain hit his hair.

By the time they'd collected Anderson and Dean and said their goodbyes, the sky had completely opened up, the rain coming down in sheets. Everyone dashed for their cars. The only time an Arizonian grabbed an umbrella was to protect themselves from the sun, not the rain.

With muddy paws, Anderson and Dean loaded into the truck, followed by Trinity and Camden.

"It's dumping." He wiped the water from his face.

Trinity's hair was sopping wet, her hat in her hand soaked through. "We need it, though."

Anderson attempted to rub the water off his coat by rolling around in the small space. Dean continually shook, unsure what all the water was about.

"At least we're on this side of town. I hope Dolores and Barrett can make it back home." Camden peered out the window.

Trinity started up the truck and clicked on the wipers. "Jennifer and Greg, too."

"Should we wait?" Camden pointed. "I don't see how you can see a thing with it coming down this hard."

Trinity glanced over at him, raising an eyebrow. "You might not be able to, but I can."

"For safety's sake, can we wait at least a few minutes?" Camden whined.

He was not one for driving in storms, especially in the dark. Continuing to observe the monsoon through the front windshield, a chill ran up his spine. His jeans and shirt were drenched through, making him cold.

"Fine." Trinity relaxed back in the seat, waiting for the rain to calm some. "I can't believe Aurora and her family didn't show up."

"That is odd. Why don't you call her?"

Trinity removed her phone and placed the call. She put the cell to her ear. Her eyes gazed out at the storm. "It's not ringing." When she looked at the phone, Trinity said, "No service."

Camden extended his arm to the headrest of Trinity's seat, blocking Dean from climbing up to the front bench seat.

"I'll drop you boys off at the house and then head over to see her. Find out what's up." Trinity put the truck into first.

"I don't know about you driving out in this alone. Try calling her again when we get home."

Trinity made it onto State Route 287. Even with everyone leaving at once, they all kept a safe distance. The water came from the sky as though someone poured out massive buckets right onto the windshield. No wiper blades could keep up.

Camden clenched his jaw, and really his entire body was tense as he gripped the handle on the passenger door, his other hand squeezing Trinity's headrest. Water from the road sprayed from the wheel wells of the large truck in front of them. Standing water stretched the width of the 287 until they turned onto Mountain View Road, where the flooding grew deeper. Mountain View Road desperately needed some form of drainage. The road was more of a river crossing, the current flowing north to south over the road.

Trinity drove the truck in second gear through the deep water, the visibility out the windshield not much better than when they'd left Shop and Save. The Hackenburgs' patio light was barely visible through the downpour as the truck inched by and turned into their driveway. The family hadn't made it to the Fourth of July celebration, either. Although, Camden wasn't sure how comfortable he would feel bringing a six-month-old out in the July heat, much less under the loud fireworks. The Hackenburgs could probably see the show from their patio, anyways.

Trinity parked the truck in the garage, and they filed out, all still very wet.

"I'll help you bathe Anderson and Dean, and then I'll try and call again." Trinity hung the truck keys on the hook just inside next to the garage door.

"No, I'll get them. You try calling your mom. She should be home by now." Camden had Anderson by the collar and Dean in his arm.

Without argument, Trinity picked up her phone and pulled up Lillian's number. She stood in her wet, dripping clothes on the mess of hardened mortar at the edge of the kitchen. Camden turned the living room lights on before ushering Anderson down the hall to the bathtub.

After loading Dean into the bathtub, he gathered two towels and placed them on the counter. Camden ran the bathwater and instructed Anderson to join his brother. He scrubbed both dogs until the water ran clean in the tub. Drying them off was more of a challenge than he expected. Anderson continued to spin in circles while Dean attempted to jump out of the tub that was far too high for him.

"Stay still, buddy," Camden instructed Anderson while kneeling. Before settling into position, he lost his balance and fell backward onto the bathroom floor. Dean took a final leap of victory, his front half out of the tub, his bottom half on the lip. The sound of paw claws scrambling to get the rest of the way over filled the air.

He started to laugh as Dean gave one last Herculean effort and made it out, stumbling onto Camden's chest, clean but sopping wet. The boys joined forces and tore down the hall. Wet paw prints smashed into the carpet along the way.

"No! Anderson, get back here! Dean!" Camden got to his feet, snatched the towels, and chased after them. "Get back here!"

When Camden reached the kitchen, he found Trinity on the phone and the boys running laps around the table. Anderson made a direction change, heading for the sofa. Dean followed, but with his larger-than-life wet puppy paws and clumsy footing, his legs went out under him. He regained his balance and shook himself off before leaping after Anderson. They rolled around on the sofa together.

"No, boys," Camden whisper-yelled, trying not to disturb Trinity's phone call. "No, off the sofa."

The dogs froze mid-play and glared at Camden. He made slow steps, approaching them without trying to spook them. Anderson caught on and jumped from the sofa, racing to his dog bed. Dean, not as skilled as Anderson, rolled over on the sofa and succumbed to the defeat of his master. Camden wrapped Dean in a towel and placed him on the floor to dry him off.

"Mom is home safe. And I finally got through to Aurora. I guess both girls are sick, so they skipped the celebration tonight. She said she texted me, but I never saw it come through." Trinity set her cell phone on the table. "What happened out here?"

She approached the sofa, wet spots everywhere. Anderson hunkered down in his dog bed, fearing the wrath of the towel coming for him.

"They escaped the confines of the tub." Camden enveloped Anderson in the towel, rubbing his fur, though most of the water had already transferred to the sofa. "What's with the look?"

Trinity covered her mouth, but he noticed she was smiling by how her eyes changed at the edges. She nodded her head. "No look. I'm going to change."

"Stop laughing," Camden called, still standing in his wet clothing, holding two relatively dry towels. "They weren't listening to me."

Once they'd both changed into their pajamas for the night, Camden and Trinity sat at the kitchen table with their feet up on the extra chairs since the sofa was still wet from the dogs.

"We need to step up the progress on the house." Trinity rubbed her fingers over the sweat forming on the outside of her water glass.

Camden sank back against the chair, examining the unfinished kitchen. "I know. We're dragging out the inevitable."

Trinity's vision locked with his. He wanted to smile, to make her eyes shine with happiness instead of disappointment. Yet, he knew his eyes looked exactly the same. He'd seen it in the mirror when he'd knotted his tie or brushed his teeth. *You're more important than having a baby.* The words danced in his thoughts, but he couldn't break her dream. She must be a mom. The world would be a better place for it.

"I picked up the sander in Cactus City days ago. I can start on that tomorrow before work," Camden offered.

"We need to remove the toilet in the spare bathroom, pull up the linoleum, and set the new tile. Since Gavin is back in town, maybe I can ask him for help. We need to hang the cabinets, too."

"I would prefer if it was you and I only, even if that means I have to learn new skills and redo them a few times before I get it right." Camden gulped water. "Although the concrete countertops . . . maybe we will need to ask Gavin for help."

"Understandable, and I do appreciate your willingness to at least allow him to help with the counters. I have no idea how to go about that." Trinity focused on the ice in the glass. "Do you know where you'll be moving to?"

"I want to stay, keep teaching. I love watching the students grow and move on to the next grade. Yet, I know I can't. It would be incredibly challenging to stay in Woolsey and no doubt see you at work and in town. I don't know where I would stay. I'm looking at some other cities nearby." Trinity nodded but didn't make eye contact with him, her vision fixed off in the distance. "And I know it's important for you to stay. You can't leave. Your mom is here, your childhood, your life."

"Yes, but I can't ask you to leave just so I can be more comfortable."

"I'm aware. I'm doing it because I love you. I always will."

"I'll always love you, too."

The rain pummeled the windows on the side of the house and slammed onto the rooftop. Bold flickers of lightning added sudden bursts of brightness through the windows; the clap of thunder immediately behind it vibrated the dishes in the sink.

Camden stared at Anderson and Dean, lying back-to-back on the carpet. He was beyond glad that neither of them were frightened by the stormy weather. As Camden closed his eyes, he absorbed the sounds of the monsoon around him and hoped he could have a few more of these nights with Trinity.

Chapter 32

Camden

"Mama, it's Camden." He stood at the door frame to Mama's bedroom with a small cream pot of Firedance Igloo mums.

Mama's head moved on the pillow in his direction. "Come in." Her voice was stronger than he expected.

"Are you feeling better?" Camden moved toward her bed and placed the mums on the nightstand.

"Indeed I am, son." Mama wiggled in the bed, trying to sit up a bit more. "Sit, son. Tell me how you're doing."

Camden wanted to come right out and ask about Dean and call her by her name, yet, something happened when he looked into Mama's eyes. Fear. He feared this feisty older woman, and a part of him worried if he was blunt with her, she might have some relapse at her age. Once she was up and moving around again, he might bring it up.

"How is your job goin' at that ridiculously long-named restaurant?"

Camden let out a singular chuckle. He hadn't thought about the length of Luis's restaurant until then. "Yes, it is a rather long name, but it's going well. The time goes by quick."

"And your wife? I heard she might be selling her wonderful cookies soon." Mama reached her hand out, and Camden held it.

"She's working on plans to see if it's possible. Our kitchen's still torn apart at home, so she'd need to wait to start it up or at least use Lillian's kitchen in the meantime."

"It's a good thing she and her mama made up. Please hand me my water. I'm feelin' parched."

Camden handed Mama her glass with a straw. She took a sip and then passed it back to him.

"I'm sorry I didn't get over to see you sooner."

"I don't want to hear excuses. How're the upgrades at the house? You'll need them. Gavin should be helping you out, I hope. How's Dean? I bet it's great preparation for—"

Camden cupped his hands together. "We're getting a divorce. Each day brings us closer to September. Mama . . . I want to ask you something." Everything in Camden's mind told him not to ask and ask at the same time.

"Oh, my." Mama placed her hand on her chest and closed her eyes. "I'm suddenly feelin' weak."

"I hope it's not my visit." Camden remained seated.

"Leave me to rest, please." Mama's eyes flickered as though trying to stay awake.

Camden rose from the bed and tiptoed out of the room, closing the bedroom door behind him. When he pivoted around, he came eye to eye with Gavin.

"Camden, I didn't know you were here."

Camden raised his finger to his lips. "Mama's trying to rest. I guess my visit hit her harder than expected." He made his way to the front door, Gavin on his heels.

The cowboy glanced back at the bedroom door. "Really? She's been doin' well all day."

Camden shoved his hands into his front pockets. "Probably best I head out, anyways. Bathroom renovation's today."

Gavin opened the front door. "Need a hand?"

"We have it under control, thanks though."

"Free of charge." Gavin rocked on his cowboy boots.

"Thank you. Honestly, the bathroom should be easy." Camden stepped out into the abundant sunshine. "The screen door turned out nice."

"Thanks. If you change your mind, let me know."

Camden waved as he climbed into his car, attempting not to burn his hands on the steering wheel.

"How is Mama, I mean Jolie Belle Dunn doing?" Trinity smirked. "I can't turn off the valve back here. It's stuck. Can you hand me a wrench, please?"

Camden grabbed the wrench out of the toolbox in the hall and handed it to Trinity. After shutting off the water, she flushed the toilet and held the handle down.

"What are you doing?"

"Trying to get all the water out." She lifted the lid off the tank and handed it to Camden. "Might want to get some gloves on."

Trinity ripped open a packet of something and sprinkled it into the toilet bowl.

"What's that for?" He pointed.

"It turns the remaining water in the bowl into a gel, so when we pull the toilet up, it doesn't leak everywhere."

He took the toilet lid to the stack out in the garage and returned wearing his gloves.

"Okay, now tell me—how is Jolie?"

"Mama is not doing well. I mean, she was when I got there, then she suddenly needed a nap."

"Maybe it's best if we wait to ask about Dean. Odd, as I thought she was getting better." Trinity kneeled on the floor and started to loosen the bolts at the base of the toilet. "Did you see Gavin? We could use his help."

"I did, but frankly, I don't want his help. Not yet. I need to learn, and we need to do this together." Camden stood awkwardly at the door.

Trinity slouched. "Then I need your full help, Mr. Not Green Hammer." She winked.

"I'm here for you." Camden pushed his shoulders up and back.

"While we wait for the gel to dry, you can help me with the vanity. You need to turn off the water supply for the hot and cold, then disconnect the P-trap."

"I'm on it. Soon, you'll be calling me Mr. Green Hammer, Mrs. Green Hammer." Camden raised an eyebrow as he reached under the sink and completed the steps. "Alright, all done."

Trinity removed the supply line from the back of the toilet and drained the little bit of water into a small bucket. "Time to pull out the vanity, then. Same as when we did the kitchen cabinets." She pointed to the crowbar.

He smiled wickedly and went to work prying it from the wall. Trinity stood to help him pull it entirely from the wall when Camden shrieked. He stumbled backward into the hall as he let go of the vanity.

"What is that!" he pointed behind the vanity.

Trinity, still holding onto her side of the vanity, peered around the back. "It looks like a dead mouse."

"I'm not here for you! Call Gavin! Call your mom!" Camden yelled from the living room. "I'm taking the boys over to see Jasmine! I'm not ever going to be Mr. Green Hammer!"

Chapter 33

Trinity

The month of July rolled in like a monsoon, fast. Tile throughout the Moore residence had been laid, two new toilets installed, and baseboards started. Gavin had proved a huge help as well. The kitchen, being the most expensive and a considerable inconvenience, remained cabinet-and counter-free. However, she and Camden hadn't asked Gavin if he knew about Mama's involvement in the sudden appearance of Dean.

Trinity stared at the calendar on the post office wall. August 16. Her heart sank as she watched Dean and Anderson roughhouse on the floor. *How can it already be mid-August?* She spent the first half of the month fighting off the courage to ditch her dreams for children and tell Camden she wanted to call off the divorce. But every time she went to tell him, she pulled back. She couldn't take his dream away.

The door opened, the bell chimed, and in shuffled Mama and Elizabeth. It was precisely 12:10. This meant the judge had left the courthouse at exactly 11:58 to make it in perfect time. She went home, loaded Mama into the car, and drove here. She must have Mama back home and eating lunch no later than 12:30. They picked up the mail, so Mama had something to go through while she ate.

"Hi, Mama," Trinity said. "Great to see you up and moving about."

"Hello, there," Mama's voice was weak but cheerful. "Good to be upright. Maybe I'll have them bury me vertically."

Since Mama's fall, she'd slowed down a great deal. Though they'd avoided most conversations and had yet to invite her and Camden back over for supper, most people in town had resorted to little if any small talk with the Moores as each day brought them closer to September 1.

Today was the day she would confront Mama. Trinity took a deep breath, her chest lifting the direction of her chin.

"Mama?" Mama and Elizabeth moved to the counter. Trinity held her hands together. *Am I trembling?* "Mama." Trinity glanced at her hands.

"Spit it out, child, I ain't got all day," Mama stated, her hand tapping the counter. "Heck, I might die walkin' back to the car."

"Mama," Elizabeth scolded.

Trinity took another deep breath. "Camden and I had Dean checked out at the vet, and he said he was registered to us by a Jolie Belle Dunn."

Mama's eyes darted to her daughter. "Well, see."

"Mama, I advise you to invoke your Fifth Amendment right." Elizabeth wrapped her arm around Mama.

"Yes, I plead the Fifth." Mama nodded.

"Elizabeth?" Trinity unlocked her hands and crossed them over her body. "This is not a courtroom. Why is your Mama taking the Fifth? Elizabeth—Your Honor?"

Elizabeth directed Mama toward the door. "Let's go, Mama."

"We plead the Fifth." Mama pivoted her feet and, like a turtle trying to win a race, shuffled her way to the door.

"Does Gavin know about this?" Trinity asked.

Mama and Elizabeth paused. The judge leaned over and whispered something to Mama.

Mama turned her head back over her shoulder. "You go right on and call all the Dunns you wish. We all plead the Fifth."

And with that, the door opened, heat crashed through like a wave, and Trinity slumped back onto the stool. "This isn't over yet."

As Trinity reached for her cell phone to text Camden, the door swung open again, and her husband came through, carrying a plate and a drink.

"Perfect timing." Trinity leaned over the counter.

"I saw Mama and Elizabeth on the way out. They were in a hurry." He set the lunch on the counter. "I have to tell you something."

"I have to tell you something," Trinity echoed. "Since you brought me lunch, you go first." Trinity took a sip from the straw.

"I swung by Hammer and Nail this morning to pick up another battery for the drill, and R. J. was taken aback. When I stepped into the store, he glanced up from his book and reached for a container on the counter. The container was rather large, and I couldn't make out the words, but I did see an image on it, a photo before he shoved it under the counter. It was a photo of us."

Trinity coughed, patted her chest, and then sipped some more before she could regain her composure. "Us? What did you say to him?"

"Nothing, I didn't know what to say. I mean, I could've been wrong. I dream about us all the time, and I swear, I see you everywhere I look. The last few nights, I've found myself smelling your jasmine scent when you're not in the room. Maybe you're a ghost, and all this has been a dream."

Trinity waved her sandwich at him. "No, this isn't a dream. Do you think you were wrong? That you mistook our photo for another couple?"

Dean and Anderson scratched at the door, and Trinity opened it so they could escape from the back room and greet Camden.

"I'm not sure. But if it wasn't us, then why did he hide it?"

Trinity shook her head and took a bite of the sandwich. *Why does a container have our picture on it?*

"What were you going to tell me?" Camden remained on his knees, petting the dogs.

"I finally gathered the courage to ask Mama about Dean. She plead the Fifth, as did the judge. Then I threatened to call Gavin and ask him if he knew about it."

"I didn't know you two were chatting." Camden rose from the floor, his hand resting on the counter.

"Only about house restoration questions."

Camden nodded and folded his arms over his chest. "That's nice of him."

"What should we do? Call a town meeting?" Trinity held her sandwich up, her elbows resting on the counter.

"And say what? This isn't *Cheers*. They might know our names, but the town of Woolsey won't be giving us any answers."

Trinity covered her mouth as she giggled. "Great analogy."

"For once, I'm looking forward to leaving this crazy town."

Trinity's giggles stopped suddenly, like pulling the reins on a horse to halt it.

"I didn't mean for that to sound harsh." Camden's eyes went to his shoes.

The stool scraped across the linoleum as she stood. "You never wanted to live here, don't start apologizing now."

"Why are you raising your voice? Of course, I didn't want to live here. It's the desert; there are snakes, scorpions, and geckos. And dead mice." Camden threw his hands up toward the ceiling. "In case you missed it, it's a billion degrees outside! I can't even drive my car without potholders on my hands. And I make sure to park in the shade!" Camden stomped his foot as though he were five years old.

"You said you wanted to move here, that you could adapt."

"Yes, because I loved you and knew how much you loved living in this dusty hole." Camden's hands flailed around like an air dancer outside a car lot.

Trinity's hand moved to her chest. "Loved?"

"You know what I mean."

"Do I?" Trinity lowered herself, weak in the knees, onto the stool. "I assumed you would grow to love it here."

"You assumed wrong." Camden made it to the door, swung it open, and disappeared into the sunshine's blinding glow.

Anderson and Dean waddled to the door just as it slammed closed. They turned around to Trinity as tears streamed down her face. She went to the dogs and kneeled on the floor as they licked her tears away. But they couldn't mend her shattered heart.

Chapter 34

Camden & Trinity

Instead of heading home, she turned left off State Route 287 and onto Wagon Circle Road toward Aurora's house. She might be able to avoid seeing her mom, who would only baby her, and right now, she needed anything but that. Hopefully, Aurora wouldn't avoid her if she stood at her front door.

Anderson and Dean climbed out of the truck as dust danced in the air. It amazed Trinity how quickly Dean had grown in the short time they had him. The puppy stage always went too fast.

The screen door creaked open, and Trinity glanced up. Even behind her sunglasses, she squinted from the sun. "Hi, girls."

Ava and Willa bolted through the entrance and rushed to hug the dogs.

The creak of the door came again and out stepped Aurora. "To what do I owe the pleasure of this visit?"

Trinity went to her best friend and embraced her. Tears streamed down her cheeks immediately.

"Oh no, sweetie." Aurora patted Trinity's back. "What happened?"

Without waiting for an answer, Aurora pulled out of the hug, took Trinity's hand, and led her inside the house, the girls and dogs following right behind.

"Girls, why don't you take Anderson and Dean into the living room and see if they want to play with any of those toys we have hidden away just for them."

The girls didn't need to be asked twice as they called the dogs, leaving Aurora and Trinity alone in the kitchen. Aurora guided her best friend to one of the swivel barstools while she retrieved a bottle of wine and two glasses.

"Do you have any chocolate?" Trinity asked, wiping her tears.

Aurora set the wine and glasses on the bar top and opened the refrigerator. Digging into the back, she removed a small bowl of assorted chocolates – the only place residents could keep it during the summer, or it would melt. Only the wealthiest, who kept their air conditioners set at seventy, could keep chocolate out all year long.

The sound of wine pouring into glasses filled the kitchen.

"Thanks." Trinity took a drink as though it was a liquor shot and then shoved a piece of chocolate into her mouth. "Camden and I got into a fight."

"You two are fighting?" Aurora snickered. "I'm sorry, sweetie. It's just that you two never fought. What could you have to fight about now?"

"How much he hates living here."

Aurora rubbed Trinity's back and moved her hair behind her ear as it stuck to her face from the tears. "He doesn't hate living here."

"No?"

"Of course not. He just can't bear the thought of leaving." Aurora rubbed her fingers over the stem of the wineglass. "What started the fight?"

"That's the thing." Trinity wiped her nose with the back of her hand. "It's because Mama pled the Fifth, and R. J. hid a container." Then she started sobbing again, lowering her cheek onto the coolness of the granite countertop.

Aurora continued to rub her friend's back and popped a chocolate in her mouth. Trinity lifted her head long enough to down several ounces of wine before returning her cheek to the counter.

"You and Camden just need a break, is all, with the entire house restoration, working, and the dogs. It's a lot to handle. Maybe you two should have a nice dinner out. Way out. Someplace special. I can take the dogs for you."

"You think Camden would want to?" Trinity mumbled.

"Yes. I think it would be great for you both."

"Okay, then. But can the dogs and I spend the night?" Trinity's voice faltered, full of tears and heartbreak.

"Yes, sweetie."

"Can we talk about why you've been avoiding me?"

Aurora topped off their wineglasses. "Shh, just drink your wine."

Camden missed Anderson and Dean. He missed Trinity. She wasn't home yet, and it was well past five thirty. He went to the front window and moved the curtains out of the way. The sun setting blinded him. If she was coming up the driveway, he couldn't see it.

Should I text her? No, if she wants to come home, she will. Maybe her truck broke down, or maybe something happened to one of the dogs. He started to text Trinity, then deleted it. He typed a few more words, then deleted them. Finally, Camden threw his phone on the sofa.

There was only one other person he could go to in this town. One person besides Trinity who understood him. The one person he could never go to come September. Camden snatched up his cell phone and headed to the garage.

As he drove past Aurora's house, he slowed the car and leaned forward in his seat. His worry finally dissipated as he spied Trinity's truck in her best friend's driveway. Camden continued until he pulled into Lillian's drive, parking somewhat hidden from view on the side of her house.

Thank goodness their fight happened on Lillian's day off from the restaurant. He glanced at the stable as he climbed from the car, locating Eastwood and Elliot. It was possible she might be out running errands. Yet, her days off were usually spent horseback riding versus errands. He rapped on the door and immediately heard footsteps inside.

"Camden." Lillian opened the door, stepping back behind it. "Come in, come in."

He wiped the dust as best he could from his shoes on the outside mat and entered the home of his mother-in-law. She closed the door, quickly moving to hug him before he escaped into the living room.

"You want a beer?" Without waiting for a reply, Lillian went to the kitchen and returned with two beer bottles and a box of crackers.

"Thanks." Camden took the beer as Lillian reached into the box and tore apart the cracker bag inside; the scent of sharp cheese filled the air. "Not bad. Not a merlot, but not bad."

Lillian leaned back in the worn tan armchair. Camden rested his right ankle on his left knee and swigged a sip of beer.

"We got in a stupid fight. I said things I didn't mean."

Lillian leaned forward and pulled a handful of crackers from the bag.

"I saw R. J. hiding this container, and I swear I saw a picture of Trinity and me on it. Then she said that Mama refused to talk. Something about pleading the Fifth." Camden shoved the fistful of crackers in his mouth, and the sound of crunching echoed in his ears. "I had just walked over in the noontime heat to bring her lunch. Maybe the temperature got to me. I can't bear to lose her."

Lillian picked at the label of her beer.

"She didn't come home from work tonight. I saw her truck next door, so at least I know she's safe. But still, I need to apologize."

Lillian nodded her head. "Maybe a nice restaurant? Outside of town? Something that has history."

Camden's eyes went to the ceiling, deep in thought. He looked at his cell phone. "Too late to go tonight, wherever we go."

"Luis can let you off early, and I'm sure the town won't mind if Trinity closes the post office a little earlier than normal," Lillian suggested.

Camden rubbed the condensation from the bottle on his pant leg. "Maybe. I can't believe we fought. We never fight."

"You're stressed, it happens. It doesn't mean you two don't love each other."

Camden nodded. "We do. I do. I love her." He wanted to tell Lillian that he tried to call off the divorce, but the words stuck in his throat.

After a few minutes of silence, all he could muster was the feeling about the town around him. "It's the oddest thing. We sense the town is hiding something from us. Are you aware of anything going on that Trinity and I may not know about?"

Lillian shifted in the chair, peeling more of the label free, her eyes everywhere but on her son-in-law. A loud rumble came from the kitchen, and they pivoted towards the noise.

"What was that?" Camden sat forward in his chair.

"The fridge, it's going out."

"Sounds like you need to buy a new one . . . maybe a week ago." Camden chucked as another moan came from the kitchen.

"Funds are a bit low; something came up. I can deal with it for a while. Besides, I eat mostly at the restaurant, so not much to keep in there other than beer and water."

Camden raised his bottle, and Lillian mirrored him.

"Cheers," they said in unison.

Chapter 35

Camden

Camden sprang from bed the following morning as the perfect place to take Trinity to dinner popped into his mind. Nothing better than the Omni. The place they'd first met.

He nearly danced into the kitchen to start the coffee. He placed a call to the resort, fingers crossed they would have a spot available for the following night. Camden would need to play it cool when Trinity arrived home for dinner, if she did come home. He'd tossed all night without her under the same roof as him. She would want to change clothes before work. She *had* to stop by.

"I'd like to make a reservation for tomorrow night, please." Camden poured coffee into a mug with a smile plastered across his face.

The garage door opened, and in burst Dean and Anderson, followed by Trinity.

"Yes, perfect. That time will work, thank you." Camden quickly disconnected. "Hi."

"Hi." Trinity's voice was low. Her clothes wrinkled, her hair unbrushed.

As she approached Camden, he saw the puffiness under her eyes from crying.

"Hi," she said again.

"Hi." Camden set his mug down and moved closer to her.

Before he knew it, Trinity wrapped her arms around him. He did the same, squeezing her body as though he could make them one person. When he released her, she didn't smile, instead, she kept her head hung down.

"Did you feed Starla and Stella?" She looked at her cell phone.

"Not yet, but I can." Camden took a sip of coffee and put on his shoes.

"It's okay. I will. You're already dressed for work. Come on, boys, wanna help?"

He watched from the kitchen slider as she approached the stall where Starla and Stella were waiting for their morning hay. He opened the slider and made his way out onto the patio. Dean and Anderson greeted the horses with a sniff fest when Starla started to neigh.

"Calm down, I'm hurrying," Trinity instructed as she entered the storage area for the hay. When Starla backed away and continued to neigh, Dean and Anderson spun in circles, unsure of the commotion. Camden turned and saw Stella react next by backing into the corral.

Trinity approached Starla, attempting to calm them all down at once. Her hands reached out, and then she froze. The dogs started to bark.

"Trinity, is everything alright?" Camden called.

He stepped off the patio and made his way toward the stalls. Then, he saw what had caused Trinity to freeze. In front of her, a rattler coiled in a defensive posture. Camden gasped, trying to find his breath. Fear spread through his limbs, paralyzing his body.

Thoughts of what to do, how to protect her and the dogs flashed through his mind. His life with Trinity scrolled by like a slideshow.

The horses continued to neigh, but the dogs remained to her right with the snake in the middle. He knew Anderson might try and protect her, but if the snake bit any of the animals, they would lose them for sure. Camden's eyes darted around.

"Can you back away without causing the dogs to lunge for the snake?"

"No, call the dogs, now!" Trinity shouted. "Now! You need to get them in the house!"

He swallowed hard. "Anderson! Dean! Come! Come!"

The dogs didn't move, they only continued to bark.

"Come! Anderson, come! Dean, come!"

The boys remained in their spots.

"Salmon treat!" Camden yelled. "You boys want some salmon?"

With that, the boys turned their heads. "Come, come!"

Dean lost focus on the rattlesnake first and rushed toward Camden. He grabbed his collar as he continued to focus on the stable.

"Anderson, come! Now!" He patted his leg.

Reluctantly, Anderson turned and trotted to Camden but stopped and turned back to Trinity.

"Anderson, come!" Camden belted again.

Finally, Anderson listened, and once within his reach, he grabbed his collar and backed up the patio steps. He yanked the slider open, shoved them inside, and shut it with more force than needed.

Camden stepped off the patio and approached the horse stall, careful not to take any steps that the rattler might perceive as threatening. The dogs' paws slammed against the slider door as they jumped up and down, barking.

Camden froze in place as the rattlesnake made a striking move toward his wife. The only prey within the rattler's reach was Trinity. His mind raced with what to do. Then, out of the corner of his eye, he saw what he needed. He crept sideways, his vision still locked on the snake.

"Camden, back off. I don't want us both getting bit." Trinity's voice was calm and poised. "I'm going to step back some more."

"I'm not letting anything happen to you." He took a deep breath, channeling his high school baseball days, and released the rock from his hand toward the snake. It hit just in front of the rattler, dirt erupting in a cloud of dust.

"Run! Now! Run!" Camden yelled at his wife.

Trinity stumbled backward, breaking her fall with her hands. She jumped up as Camden backed away, running for the patio also. Once safe, Camden wrapped Trinity up in his arms.

"You saved me." Trinity shuttered.

"Did you not see it there?"

"I wasn't paying any attention. I think Starla saw it, and that was why she was neighing. I was just an innocent bystander arriving late." Her hand wrapped around Camden. "Thank you. Throwing a rock at it was risky, though. It could've ticked it off more."

They held each other for a few more seconds before separating.

"You're safe. That's all that matters. Where do you think it slithered off to?" Camden questioned. "Or did I kill it?"

"It's long gone." She pressed her hand onto his chest to feel how his heartbeat raced.

Trinity looked over at the horses that were now calm. "I'll call Wallace, have him come over and make sure it doesn't come back."

Wallace was an expert on desert life and had trapped many rattlesnakes, transplanting them far away from town in the wilds of the desert.

"I think I might need to add some liquor to my morning coffee." Camden reached for the slider. He wiggled the handle, but it didn't budge. "Great."

Trinity glanced at Anderson and Dean, sitting patiently on the other side of the glass door. "Did they lock it again?"

Camden nodded. "We should replace that lock with something a dog can't slide down with a paw bump."

Holding hands, they made their way around to the front door to let themselves inside.

Chapter 36

Trinity & Camden

"It's Mama." Trinity appeared at the newly renovated spare bathroom door.

Camden shut off the electric razor but held it tight in his hand. They stared at each other in the reflection of the framed mirror hanging over the new vanity. Trinity didn't smile, her lips creating a flat line.

She covered her mouth, sadness formed in her eyes. "It's not good. We need to leave now."

Camden set the razor down, hit the light switch, and quickly changed out of his pajamas, meeting Trinity in her truck as she pulled out of the garage.

As they made their way down the road, she glanced in her rearview mirror and spotted the Hackenburgs' SUV. After crossing State Route 287, a line of cars followed behind and in front of Trinity's truck. The entire town was headed to see Mama.

The line of residents ran out the front door, and Gavin busied himself by handing out homemade lemonade. Trinity took a glass and felt guilty enjoying it as much as she did. Camden reached for Trinity's hand, and she took hold of it, not wanting to let go.

For as many residents as were shoved into Elizabeth's house, it was quiet as could be. Trinity could even make out Mama's soft cough coming from her room. Camden squeezed her hand, and she squeezed back.

"I hope this is a false alarm," Trinity whispered at Camden.

He nodded his head as they were finally next.

Mama's eyes were heavy, and she held a tissue up to her mouth when she coughed. Camden guided Trinity to Mama, and he took up the edge of the bed directly behind his wife.

"Mama, we're here. Camden and I." Trinity took hold of Jolie's weak and soft hand.

Mama's lips upturned at the edges. "Thank you for comin'."

"You'll be just fine, Mama. I'm sure I'll see you at the post office in a few days. You'll be up and about." Trinity rubbed Mama's shoulder with her other hand.

"Hush, now," Mama whispered. "Your children are going to be so blessed to have you."

Trinity glanced at Camden. It would be best not to correct Mama, and she knew it. "You focus on resting, Mama."

"Promise me you'll give them strong names," Mama spoke, her eyes closed. "Don't be namin' them after fruits or cars."

Trinity grinned even as tears started to form. "Camden and I are so grateful to have spent as much time with you as we have."

"We want more time with you," Camden added. "So you hang in there and get well."

"Cookies," Mama squeaked. "Cookie sales."

"Yes, Mama. Once September comes, I'll start to sell my cookies at the grocery store, post office, and restaurant. They all agreed."

Mama grinned as wide as she could with such weakness.

"There's a long line of residents here to see you. We'll see you again soon, Mama." Trinity leaned over and kissed her on the forehead, then headed out of the bedroom.

Camden and Trinity climbed into the truck but didn't start it. The heat cooked them for a few minutes through the windows before Trinity finally turned the key.

"I'm going to miss her." Trinity pushed the clutch in and shifted into first gear.

"Me too." Camden rested his hand on her shoulder as they made their way back home.

"Let's go around back." Camden motioned with his head towards the backyard.

Trinity raised an eyebrow. "What's going on?"

He shoved his hands in his pocket to keep from reaching for her hand to guide her. Excitement revved through his veins as she followed him without hesitation around the side of the house to the backyard.

"Is that a firepit?" Trinity's hand went to her heart. "From the bricks at—"

"I figured we could enjoy it for at least a few nights."

She didn't respond, but he so badly wanted her to be thinking what he was thinking. That, like the fireplace surviving one hundred years, so could their love.

Chapter 37

Camden

Camden straightened out his solid black tie. Everything needed to be perfect tonight. Everything. Not only would he hold the memory of tonight in his mind forever, but he also hoped Trinity would, too.

"Trinity, are you ready to go?" He stepped away from the dresser mirror.

"One more minute," she called from the crack in the bathroom door.

Trinity had dropped off the dogs at Aurora's after work before coming home to get ready.

"How do I look?" Trinity asked, entering from the hallway. She glanced down at her clothes, but when their eyes met, she smiled. And Trinity took his breath right from his lungs.

"You're beautiful. Absolutely perfect."

Trinity wore a sleeveless black dress that fell to her knees, but the fabric was thinner with a knit appearance at the neck and bottom. She wore tan heels, which she rarely wore, except for weddings.

"Not too fancy? I feel over-fancy."

Camden went to her and reached his hand out. "No, you're perfect."

The drive to the Omni in Scottsdale took about two and a half hours, and the nervousness and sadness filled the car the entire way. Mama had passed away shortly after the caravan of Woolsey residents dissipated last night, and the silence of the town in mourning stuck with them all.

"I'm starving," Trinity mentioned as Camden parked the car in the parking garage.

"Me too. Stay there."

The door popped open, and Camden's hand reached inside. Trinity took it and climbed from the car.

Trinity's first few steps were wobbly, but Camden held her hand and held her steady.

"I'm horrible at walking in these," Trinity laughed.

"You should have worn your boots."

"I should have, but I wanted to dress up to be on par with you. At least once." Trinity bumped Camden's arm with hers.

They made their way, hand in hand, to the main entrance of the resort and entered the restaurant. The grounds were lit with the warm glow of lanterns and lush green vines ran up the pillars. Water sculptures muffled the sound of guests mingling in the courtyard.

When they reached the hostess stand, she asked, "Do you have a reservation?"

"Yes. Moore," Camden stated.

"We do? I thought this was last minute," Trinity whispered.

"Not completely last minute." Camden winked.

"This way, please," the hostess announced and they followed her to their table.

Off in the distance, a striking view of Camelback Mountain was bathed in the golden sunset light as Camden pulled out Trinity's chair, and they took a seat. The hostess placed the menus in their hands and walked away. Candlelight danced in the middle of the small table as they looked over their menus, and the waitress approached.

"I'm Laura, and I'll be your server this evening." She held a wine bottle in hand. "Mr. Moore, here is the 2010 Malbec, shall I?"

Camden nodded as Laura poured them each a glass.

"I'll be back to take your order, unless you're ready now?"

"A few more minutes, please," Trinity stated.

Laura left, and Camden raised his wine glass. "To us."

"To us." Their glasses clinked. "Excellent choice," Trinity said. "You always pick the best wines."

After Laura returned to jot down their orders, she left them with fresh sourdough bread.

"I could eat this entire loaf before she returns with our meals." Trinity took a slice and tore it apart.

Camden sighed and set down his wineglass. His pincer grasp remained loose around the stem, twisting it back and forth.

"This is so much harder than I thought. It's as though the entire town is shutting down as each day passes."

Trinity tore off more bread. "Sure feels that way. Everyone is hiding from us, avoiding conversation. And eye contact, too. I'm sure Mama's passing will only add to it."

Camden held the wineglass to his lips, pausing. Trinity gazed out at the view, and the light caught her profile. His breathing deepened as his heart ached. He sipped the Malbec and returned his glass to the table as Trinity turned back around.

"We're avoiding things, too."

Camden nodded. *Tell her you want to stay married more than having kids. Tell her!*

"Dividing everything up. Discussing Anderson and Dean." Trinity made fleeting eye contact with him.

You big baby! "Take anything you want. I'm not going to worry about DVDs, plates, and bed linens while I'm sitting around in my boxers depressed."

Trinity pressed her lips together, holding the laughter inside.

"It's not funny," Camden warned.

Trinity covered her mouth. Her body trembled with laughter. "Yes, it is, Camden. You, sitting around in boxers? Come on. You've never done anything so informal in all your life."

A smile crested on Camden's lips. "Maybe you're right. Wait." He sat up straighter. "What about New Year's Eve two years ago?"

Trinity slapped her hand on the table, and the Malbec rippled in the glasses. "You're right!"

Camden took a slice of bread. "I'd forgotten to put the clothes in the dryer like you asked."

Trinity nodded and raised her eyebrows.

"We'd just moved in and had only a few pairs of clothes, *everything* was in the washing machine. I was naïve to assume that temperatures in the desert never dropped below eighty degrees, ever."

"You should've known better. I warned you."

"You shouldn't have hidden all the blankets. I nearly froze to death trying to cover my cold body up with the couch pillows."

"Good thing we had furniture delivered."

Camden's smile faded. "I'm going to miss our house."

"I will too. I'm not thrilled about moving back in with Mom."

"Is anyone ever?" Camden laughed.

"No." Trinity gazed out at the view again. "Do you know where you plan to move to?"

"I should probably have an answer for that. Maybe. I guess it comes down to interviews. I haven't heard back from any of the schools in Arizona."

"That's right, you're interested in the Saddle Mountain school district and Glendale, right?"

"Plus, one more in Buckeye. I'd still like to see Anderson and Dean. And I can't do that if I'm in Chicago."

"Yes, of course. We'll make some arrangements. I mean, if parents can do it with kids, we should be able to do it with dogs."

Camden's phone vibrated in his pocket. "It's Aurora. She wants to know when we'll be home?" He turned the phone to show her the message.

"She texted me the same question on the way here."

"Do you think the dogs are causing problems?"

"I doubt it."

Dinner arrived—wild mushroom linguine for Trinity and paella a la Valenciana for Camden.

"It looks delicious!" Camden leaned over his plate.

"It better be for the price."

"No discussion about that. We're allowed to splurge. We've earned it."

"To divorce." Trinity's voice cracked as she raised her glass.

"No," Camden said. His eyes blinked rapidly. "No, I want to call it off."

Trinity lowered her glass to the table. "You want to stop the divorce?"

"Yes." He leaned forward and reached for her hand. "I want to stay your husband. Baby or no baby. You're my dream. You're my future."

Trinity's mouth hung open. "I . . . I . . ."

"You don't feel the same, do you?" Camden nearly dropped his head onto his plate.

"No." Her hand reached out. "Cam, I do too. You and me. I want nothing more than to raise a family with you, but if staying with you means no kids, then that's what it means."

When his eyes met hers, he saw the tears. Camden reached over and wiped them with his thumb. "I love you, Trinity Moore."

"I love you, too, my sweet hubby."

"But we need to eat. We can talk this over after dinner because I don't need you getting hangry."

Trinity blushed and dove into her meal but didn't let go of his hand. After dinner and dessert, Camden pulled out her chair, and they made their way around the resort, past the pool to where the water caused the summer night air to cool slightly. The fountains trickled and splashed over the royal-blue tiles, and the bloom of pink-and-orange flowers sprinkled the area.

Trinity turned to Camden, the moonlight casting their shadows across the grass. They stood face-to-face in an area of the resort where the path lights were sparse.

She dropped her heels in the grass and took his other hand in hers. "Are you sure?" Trinity's voice was soft.

Camden locked eyes with his wife. "I'm absolutely positive. No divorce."

"But it means—"

He moved his finger over her lips. "It means we stay together. Don't get me wrong, the pain of not having kids will be hard, but we can find other ways to love and be a family. Maybe more dogs?"

"Always more dogs. I wish my cookie sales could be enough."

"Shh." Camden touched his lips to his wife's before gently pulling her closer to him.

When they parted, she said, "Maybe a miracle will happen."

"A Hail Mary."

Their foreheads touched. Camden brushed her cheek with his fingertips.

"A ninth-inning miracle."

"If you can keep throwing more sports terms around, it might work."

"In the final lap."

"Just before the buzzer." Trinity winked.

"I love you, Mrs. Moore." Camden wrapped his hand around the side of her neck and his other hand around her waist. They stood in the spot where they'd first kissed.

They pulled back enough for their eyes to meet.

"I love you more," Trinity whispered and kissed him.

Chapter 38

Trinity & Camden

"What's going on?" Trinity leaned forward in the passenger seat.

A line of residents flanked both sides of their driveway. They waved with broad smiles, which were seen thanks to the full moon's glow and Camden's headlights.

"Do you think this is why Aurora wanted to know when we would be home?" Trinity gave a half-wave out the window. Confusion plain across her face.

Camden pulled the car into the garage, and they climbed out. Anderson and Dean greeted them as they rounded the garage.

Beyond the dogs were Lillian, Luis, Gavin, Jennifer and Greg, William, Charlie, Alexander, R.J., Dolores and Barrett, and Elizabeth. Aurora, her girls, and Mike stepped into the middle of the crowd, followed by the Hackenburgs with Jasmine.

"What's everyone doing here?" Trinity asked as fear rattled through her voice.

"Elizabeth, what's going on?" Camden echoed, glancing at the townspeople behind her. He'd started to sweat—apart from the hot summer night air—the unknown made him nervous.

"We wanted to keep this a secret until just before your September 1 court date. Yet, Mama insisted before we lost her to the angels that we shouldn't wait a minute longer. And seein' as though every resident standin' here was fallin' apart trying to keep it a secret from y'all—"

"We couldn't bear to see your hearts breaking any longer, either," Aurora added.

Elizabeth clutched her necklace between her fingers. "I'm just so sorry Mama isn't here to see this. After all, it was her plan."

Camden and Trinity reached for the other's hand, and he squeezed her tightly. They glanced at each other, clueless.

"Mama's idea?" Trinity asked.

"It might have been Mama's idea, with her providing the largest contribution, but every single wonderful resident of Woolsey came together and made it happen." Elizabeth held out a small white envelope, and Trinity took it in her right hand as her other was still clamped onto Camden's.

"What's this?" Trinity asked.

"Open it!" Ezra yelled.

Then every resident standing in the front yard of the Moore's home started to chant, "Open it! Open it!"

Elizabeth held out her cell phone, using the flashlight feature so Camden and Trinity could see what was inside.

Trinity and Camden pivoted towards each other, their hearts beating so loud they threatened to drown out the chanting.

Trinity tore a slit on the top and ripped open the envelope. She reached inside and pulled out the single piece of paper and held it out for Camden and her to see together.

"It's a check," Trinity whispered.

"A check made out to us," Camden added.

Their eyes saw the total and then darted to the memo section: *Adoption Fee.*

"I don't understand," Trinity mumbled.

"The residents of Woolsey wanted to make sure that you could stay."

"Stay married!" Jennifer yelled.

"Stay in town!" Lillian shouted.

Trinity faced the crowd. "Camden and I decided to call off the divorce at dinner tonight. We couldn't be without each other, even if that meant our dreams didn't happen. But now, it looks like we can have everything we've ever dreamed of!"

The townspeople clapped and shouted cheers of joy. Trinity and Camden's eyes filled with tears as they hugged each other.

"I can't believe you kept this a secret—all this time. Wait—" Trinity turned to Elizabeth. "What about forcing Gavin on me?"

"Nothing better than a little jealousy." Elizabeth winked.

"R. J.!" Camden shouted. "The container, with our picture on it . . .?"

R. J. stepped forward. "Always good to encourage a few more donations we might have missed."

"What about the wine from Utah?" Trinity called out to the Hackenburgs.

"No fire up north," Wyatt raised his voice. "We had a lovely anniversary trip to Utah and stayed at a spa resort. And you two enjoyed a firsthand parenting experience together."

Trinity and Camden turned to each other.

"Well, Mr. Not Green Hammer," Trinity oozed, "what do we say to everyone? Thank you is not enough. Do we have a sports term for this?"

He took her hand in his, tilted his head back, and screamed, "GOOAAAALLLL!"

Epilogue

One Year Later

"Camden!" Trinity called from the bedroom. "Can you grab the cookies? The timer's going off."

"Got 'em!" Camden shouted back.

He snatched the pot holder off the counter and removed the baking sheet full of coconut chip cookies from the oven. Then, taking a spatula, Camden placed each cookie to cool on the wire racks spread over the concrete countertop of the kitchen island.

Summer was back, yet again, and the sunlight filtered through the kitchen windows and slider, bouncing off the white subway tile backsplash. The kitchen turned out better than he or Trinity had expected, and he knew that some of it was due to Gavin's professional handyman skills.

"What's taking you two so long?" Camden asked, leaning down the hall. "I'm going to check Starla and Stella's water."

"We'll be out in a minute," Trinity called out.

Camden opened the slider, leaving Anderson behind, and made his way to the stalls. He filled up the water basin and returned to the back patio slider to find Anderson and Dean sitting with goofy smiles as their tongues hung out of their mouths.

He reached to pull open the sliding door, but it didn't budge. "Boys, did you jump up and lock this door?" Camden rubbed his forehead and threw his head back. They should've replaced the lock a year ago after the rattlesnake incident.

Camden stepped off the patio and made his way around to the front door.

"Camden!" Wyatt's voice came from across the way. "How is it going with Jasmine? Is Trinity almost done?"

He waved his hand. "Yes, she should be just about done. Come inside."

Wyatt followed Camden inside and was quickly greeted by the boys.

"Trinity, Wyatt is chomping at the bit out here."

"We're ready," Trinity stated as she carried Jasmine out to see her dad.

Wyatt gasped and put a hand over his mouth. "She's beautiful."

Trinity had offered to do Jasmine's hair for the family portraits the Hackenburgs were getting done to celebrate the addition of Jasmine's older brother, Jeter, whom they adopted a few months ago. Jeter had bounced around foster homes for the first two years of his life, and the Hackenburgs could not be any happier to welcome him into their expanding family.

"The curls should hold for a few hours." Trinity handed over Jasmine to Wyatt.

"Thank you so much. She looks darling!" he squealed.

Camden side-hugged his wife and kissed the top of her head. Trinity hugged him back.

As soon as Wyatt left, Camden said, "The boys locked me out again."

Trinity rolled her eyes. "We must remember to switch out the lock on that."

Then a cry came from down the hall.

"I'll go." Camden headed out of the living room.

Trinity busied herself by washing her hands and wrapping up the cookies for sale.

"Someone had a great nap." Camden entered the kitchen with his arms full of a four-month-old baby girl. Her short hair was such a dark brown it appeared black in certain light. "Mommy cannot wait to curl your hair someday." Camden kissed his daughter's forehead.

"Did you have a great nap, Jolie?" Trinity oozed and made her way over to kiss her daughter's cheeks.

One kiss was never enough for Trinity. She needed to kiss each cheek at least twice, which caused Jolie to giggle each and every time.

Trinity couldn't have fathomed the outcome of their life would mean all her dreams came true. But having Camden, their baby, and their beautiful kitchen, was only as perfect as the town of Woolsey.

The End

Did you LOVE, LIKE, or DISLIKE this novel? Let me know by leaving a review, please and thank you.

Don't miss out on what happens next in Woolsey!
A Desert Romance - Book 2
A Desert Rivalry - Book 3

Eggless Coconut-Chip Cookies

Preheat oven to 350° F

IN A LARGE BOWL MIX

2 tablespoons chia seeds soaked in 6 tablespoons of water for 10 minutes

AND THEN ADD

2 ½ cups unbleached flour

2 cups packed brown sugar (golden)

1 teaspoon baking soda

1 ½ teaspoons vanilla extract

8 tablespoons SALTED butter (room temperature)

1/3 cup of water

MIX ALL THIS TOGETHER, AND THEN ADD THE FOLLOWING

1 cup semi-sweet chocolate chips (I get ones with 43% cocoa)

1 cup dried cranberries

½ cup chopped walnuts

½ cup unsweetened shredded coconut flakes

MIX

LINE BAKING SHEET WITH PARCHMENT PAPER

PLACE HEAPING 1 TABLESPOON SIZE BALLS ONTO THE SHEET

BAKE FOR ABOUT 12 MINUTES (ovens may vary)

*makes about 20-25 cookies

About the Author

Savannah Hendricks (born in California, raised in Washington, and resides in Arizona) is a full-time social worker and fills as much of her weekends as possible with writing. She loves all things dog-related and has a passion for red wine. Savannah enjoys gardening, baking, and creating yummy recipes. You'll often find her hollering at the TV during restoration shows when they paint over red bricks.

If you'd love a digital personalized autograph or bookplate, you can request one by visiting: savannahhendricks.com
Please discover more about Savannah by interacting with her on:

Instagram: savannahhendricks_author
Facebook: AuthorSavannahHendricks

Also By Savannah

Heartfelt Coming of Age/Women's Fiction

Sun City, 85373

The Album (Multi-Award-Winning)

I Adopted My Mom at the Bus Station (Multi-Award-Winning)

Humorously Wholesome Romance

Route to Romance

A Hearts of Woolsey series: A Desert Restoration, A Desert Romance, A Desert Rivalry

The Christmas Rental

Grounded in January (Award-Winning)

Grounded in July

To Work Out or to Wed

Meaningful Picture Books

SAVANNAH HENDRICKS

Where Does "I Love You" Go?
The Needle-less Christmas Tree & Other Tree Tales
Winston Versus the Snow (Multi-Award-Winning)
Nonnie and I (Available in English, Spanish & Bilingual)

www.ingramcontent.com/pod-product-compliance
Lightning Source LLC
LaVergne TN
LVHW091122080826
845145LV00008B/2017